7

JAMES PATRICK KELLY salutes Johnny America in a landmine called "Home Front." Watch your step.

ROBERT FRAZIER offers "Tags" to the snuffed. Rejuice and die again. Got a problem with that, Private?

MOLLY GLOSS walks you through a "Personal Silence" till you come to the end of the war. Make a left and keep dreaming.

JOHN BARNES gives "My Advice to the Civilized" on the eve of the Last Battle. Read it and weep, soldier.

GENE WOLFE hires "The Peace Spy." He grants unusual requests for unusual clients in a strange country called America.

Isaac Asimov's
WAR

ISAAC ASIMOV'S

WAR

**EDITED BY
GARDNER DOZOIS**

ACE BOOKS, NEW YORK

This book is an Ace original edition
and has never been previously published.

ISAAC ASIMOV'S WAR

An Ace Book / published by arrangement with
Bantam Doubleday Dell Direct, Inc.

PRINTING HISTORY
Ace edition / September 1993

ISBN: 0-441-37393-3

ACE ®
Ace Books are published by The Berkley Publishing Group,
200 Madison Avenue, New York, NY 10016.
ACE and the "A" design
are trademarks belonging to Charter Communications, Inc.

PRINTED IN THE UNITED STATES OF AMERICA

10 9 8 7 6 5 4 3 2 1

Grateful acknowledgment is made to the following for permission to reprint their copyrighted material:

"My Advice to the Civilized" by John Barnes, copyright © 1990 by Davis Publications, Inc., reprinted by permission of Ashley Grayson, Literary Agent;

"Hardfought" by Greg Bear, copyright © 1982 by Greg Bear, reprinted by permission of the author;

"Warstory" by Gregory Benford, copyright © 1989 by Davis Publications, Inc., reprinted by permission of the author;

"Tags" by Robert Frazier, copyright © 1988 by Davis Publications, Inc., reprinted by permission of the author;

"Personal Silence" by Molly Gloss, copyright © 1989 by Davis Publications, Inc., reprinted by permission of Virginia Kidd, Literary Agent;

"Home Front" by James Patrick Kelly, copyright © 1988 by Davis Publications, Inc., reprinted by permission of the author;

"Madness Has Its Place" by Larry Niven, copyright © 1990 by Davis Publications, Inc., reprinted by permission of the Spectrum Literary Agency;

"Fire Zone Emerald" by Lucius Shepard, copyright © 1986 by Davis Publications, Inc., reprinted by permission of the author;

"The Peace Spy" by Gene Wolfe, copyright © 1986 by Davis Publications, Inc., reprinted by permission of Virginia Kidd, Literary Agent.

All stories previously appeared in *Asimov's Science Fiction*, published by Dell Magazines, a division of Bantam Doubleday Dell Magazines.

ACKNOWLEDGMENTS

The editor would like to thank the following people for their help and support: Susan Casper, who helped with the wordcrunching involved in preparing this manuscript, and who lent the use of her computer; Shawna McCarthy, for having the good taste to buy some of this material in the first place; Sheila Williams, who has labored behind the scenes on *Asimov's* for many years and played a part in the decision-making process involved in the buying of some of these stories; Ian Randal Strock, Scott L. Towner, and Adam Stern, who did much of the thankless scut work that was necessary; Constance Scarborough, who cleared the permissions; Cynthia Manson, who set up this deal; and thanks especially to my own editor on this project, Susan Allison.

CONTENTS

WARSTORY
  Gregory Benford   1
FIRE ZONE EMERALD
  Lucius Shepard   41
HOME FRONT
  James Patrick Kelly   71
TAGS
  Robert Frazier   89
PERSONAL SILENCE
  Molly Gloss   93
MADNESS HAS ITS PLACE
  Larry Niven   119
MY ADVICE TO THE CIVILIZED
  John Barnes   151
THE PEACE SPY
  Gene Wolfe   171
HARDFOUGHT
  Greg Bear   181

ISAAC ASIMOV'S WAR

WARSTORY

Gregory Benford

"Warstory" was purchased by Gardner Dozois, and appeared in the January 1990 issue of Asimov's, *with an evocative cover and interior illustration by Gary Freeman. Benford published a string of strong stories in* Asimov's *during the '80s, all of them marked by that mixture of humanistic insight and shrewd technological speculation that has always been his forte. The story that follows was no exception, as he takes us to the frozen landscape of Ganymede for a fast-paced and thrilling tale of the high-tech warfare of the future—a tricky one, however, where nothing is quite what it seems. . . .*

Gregory Benford is one of the modern giants of the field. His 1980 novel Timescape *won the Nebula Award, the John W. Campbell Memorial Award, the British Science Fiction Association Award, and the Australian Ditmar Award, and is widely considered to be one of the classic novels of the last two decades. His other novels include* The Stars in Shroud, In the Ocean of Night, Against Infinity, Artifact, *and* Across the Sea of Suns. *His most recent novels are the bestselling* Great Sky River, *and* Tides of Light. *He has recently become one of the regular science columnists for* The Magazine of Fantasy and Science Fiction. *Benford is a professor of physics at the University of California, Irvine.*

1

Russ flexed his four-fingered clamp hands and surveyed the landscape. They were on the nightside of Ganymede. Pale crescents of the other moons sliced the darkness. Jupiter hung like a fat, luminous melon above the distant horizon. He counted three distinct shadows pointing off at angles, each differently colored.

Well, so he'd lost his ship. Worse things could happen. He could be dead.

Co-pilot Columbard already was. They had left her in the wreck, not even able to get the body out. Not that they could have buried it in this damned ice.

"Maybe these'll help us sneak by optical pattern-recog detectors," he said to Zoti, pointing.

"Shadows?" she asked, puffing up a slope even in the light gravity. She carried a big supply pack. "Think so?"

"Could be." He didn't really think so but at this point you had to believe in something.

"Better get away from here," Zoti said.

"Think the Feds got a trace on us?"

She shook her head, a tight movement visible through her skinsuit helmet. "Our guys were giving them plenty deceptors, throwing EM jams on them—the works."

Russ respected her tech talents, but he never relied on tricks alone. Best thing was to get away before some bat came to check the wreck.

"We'll hoof in three minutes," Russ said.

He looked back at the crushed metal can that a big blue-black ice outcropping had made of *Asskicker II*. It didn't look like a fabulously expensive, threatening bomber now, just a pile of scrap. Nye and Kitsov came up the hill, lugging more supplies.

"Got the CCD cubes?" Russ asked Nye.

"Yeah, I yanked them." Nye scowled. He never said much, just let his face do his complaining for him.

"Think they've got good stuff?" Russ asked.

"Some fighter shots," Nye said. "Then a big juicy closeup of the snake that got us."

Russ nodded. Snakes were the thin, silvery missiles that their Northern Hemisphere tech jockeys couldn't knock out. "Well," he said, "maybe that'll be worth something."

Kitsov said, "Worth to Command, could be. To Natwork, no."

Zoti said, "Natwork? Oh—look, *Net*work can't use anything that's classified. A snake shot will have TS all over it."

Russ asked, "TS?"

Zoti grinned. "They say it means Top Secret, but as far as we're concerned, might as well be Tough Shit. Means we make no loot from it."

Russ nodded. He hated this mercenary shit. If everything had gone right, *Asskicker II* would have lobbed a fusion head smack onto Hiruko Station. Earthside network royalties for the shot would've gone to them all, with Russ getting twice the share of the others, since he was Captain and pilot.

Had that made any difference? You could never really be sure that some subconscious greed hadn't made you rush the orbit a little, shade the numbers, slip just a hair off the mark. Could that be what had let the snake through?

He shook his head. He'd never know, and he wasn't sure he wanted to.

"Still think we'll see a single Yen out of it?" Zoti asked him. He realized she had interpreted his shaking head as disagreement. They would be reading him closely now. The crew wanted reassurance that they weren't doomed and he was the only authority figure around. Never mind that he'd never led a ground operation in his life.

"I think we'll get rich," Russ said, voice full of confidence he had dredged up from somewhere. He wondered if it rang hollowly but the others seemed to brighten.

"Is good!" Kitsov said, grinning.

"It'll be better if we get out of here," Russ said. "Come on."

"Which way?" Nye asked.

"Through that notch in the hills there." Russ pointed.

Nye frowned, black eyebrows meeting above his blunt nose. "What's that way?"

"More important, what *isn't* that way," Russ said. "We'll be putting distance between us and Hiruko Station."

Nye's forehead wrinkled. "You sure?"

"We don't have any nav gear running. I had to sight on the moons." Russ said this confidently but in fact he hadn't done a square, naked eye sighting since tech school.

Zoti said tentatively, "How about a compass?"

"On ice moon?" Kitsov chuckled. "Which way is magnetic pointing?"

"That's the problem," Russ said. "Let's go."

They moved well in the low gravity. None were athletes but they had kept in shape in the gym on the voyage out. There wasn't much else to do on the big carriers. Columbard had said that Zoti got all her workout in the sack, but then Columbard had always been catty. And not a great enthusiast in the sack herself, either. Not that her opinion mattered much, Russ thought, since she wasn't around any more to express it.

A storm came sweeping in on them as they climbed away from the wreck. It was more like a sigh of snowflakes, barely buoyant in the thin, deadly methane air. It chilled them further and he wondered if they would all get colds despite the extra insulation they all wore over their combat skinsuits.

Probably. Already his feet tingled. He turned so that his bulky pack sheltered him from the wind. They'd all get frostbite within a couple of days, he guessed.

If they could survive at all. A man in a normal pressure suit could live about an hour on Ganymede. The unending sleet of high energy protons would fry him, ripping through delicate cells and spreading red destruction. This was a natural side effect of Jupiter's hugeness—its compressed core of metallic hydrogen spun rapidly, generating powerful magnetic fields that whipped around every ten hours. These fields are like a rubbery cage, snagging and trapping protons spat out by the sun. Io, the innermost large moon, belched ions of sulfur and sodium into the magnetic traps, adding to the sleet. All this rained down on the inner moons, sputtering the ice.

Damn it, he was a sky jock, not a grunt. He'd never led a crew of barracks rats on a mud mission.

He kept his mind off his bulky pack and chilled feet by guessing what the Feds were doing. The war was moving fast, maybe fast enough to let a downed bomber crew slip through the Fed patrols.

When Northern Hemisphere crews had held Hiruko Station, they'd needed to work outside, supervising robot icediggers. The first inhabitants of Ganymede instead used the newest technology to fend off the proton hail: superconducting suits. Discovery of a way to make cheap superconducting threads made it possible to weave them into pressure suits. The currents running in the threads made a magnetic field outside the suit, where it brushed away incoming protons. Inside, by the laws of magnetostatics, there was no field at all to disturb instrumentation. Once started, the currents flowed forever, without electrical resistance.

He hoped their suits were working right. *Asskicker II*'s strong magnetics had kept them from frying before, but a suit could malf and you'd never know it. He fretted about a dozen other elements in a rapidly growing list of potentially deadly effects.

Already he had new respect for the first Hiruko crews. They'd been damn good at working in this bitter cold, pioneering against the sting and bite of the giant planet. They had carved ice and even started an atmosphere. What they hadn't been so good at was defending themselves.

No reason they should've been, of course. The Southern Hemisphere had seen their chance and had come in hard, total surprise. In a single day they had taken all Ganymede. And killed nearly every Northerner.

The bedraggled surviving crew of *Asskicker II* marched in an eerie dim glow from Jupiter. Over half of Ganymede's mass was water-ice, with liberal dollops of carbon dioxide ice, frozen ammonia and methane, and minor traces of other frozen-out gases. Its small rocky core was buried under a thousand-kilometer-deep ocean of water and slush. The crust was liberally sprinkled by billions of years of infalling meteors. These meteorites had peppered the landscape but the atmosphere building project had already smoothed the edges of even recent craters. Ancient impact debris had left hills of metal and rock, the only relief from a flat, barren plain.

This frigid moon had been tugged by Jupiter's tides for so long that it was locked, like Luna, with one face always peering at the banded ruddy planet. One complete day-night cycle was slightly more than an Earth week long. Adjusting to this rhythm would have been difficult if the sun had provided clear punctuation to the three-and-a-half-day nights. But even without an atmosphere, the sun seen from Ganymede was a dim twenty-seventh as bright as at Earth's orbit.

They saw sunup as they crested a line of rumpled hills. The sun was bright but curiously small. Sometimes Russ hardly noticed it, compared to Europa's white, cracked crescent. Jupiter's shrouded mass flickered with orange lightning strokes between the roiling somber clouds.

Ganymede's slow rotation had been enough to churn its inner ocean, exerting a torque on the ice sheets above. Slow-motion tectonics had operated for billions of years, rubbing slabs against each other, grooving and terracing terrain. They leaped over long, strangely straight canyons, rather than try to find ways around. Kitsov proved the best distance man, remorselessly devouring kilometers. Russ watched the sky anxiously. Nothing cut the blackness above except occasional scruffy gray clouds.

They didn't stop for half a day. While they ate he ran an inventory on air, water, food. If their processors worked, recycling from the skinsuits, they could last nearly a week.

"How much food you got?" Nye wanted to know while Russ was figuring.

"I'm not carrying any," Russ answered levelly.

"Huh?" Like most cynics, Nye was also a little slow.

"I'm carrying the warhead."

"What!" Nye actually got to his feet, as though outraged.

"Regs, Sergeant," Russ said slowly. "Never leave a fusion head for the enemy."

"We got to survive out here! We can't be—"

"We are," Russ said. "That's an order."

Nye's mouth worked silently. After a while he sat back down, looking irritated and sheepish at the same time.

Russ could almost sympathize with him, perhaps because he had more imagination. He knew what lay ahead.

Even if no patrol craft spotted them, they couldn't count on their carrier to send a pickup ship. The battle throughout the inner Jovian system was still going on—he had seen the flashes overhead, far out among the moons. The Northern Hemisphere forces had their hands full.

He looked down at his own hands—four clamp-fingers with delicate tools embedded in the tip of each. Combat pilot hands, technological marvels. Back on the cruiser they could detach these ceramo-wonders and his normal hands would work just fine.

But out here, in bitter cold and sucking vacuum, he couldn't get them off. And the chill seeping into them sent a dull ache up his arms.

The pain he could take. The clumsiness might be fatal.

"Get up!" he called. "Got klicks to go before we sleep, guys."

2

They spotted the autotruck the next day at noon.

It came grinding along beside a gouged trench. The trench looked manmade but it was a stretch mark. Ganymede's natural radioactive elements in its core had heated the dark inner ocean, cracking the ice shell.

But the strip beside the natural groove was a route the automated truck used to haul mined ores.

Or so Russ figured. He did know that already, after just over a day of hard marching, his crew was wearing out fast. Zoti was limping. Maybe she *had* spent her gym time on her back. He didn't give a damn one way or the other but if she slowed them down they might have to leave her behind.

But the truck could change all that. He stopped, dead still, and watched it lumber along. Its treads bit into the pale blue ice and its forward sensors monotonously swept back and forth, watching for obstructions.

Russ was no infantry officer. He knew virtually nothing about flanking and fire-and-maneuver and all the other terms that raced through his head and straight out again, leaving no residue of useful memory.

Had the Feds put fighting machines in the trucks? The idea suddenly occurred to him and seemed utterly logical. He could remember nothing in the flight briefing about that. Mostly because the briefing officer expected them to either come back intact or be blown to frags. Nobody much thought fighter-bombers would crash. Or have surviving crew.

Could the truck hear his suit comm? He didn't know.

Better use hand signals, then. He held up a claw-hand. Nye kept walking until Kitsov grabbed his arm. They all stood for a long moment, looking at the orange-colored truck and then at Russ and then back at the truck again.

One thing was sure, Russ thought. If the truck was carrying a fighting machine, the fighter wasn't so hot. His crew made beautiful targets out here, standing out nice and clean against the dirty ice.

He waved with both arms. *Drop your packs.*

Somewhat to his surprise, they did. He was glad to get the bulk off his shoulders.

The truck kept lumbering along, oblivious. He made broad gestures. *Pincer attack.*

They closed the distance at a dead run. The truck didn't slow or turn.

They all leaped the deep groove in the ice with no trouble. They cleared the next forty meters quickly and Nye had reached the truck when a small popping sound came from the truck rear and Kitsov fell.

Russ was headed for the hatch in the front so he couldn't see the rear of the truck at all. The popping came again and Nye fired his M18 at something, the whole clip at once, *rrrrrrrttttt!*

The popping stopped. Russ ran alongside the truck, puffing, Zoti beside him. Nye had the back of the truck open. Something came out, something all pipes and servos and rippled aluminum. Damaged but still active. Zoti brought up her M18. Nye hit the thing with the butt of his M18 and caved in an optical sensor. The fighter didn't stop. It reached for Nye with a knife that suddenly flipped up, standing straight out at the end of a telescoping arm. Zoti smashed the arm. The fighting machine tumbled out and went face down on the ice. Russ shot it in the back of its power panel. It didn't move any more.

"Damn!" Nye said. "Had a switchblade! You ever—"

"Get in front!" Russ yelled, turning away.

"What? I—"

"It's still armed," Russ called, already running. If Nye didn't want to follow orders that was fine with him.

They had all nearly reached the front of the truck when the fighter went off, a small *crump*. Shrapnel rattled against the truck.

"Think it's dead now?" Zoti asked, wide-eyed.

"Leave it," Russ said. He walked to where Kitsov lay face down.

The man had a big hole in his chest and a bigger one in back. It was turning reddish brown already. The thin atmosphere was sucking blood out of the body, the stain spreading down the back and onto the mottled ice. It made a pool there which fumed into a brown vapor. He looked at it, his mind motionless for a long moment as he recalled Kitsov once saying some dumb reg made his blood boil. Well, now it was. Clichés had a way of coming true out here.

Russ knew that even the skimpy gear on *Asskicker II* could have kept Kitsov running long enough to get back to the cruiser. Out here there was utterly no hope.

Two days, two crew. Three remaining.

And they had maybe six days of air left. Plenty of time to get their dying done.

3

They got the truck started again. Its autosystems had stopped at the command of the fighting machine. Apparently the machine didn't send out an alarm, though, so they probably had some time to warm up inside.

He checked the general direction the truck was heading and then let himself relax. They were all exhausted.

"Nye, you're first watch," he said.

"Damn, Cap'n, I can hardly—"

"We're all that way. Just watch the board and look out the front port. I'll relieve you in two hours."

Zoti had already dozed off, sprawled on the deck.

He laid down beside her. Two hours would do more for him if he used the syntha-narrative. He plugged it in and selected a storyline. No porno, no. Something as far from this war as he could get, though. It would give him the combined benefits of subconscious combing and action-displacement.

He settled back and felt the soft buzz of electro-input. First, music. Then a slow, gentle edging into another life, another world . . .

The phone barked her awake. Tina liked the Labrador's warm woofing but her mate did not. She slapped the kill switch and cupped the receiver to her ear, then stumbled in darkness into the bathroom.

It was Alvarez from Orange County Emergency Management. The news was worse than anything she had expected: a break in the Huntington Beach dike.

"I'll send a chopper," Alvarez said in her ear, his tinny voice tight with tension.

"Don't bother—use your choppers to evacuate people. How far is the Metro running from Laguna?"

"To the stop by the river. Traffic's pilin' up there."

She leaned forward in the predawn gloom, letting her forehead press against the cool tile of the bathroom, allowing herself ten seconds of rest.

In four minutes she was walking swiftly toward the bus stop near her apartment in Aliso Viejo. Her hand comm said the next bus was due in two minutes and here it came, early, headlights spiking through the pre-dawn murk.

On the short run into Laguna Beach Tina called the County Overview officer and got the details. The dike had broken badly and the sea was rushing inland, driving thousands before it. Three dead already and calls coming in so fast Operations couldn't even log them.

Tina yanked open a window and looked at the sky. Cloudless. A lucky break—the storm with its high winds had blown through. Had the tail end of it broken the dike?

She sensed flowing by outside the last long strip of natural greenery in the county—the hushed, moist presence of Laguna Canyon. Then Laguna's neon consumer gumbo engulfed the bus and she got off at the station. Walking to Pacific Coast Highway calmed her jittery nerves. As chief structural engineer she had to find out what broke the dike, whether the trouble was a fluke. A thousand lawsuits would ride on the details.

The Metro came exactly on time, humming on its silvery rails. Tina watched the thin crescent of Main Beach vanish behind in the gathering glow of dawn as she called up more details from OC Operations on her comm. The Metro shot north on Pacific Coast Highway in its segregated lane, purring up to high speed. They passed the elite warrens bristling with guard stations. The Metro overtook a twencen car, a big job from the '70s with the aerodynamics of a brick. It sluggishly got out of the way. A bumper sticker underlined its splendid chrome extravagance, proclaiming THINK OF THIS AS A KIND OF PRO-TEST. It trailed greasy smoke.

Heavy traffic buzzed over the helipad at Newport. Cars came fleeing south, horns honking. The Metro slowed as it neared the overpass of the Santa Ana River. Helicopters swooped over a jam up ahead. They blared down orders to the milling crowd that seemed to want to stay, to watch the show.

Tina got off the Metro and walked down the light rail line. People were moving aimlessly, frightened, some stunned and wet.

The dike began here, ramparts rising toward the north as the land fell. Surf burst against the outer wall as she climbed up onto the top walk. She could see all the way to Palos Verdes as daybreak set high clouds afire with orange. A kilometer north the smooth curve of the dike abruptly stopped. She watched ocean currents feeding the break, eagerly exploiting this latest tactical victory in a vast war.

A hovercraft sped toward her along the segmented concrete top of the dike. Alvarez, Tina realized; the man had simply traced the Metro. Alvarez's dark face, split by a grin, called "Ready for some detective work?" as Tina got aboard.

"I need a good look before the block-droppers get here," Tina said. Alvarez nodded. The hovercraft spun neatly about and accelerated.

The ocean had already chewed away a lot of pre-stressed concrete. Currents frothed over gray chunks and twisted steel that jutted up like broken teeth.

"A whole segment gave way," Tina said tightly.

"Yeah, not just a crack. Somethin' big happened."

Something deep and serious, she thought. This was the first major break in a chain that ran all the way to Santa Barbara. If there was a fundamental flaw they'd overlooked . . .

Tina clambered down the landward slope of the dike, studying the stubby wreckage, measuring with a practiced eye the vectors and forces that should have held. The sea murmured and ran greedily, the tide rising like an appetite. There were no obvious clues; currents had already erased most evidence. A thin scum clung to the broken slabs and Tina slipped on it.

"Hey!" Alvarez called uselessly. Tina slid down the steep slope. She caught herself at the edge of the rushing, briny flow.

The scum was pale gray goo oozing from fresh cracks in the concrete. It smelled like floor cleaner and stung her fingers. She inched her way back up, hands rubbed raw.

"Been any maintenance here lately?"

"No, I checked," Alvarez said. "Just the biofilm treatment half a year back."

"Any modifications here?"

"Nope." Alvarez answered his comm, listened, then said, "Big choppers on the way. We better zero outta here."

She disliked losing what frail leads she had. She took a 3D camera from Alvarez and began snapping holographic shots of the gap. She was still clambering over ruptured concrete when six enormous helicopters came lumbering in from the east, a great rectangular block swaying on cables below each.

Alvarez took the hovercraft down the inward curve of the dike and onto the frothy flood waters. They sped away, heading inland toward half-submerged buildings. The choppers hovered one at a time and dropped their concrete plugs.

Tina listened to the pilots' running crosstalk on the hovercraft comm. They gingerly released their plugs, neatly jamming up the break.

"Think it'll hold?" Alvarez asked, swinging the craft in close for an inspection.

Tina squinted. "Better." No plug was perfect, but this had stopped most of the gushing white plumes of the sea.

They turned inland. Pacific Coast Highway was meters below the water. Signs poking above the swirling water proclaimed that this was Main Street—a district, she remembered, devoted to boutiques and memorabilia from the lost days when this had been a sandy daydream land, blissful surfer country.

They sped along Main, ignoring the shouts of people marooned on roofs. "Safe enough where they are," Tina said.

A man in a dirty T-shirt with HOT TO TROTSKY printed on it gave them an obscene gesture. She turned away, trying to think.

The hovercraft growled, cutting toward the north, but the water did not get more shallow. Bedraggled people perched atop cars and houses, looking like drowned rats.

"Hey!" Alvarez pointed. A body floated face down in a narrow alley. They edged down between garages, water lapping against peeling paint.

Tina hauled in the body, an elderly woman. The arms were already stiffening. Until now Tina had been abstractly precise, gathering data. The woman's sad, wrinkled face sobered her. The brown eyes were open, staring out across the Pacific floodwaters at a distant shore only the dead can see.

They kept on.

Somehow the salty tang of the air lulled her momentarily, as if a part of her wished to withdraw from a world made abruptly raw and solid. She stared into the murky, muddy-brown waters as they skimmed over lawns. She thought of all the sopping rugs and stained furniture inside these elegant homes, the damage from the sea's casual embrace. Hunger and an old lethargy came upon her. The purring hovercraft seemed to drag her down into a soft, gauzy daydream. She often used this dazed state, allowing her subconscious to fumble with a problem when her more alert self could not make progress. The blurred sounds and smells dropped away around her and she let go. Only for a moment.

4

Russ wondered what shape and size of man had designed the forward seat. He peered forward through a smeared viewport, which barked his knees against the rough iron. The autotruck had been fashioned from Ganymede ore and nobody had bothered to polish rough edges. The seat bit into him through his skinsuit and somehow the iron cabin smelled bitter, as if some acid had gotten in at the foundry.

But, far more important, the cabin was *warm*. The Ganymede cold had seeped into them on the march. They kept the interior heaters on high, basking in it.

He had slept well with the narrative line running in his head. Three watch changes had refreshed them all and had carried him partway through Tina's vexing puzzle. The detail in the story was riveting—all sights and sounds seemed real, crisp, vivid. It took longer to dream than the "real" time of the story.

The experience was always strange, like drifting through a moist, silky world. The symphony of intricately realized dreaming did something real dreams could not—tap deep wellsprings of the unconscious, while imposing the closure of a concrete story line. He had felt himself caught up in the problems of Tina—real ones, yes, but comfortably distant all the same.

Adventure, he thought wryly, was somebody else doing something dangerous a long way off. Earthside's continuing struggle against the greenhouse effect was quite pleasant, compared with Ganymede.

He sighed and watched the rutted terrain ahead closely. There had been no sign of activity during the day they had ridden in the autotruck. The truck was sluggish, careful, dumb. It had stopped twice to pick up ore canisters from robot mines. The ore came out of a hole in the ground on a conveyor belt. There were no higher order machines around to notice three stowaway humans.

Russ got out of the seat, having to twist over a cowling, and jerked a thumb at Nye to take over. They switched every half hour because after that you couldn't stay alert. Zoti was asleep in the back. He envied her. He had caught some down time but his nerves got to him after a few hours.

"Helmet," he called. Russ pulled his on and watched Nye zip up. Zoti slept with hers on, following orders. The pleasure of being under pressure was hard to give up.

He climbed out the broken back hatch. Nye had riddled it but the pressure seal inside self-healed. Russ used hand-holds to scramble onto the corrugated top of the truck. He could see much further from here. Watching the rumpled hills reassured him somehow. Scrunched down below, staring out a slit, it was too easy to imagine Feds creeping up on them.

Overhead, Jupiter eclipsed the sun. The squat pink watermelon planet seemed to clasp the hard point of white light in a rosy glow, then swallowed it completely. Now Europa's white, cracked crescent would be the major light in the sky for three-and-a-half hours, he calculated. A rosy halo washed around the rim of Jupiter's atmosphere as sunlight refracted through the transparent outer layers.

He wished he could get the crazy, whirling geometry of this place straight in his head. The Feds had knocked down all navsats, and he couldn't stay on the air long enough to call for a position check with the carrier. This truck was carrying them away from Hiruko Station, he thought. It would be reassuring to get some sort of verification, though. No pickup mission would risk coming in close to Hiruko.

He took out his Fujitsu transponder and tapped into the external power jack. He had no idea where the carrier was now so he just aimed the pistol-grip antenna at the sky and got off a quick microwave MAYDAY burst. That was all the carrier needed to know they were alive, but getting a fix on them would be tough.

Job done, he sat and watched the slow swirling dance of the sky. No flashes, so maybe the battle was over. Only for a while, though. Neither side was going to give up the inner moons.

Russ grinned, remembering how just a few years back some of his Earthside buddies had said a real war out here was pointless. Impossible, too.

Too far away, they said. Too hard.

Even after the human race had moved into the near-Earth orbits, scattering their spindly factories and cylinder-cities and rock-hopping entrepreneurs, the human race was dominated by nay-saying groundhogs.

Sure, they had said, space worked. Slinging airtight homes into orbit at about one astronomical unit's distance from the sun was—in retrospect—an obvious step. After all, there was a convenient moon nearby to provide mass and resources.

But Earth, they said, was a benign neighborhood. You could resupply most outposts within a few days. Except for the occasional solar storm, when winds of high energy particles lashed out, the radiation levels were low. There was plenty of sunshine to focus with mirrors, capture in great sheets of conversion wafers, and turn into bountiful, high quality energy.

But Jupiter? Why go *there*?

Scientific teams had already touched down on the big moons in the mid twenty-first century, even dipped into the thick atmosphere. By counting craters and taking core samples, they deduced what they could about how the solar system evolved. After that brief era of quick-payoff visits, nobody had gone back. One big reason, everyone was quick to point out, was the death rate in those expeditions: half never saw Earth again, except as a distant blue-white dot.

Scientists don't tame new worlds; pioneers do. And except for the bands of religious or political refugee/fanatics, pioneers don't do it for nothing.

By 2050 humans had already begun to spread out of the near-Earth zone. The bait was the asteroids—big tumbling lodes of metal and rock, rich in heavy elements. These flying mountains could be steered slowly from their looping orbits and brought into near-Earth rendezvous. The delta-V wasn't all that large.

There, smelters melted them down and fed the factories steady streams of precious raw materials: manganese, platinum, cadmium, chromium, molybdenum, tellurium, vanadium, tungsten, and all the rare metals. Earth was running out of these, or else was unwilling to pollute its biosphere to scratch the last fraction out of the crust. Processing metals was messy and dangerous. The space factories could throw their waste into the solar wind, letting the gentle push of protons blow it out to the stars.

For raw materials, corporations like Mosambi and Kundusu grub-staked loners who went out in pressurized tin cans, sniffing with their spectrometers at the myriad chunks. Most of them were duds, but a rich lode of vanadium, say, could make a haggard, antisocial rockrat into a wealthy man. Living in zero-gravity craft wasn't particularly healthy, of course. You had to scramble if a solar storm blew in, and crouch behind an asteroid for shelter. Most rock-hoppers disdained the heavy shielding that would ward off cosmic rays, figuring that their stay would be short and lucky, so the radiation damage wouldn't be fatal. Many lost that bet.

One thing they could not do without, though, was food and air. That proved to be the pivot-point that drove mankind still further out.

Life runs on the simplest chemicals. A closed artificial biosphere is basically a series of smoldering fires: hydrogen burns with oxygen to give water; carbon burns into carbon dioxide, which plants eat; nitrogen combines in the soil so the plants can make proteins, enabling humans to be smart enough to arrange all this artificially.

The colonies that swam in near-Earth orbits had run into this problem early. They needed a steady flow of organic matter and liquids to keep their biospheres balanced. Supply from Earth was expensive. A better solution was to search out the few asteroids which had significant carbonaceous chondrites—rock rich in light elements: hydrogen, oxygen, carbon, nitrogen.

There were surprisingly few. Most were pushed painfully back to Earth orbit and gobbled up by the colonies.

By the time the rockhoppers needed light elements, the asteroid belt had been picked clean.

Besides, bare rock is unforgiving stuff. Getting blood from a stone was possible in the energy-rich cylinder cities. The loose, thinly spread coalition of prospectors couldn't pay the stiff bills needed for a big-style conversion plant.

From Ceres, the largest asteroid, Jupiter loomed like a candy-striped beacon, far larger than Earth. The rockrats lived in the broad band between two and three astronomical units out from the sun—they were used to a wan, diminished sunshine, and had already been tutored in the awful cold. For them it was no great leap to Jove, hanging there 5.2 times further from the sun than Earth.

They went for the liquids. Three of the big moons—Europa, Ganymede, and Callisto—were immense iceballs. True, they circled endlessly the most massive planet of all, 318 times the mass of Earth. That put them deep down in a gravitational well. Still, it was far cheaper to send a robot ship coasting out to Jupiter, and looping into orbit around Ganymede, than it was to haul water up from the oceans of Earth. The first stations set up on Ganymede were semi-automatic—meaning a few unlucky souls had to tend the machinery.

And here came some of that machinery now.

Russ slid back and lay down on the truck's flat roof. Ahead a team of robos was digging away. They had a hodgepodge of tracks and arms and didn't look dangerous. The biggest one threw out a rust-red stream of ore which the others were sampling.

One of the old exploration teams, then. He hoped they'd just ignore the truck.

"What'll we do?" Nye whispered over comm.

"Shut up," Russ answered.

The truck seemed to hesitate, deciding whether to grind over to the robos. A small robo noticed this and came rolling over on balloon tires.

Russ froze. This robo looked intelligent. It was probably the team leader and could relay an alarm.

Still lying flat, Russ wormed his way over to the edge of the truck roof. He brought his heavy pilot's hands forward and waited, hoping he blended into the truck's profile.

The robo seemed to eye the truck with swiveling opticals. The truck stopped. The robo approached, extended a telescoping tube. Gingerly it began to insert this into the truck's external socket.

Russ watched the robo's opticals focus down on its task. Then he hit it carefully in the electrical cowling. His hand clanged on the copper cowling and dented it. The robo jerked, snatching back its telescope arm.

The robo was quick. It backed away on its wobbly wheels, but just a little too fast. They spun. It slewed around on the ice.

Russ jumped down while the robo was looking the other way. It might already be transmitting an image. He hit the cowling again and then pried up the copper sheet metal. With two fingers he sheared off three bundles of wire.

The robo stopped. Its external monitor rippled with alarm lights. Russ cut some more and the alarms went off. MECHANICAL DAMAGE, the robo's status digitals said.

The other robos just kept on studying the soil.

Zoti was coming out of the rear hatch when he climbed back on the truck. "Back inside," he said. "Let's go."

They got away fast. Those robos had been easy only because no Feds had gotten around to reprogramming them.

Soon enough, somebody would. They were in for a long war out here. He could feel it in his bones.

Trouble was, Earthly interests swung plenty of weight—and mass—even out here. The old north-south division of wealth and ability was mirrored in the solar system, though warped. The Southern Confederation Feds wanted a greater share of the Jovian wealth. So they had seized a few Northern Hemisphere ice-eating bases, like Hiruko Station. Those robos now labored for the Fed factories waiting in near-Earth orbit for the ore.

The shock of actual war, of death in high vacuum and biting, unearthly cold—that had reverberated through Earthside politics, exciting public horror and private thrills.

Earth had long been a leafy preserve, over-policed and under-armed. Battle and zesty victory gave the great publics of the now-docile planet a twinge of exquisite, forbidden sin.

Here was a gaudy arena where civilized cultures could slug it out, all the while bitterly decrying the beastly actions, the unforgivable atrocities, the inevitable horrific mischances.

And watch it all on 3D. In full, glossy color.

The economic motivations sank beneath the waves of eager surrogate participation. Unfortunately, the two were not so easily separated in the Jovian system. The first troops guarded the automatic plants on the moons. Thus they and the plants became first targets for the fleets that came accelerating into the system. Bucks blended with blood. Hiruko Station was the first to fall to the Feds. Now the only way to root them out was to blast the surface, hoping the ice mines would escape most of the damage. That had been *Asskicker II*'s job.

Russ wished he could get news of the fighting. Radio gave only meaningless coded buzzes, flittering through the hiss of the giant Van Allen belts. News would have distracted him from his other preoccupation: food. He kept remembering sizzling steaks and crisp fries and hot coffee so black you had to sip it slow.

Already he had to be careful in dividing up their rations. Last meal, Nye and Zoti had gotten into a petty argument about half a cereal bar. They knew there wasn't much left, even with the packs of Kitsov and Columbard.

He rode along, not minding the cold yet, thinking about fried eggs and bacon. Zoti came topside. She had been weapons officer and she shared his dislike of the cramped, blind cabin, even if it was warm. They were used to fighting from a cockpit, enveloped in 3D graphics, living in an all-seeing electronic world.

"I could do without this mud-hugger stuff," Zoti said on short-range suit comm.

"Mud, now that I'd like," Russ said.

"Yeah, this ice gets to me. Brrrr! Pretty, though."

Russ studied the gray-blue valley they were entering. Gullies cut the slopes. Fans of rusty gravel spread from them across the rutted, rolling canyon floor. It did have a certain stern beauty. "Hadn't noticed."

"Wouldn't mind living here."

He blinked. "Really?"

"Look, I grew up in a ten-meter can. Rockrats for parents."

"How you like this grav?"

"A seventh of a g? Great. More than I ever got on a tether."

"Your parents ever hit it big?"

"Last time I was home, we still measured out our water in cc's."

He waved at an ice tower they were passing. He hadn't been able to figure whether they were eroded remnants or some kind of extrusion, driven by the oddities of ice tectonics. "So to you this is real wealth."

"Sure." She gave him a quizzical glance. "What else is better'n ice? You can make air with it, burn the deuterium for power, grow crops—even swim."

"You ever done that?"

"In grav? Naw—but I sneaked into the water reserve tanks at Ceres once. Strangest thing I ever did."

"Like it better than zero g?"

She nodded enthusiastically. "*Every*thing's better in gravs."

"Everything?"

"Well," she gave him a veiled glance. "I haven't tried everything yet."

He smiled. "Try Earth normal sometime."

"Yeah, I heard it's pretty bad. But grav keeps everything steady. It *feels* better."

He had wrenched his back carrying the fusion warhead and felt a twinge from it as the truck lumbered through a depression. "Not so's I'd notice," he said moodily.

"Hey, cheer up. This's a holiday, compared to fighting."

"This *is* fighting. Just slow-motion, is all."

"I love it, ice and gravs."

"Could do with some better rations." It was probably not a good idea to bring up food, but Russ was trying to find a way to keep the talk going. For the first time he was feeling differently about Zoti.

"Hell, at least we got plenty water."

The truck lurched again and Russ grunted despite himself. "Maybe we should carve out some more?"

"Sure," she said lightheartedly. "I'm getting so I can spot the pure water. Tastes better'n cruiser supply."

"Wait'll we get onto the flat. Don't want this truck to speed up and leave you behind."

"Take it off auto." They had already nearly left Zoti once when she laser-cut some water ice.

"Don't want the risk. We override, probably'll show up in a control system back at Hiruko."

"I don't think the Feds have had time to interface all these systems. Those Dagos don't know zip."

"They took Hiruko pretty easy."

"Snuck up on it! Listen, those oily bastards—" and she was off on a tirade. Russ was a Norther, too, born and bred, but he didn't have much feeling about political roots that ran back to lines drawn on Earth's old carcass. He listened to her go on about the filthy Feds and watched the lurching view and that was when he saw the bat.

It came over the far ice hills. Hard black against the slight haze of a yellow ammonia cloud, gliding when it could, jetting an ivory methane plume when it couldn't.

"Inside!" he whispered.

They scrambled off the truck roof. Zoti went in the rear hatch. He looked over the lip of the roof and saw the bat veer. It had seen them. It dove quickly, head on toward them.

The M18s were lashed to the roof. There wasn't time to get Zoti back out so he yanked an M18 free—making sure he got the one loaded with HE—and dropped off the back of the truck, slipping and landing on his ass. He stooped far over and ran by kicking back on the ice, so that he didn't bounce in the low gravity. He used the truck for cover while he got to the shelter of some jagged gray boulders.

It made one pass to confirm, sweeping in like an enormous thin bird, sensors swiveling. He wedged down among the rocks as it went over. It banked and turned quickly, coming back. Russ popped his helmet telescope out to full extension and saw that it carried rockets under the wings.

The bat lined up on the truck's tail and swooped down. It looked more like a kite from this angle, all airfoil and pencil-thin struts.

The bat was looking at the truck, not at him. He led it a full length and opened up with the HE shells. They bucked pretty bad and he missed with the first two rounds. The third caught it in the narrow fuselage. He saw the impact. Before he could grin a rocket fired from under the right wing and streaked straight for him, leaving an orange trail.

He ducked. The rocket fell short of the truck but close to him. The impact was like a sudden jar. He heard no sound, just found himself flat on his back. Mud and ice showered him.

The bat went on, not seeming to mind the gaping hole

in its thin fuselage, but it also didn't rise any more. Then it started a lazy pitch, yawed—and suddenly was tumbling end over end, like a thrown playing card.

It became a geyser of black fragments against a snowy hill.

5

Russ had caught all the right signals from her, he thought.

It was dumb, he knew that, and so did she. But somehow the tension in them had wound one turn too many and a mere glance between them set all the rest in motion.

Sure enough, as soon as Nye left by the forward hatch to reconn over the hill, Zoti started shucking her skinsuit. Then her thin green overalls.

He wasn't far behind her. They piled their clothes on the deck and got down on them. He suggested a sitting position but she would have none of it. She was feverish and buoyant in the muted phosphor glow of the cabin, swiveling on him with exuberant soft cries. Danger, sweat, piercing cold—all wedded into a quick, ferocious, hungry battering that they exacted from each other, rolling and licking and slamming among the machine-oil smells and rough iron rub. Fast and then mysteriously, gravely slow, as though their senses stretched time in pursuit of oblivion.

It was over at last and then maybe not and then definitely not and then, very fast this time, over for sure. They smiled at each other through a glaze of sweat and dirt.

"Lord!" she gasped. "The best!"

"Ever?" Frank disbelief.

"Sure . . ." She gave him a sly smile. "The first, too."

"Huh? Oh, you mean—"

"First in real gravity, sure."

"Gravity has a way of simplifying your choices."

"I guess. Maybe everything really is better in gravs."

"Deck of an autotruck isn't the best setting."

"Damn straight. We'll give it a try in someplace better."

"You got a date." He got to his knees and started pulling on his blue longjohns.

Automatically he reviewed their situation, shifting back into reality after a blissful time away. He replayed events, trying to see it whole, to look for problems, errors.

They had been forced to override the truck's controls. The bat had undoubtedly reported something, maybe even direct vid images of them. So Zoti and Nye had conferred over the board and got the truck off its designated route.

They left the marked track and ground gears to work their way up among the jagged hills. An hour later two bats came zooming over. By that time Nye had gotten the truck back into a cave. They had left the snow two klicks back, picking their way over rocky ridges, so the bats had no tracks to follow.

They sat there edgily while the bats followed a search pattern, squaring off the valley and then other valleys, gradually moving away.

That had given Russ time to think and get hungry and eat. They didn't have much food left. Or time. Unless the Norther fleet kept Hiruko busy, the Feds would have time to send a thorough, human-led search party.

So they had to change tactics. But keep warm.

Hiruko probably had this truck identified by now.

Which meant they needed another truck. Fast.

Once they'd broken the code seal on the truck's guidance, they had access to general tracking inventory. Nye had found the nearest truck, about fifteen kilometers away. They had edged out of the cave when an ivory fog came easing in from the far range of rumpled mountains.

The truck moved pretty fast when its cautious nav programs were bypassed. They had approached the target truck at an angle, finally lying in wait one hill over from its assigned path.

And when Nye went out to reconn the approaching

truck, Russ and Zoti had taken one swift look at each other, one half-wild glance, and had seized the time.

Nye came back through the hatch as Zoti tucked her black hair into her neck ring.

"It's coming. No weapons visible." Nye looked from Zoti to Russ, puzzled.

Russ realized he was still flushed and sweaty. "Good," he said energetically. "Let's hit it."

"Better hurry," Nye said, his face narrowing again as he concentrated on tactics. "It just loaded up at a mine."

"Okay. Come out and help me on with my pack," Russ said.

Nye looked surprised. "You still gonna carry that warhead?"

Russ nodded. "Regs."

"Look, we gotta *move*. Nobody'd expect—"

"You want to pay for it when we get back?"

Nye shrugged. "Your hassle, man."

"Right," Russ said evenly.

The second truck was moving stolidly down a narrow canyon. It had the quality of a bumbling insect, dutifully doing its job.

"Flank it?" Zoti asked as they watched the truck's approach.

"Okay," Russ said. "You two take it from the sides, just after it passes."

"And you?" Nye asked sarcastically.

"Hit it right where the canyon necks in. See? I'll come in from the top."

It had finally occurred to him that the light gravity opened the choices of maneuver. He leaped from the nearest ledge, arcing out over the canyon and coming down on the top of the truck.

Zoti and Nye fired at the rear hatch, rounds skipping off the thick gray iron. A fighting machine, Class II infantry, popped out the front hatch.

It clanked and swiveled awkwardly. It had heavy guns

built into both arms and started spraying the rear of the
truck, chipping the metal corners. It hadn't registered Russ
yet. When it did a small gun popped out of the machine's
top and fired straight at him. He shot the machine three
times and it tumbled over and broke in half.

Russ didn't get to see it fall. A heavy round went
through his shoulder. It sent a white-hot flower of agony
through him and knocked him off the truck. He landed on
his neck.

6

Ironies abounded here. Once a sleepy beach town
devoted to the elixirs of sun and surf, Huntington
Beach's major problem had been the traffic trying
to reach the sand on Saturday afternoons. Now the
problem was stopping the Pacific from getting to the
people.

Tina was thinking furiously, her brow knitted sternly,
when the Orange County observation dirigible came
humming into view, skimming over a stucco apartment
complex. The silvery bullet gleamed in the dawn's
crisp radiance.

Nguyen, the head of the Federal Emergency Management Agency, called her on comm and ordered
them to come up. Tina had never liked the ride up
the spindly cable, but this time she was so interested
in the spectacle she scarcely noticed. In the gondola
beneath the great silvery belly Nguyen stood stiffly
watching the disaster below.

He was short, intense, direct. His first words were,
"What happened?"

"Something structural," Tina said. "I want to look at
the whole dike from the sea side."

"Okay." He gestured to the pilot. The dirigible purred
and moved sluggishly seaward. "Should I declare an
emergency all along the line?"

"Wait'll I think this through. And check this out." She handed him a flake of concrete with a dab of the gray goo on it.

"From here?" Nguyen sniffed at it.

"You've got a portable chem lab in the next deck, right?"

"Yes, but this is plainly an engineering malfunction. What—"

"Just do it."

She put off further questions by moving to the windows. The dark waters reached far inland to Talbert Avenue, sweeping north as far as the wetlands where the Naval Weapons Depot had been. Most buildings had their first floors submerged. Trees ringed most buildings as energy-conserving measures—shade in summer, shelter against cool winds in winter.

She thought wryly about how linked the human predicament was. The worldwide greenhouse effect had forced energy conservation to save burning oil. Global warming had also made the oceans expand and melted ice at the poles, bringing on this flood. And now people were perched in the trees, keeping dry. Maybe the hominids should never have left the trees in the first place.

The dirigible swooped along the dike's northward curve. They could stay up here forever, burning minimal fuel, another saving measure mandated by the Feds. As they swung lower Tina picked out the pale green of the biofilm protectant which was regularly applied to the dike's outer ramparts.

She asked Alvarez, "Anything new about that last painting?"

He consulted his portable data screen. "Nope. Supposed to be better, was all."

"How?"

"Stops barnacles and stuff from eatin' away at the concrete."

"Just a cleaner?"

"Lays down a mat, keeps stuff from growin'."

Now she recalled. Tina knew little about biotechnology, but she understood as an engineer what corrosive seawater did. Biofilm was a living safeguard that stopped sea life from worming its way into porous concrete. It pre-empted surfaces, colonizing until it met like biofilm, forming a light green shield which lasted years.

"See those splotches?" She pointed at the sea bulwarks near the break in the dike. Gray spots marred the green biofilm.

Nguyen asked, "Seaweed?"

"Wrong color."

Alvarez frowned. "How could li'l microorganisms . . . ?"

"Burrowing back into cracks, growing, forcing them open," Tina said, though her voice was more certain than she felt.

Nguyen countered, "But this product has been tested for over a decade."

"Maybe it's changed?" Alvarez asked.

Nguyen shook his head. "You said this last painting was even better. I don't see how—"

"Look," Tina said, "biotech isn't just little machines. It's *alive.*"

"So?" Nguyen asked.

"Life keeps changing. It evolves. Mutates."

Nguyen blinked, disconcerted. "At this one spot?"

"Some microbe goes awry, starts eating concrete," Tina said. "And reproduces itself—there're plenty of nutrients in seawater."

The chemlab report came in then, appearing on the central screen beside the pilot's chair. Even she, an engineer, could see the gray goo wasn't the same as the biofilm.

"We're right," Nguyen said.

She eyed the long curve of the dike toward Long

Beach, where offshore wedges protected the beaches. Vast stretches of anchored defenses. Were all these great earthworks being chewed up by the very biotech engineered to protect them? Ironies abounded today.

"Perhaps this is a local mutation," Nguyen said.

"For now, yes," Tina said.

"Means the product's vulnerable, though," Alvarez said, his eyebrows knitted together in worry. "Happened here, could happen anywhere. Those dikes they're puttin' in the Potomac, right by the Lincoln monument, f'instance."

Tina looked inland, where the monumental energies of Orange County had filled in the spaces left by 'quake damage. The Big One and the greenhouse effect had hardly slowed down these people.

Their gesture of uncowed exuberance rose in Irvine to the south: the Pyramid. Four-sided and the size of the Pharaohs' tombs, but inverted. Its peak plunged into the ground like an impossible arrowhead, gossamer steel and glass, supported at the corners by vertical burnt-chrome columns. Impossible but eerily real, catching the cutting sunrise glow. Its refracting radiance seemed to uplift the toylike buildings that groveled around it.

A brown splotch coated one side of the Pyramid. She saw that it was one of the new biofilm cleaners, working its way around the Pyramid while it absorbed dirt and tarnish. Could that moving carpet go awry, too? Weaken the walls?

"There's going to be plenty of questions to answer," she said distantly.

"Be expensive to replace that biofilm," Nguyen said. "But essential, to avoid such incidents."

"How much you figure this little 'incident' will cost?" Alvarez asked.

"Five, six billion."

"Really?" Tina was surprised. "Six billion Yen?"

"Or more," Nguyen said.

Tina hoped there were few dead. This whole incident was dumb, because somebody should have foreseen this biotech weakness. But engineers could not foresee everything, anymore than geologists could predict earthquakes. Technology was getting to be as vast and imponderable as natural forces. The world kept handing your dreams back to you as reworked nightmares.

But they had no choice but to use technology— imperfect, human crafts, undaunted gestures before the infinite. The county lived by that belief, and today some died by it. But she knew in her bones that these people blessed by sun and ocean would keep on.

7

Russ still had to shake his head to jerk himself out of the sunny, airy spaces of Huntington Beach. He had never been there, never even been in North America, but now he longed to be lying on a beach beneath a fireball sun.

Story-sleep wasn't supposed to cling to you like that. Maybe the extremity of his pain had screwed up the effects. Zoti had given him the sleepstory plug in an effort to supplement the autodoc as it worked on him. He could feel the hours of repair work in his left shoulder socket. A patch job, but at least the worst of the pain had ebbed.

Worse, his own memories were warped when he tried to review them. He blinked and could not bring the stale, sweaty cabin into focus. He knew Nye was saying something, but he couldn't make out what it was.

A single picture flitted through his mind. He had crashed in *Asskicker II*, but not on Ganymede. Saturn hung in the black behind the ship. And his helmet was metal, no faceplate. Comically, a road sign pointed to Earthly destinations.

Disturbing. Was the sleepstory intruding into his longterm memory? Rewriting his life, rubbing out some features, heightening others? He would have to watch himself. If the other two caught on, he wouldn't have much conviction as a commander.

Not that he had a whole lot right now. His head dipped with fatigue and he barely caught himself before his chin struck his chest. He wiped feverish sweat from his eyes with a claw-hand.

Nye, yes, Nye was talking. What . . . ?

"Actually," Nye said with a sly sort of humor, "that shoulder may not be the worst news you got."

Russ let his head clear. He was not in a terrific mood. Nye's wit went unremarked. "What?"

"I got a readout on this truck's itinerary. Didn't have to bust into the command structure to do it, either." Nye grinned proudly.

"Great." His neck hurt worse than his shoulder. The truck's rumbling, shifting progress seemed to provoke jabbing pains all down his spine. The bandage over his shoulder wound pulled and stung. Aside from this he was merely in a foul mood.

"We're going to Hiruko Station," Nye said. "Drop off the ore."

"Well, that doesn't matter," Zoti said. "We'll just jump off somewhere."

Russ nodded blearily. His mouth was dry and he didn't feel like talking. "Right. Steal another. Play musical trucks with the Feds."

"Better hurry. We're less than twenty klicks from Hiruko."

"What?" Russ barked.

Zoti's mouth made a precise, silent O.

"Looks like you had us pointing the wrong way all along," Nye said, his humor dissolving into bitterness.

Russ made himself take a breath. "Okay. Okay."

There didn't seem much more to say. He had probably screwed up the coordinates, gotten something backward. Or maybe the first truck took a turn that fouled up his calculations.

It didn't matter. Excuses never did, not unless you got back to the carrier and a board of inquiry decided they wanted to go over you with a microscope.

Zoti said carefully, "So close—they will pick us up easily if we leave the truck."

"Yeah," Nye said. "I say we ride this truck in and give up. Better'n freezing our tails, maybe get shot at, then have to give up anyway."

"We bail out now," Russ said.

"You hear what I said?" Nye leaned over Russ, trying to intimidate him. "That's *dumb!* They'll—"

Russ caught him in the face with a right cross that snapped Nye's head around and sent him sprawling. For once his pilot's hands were an advantage, heavy and hard.

Russ was sitting on the floor of the truck cabin and he didn't want to bother to get up. He also wasn't all that sure that he could even throw a punch while standing anyway. So when Nye's eyes clouded and the big man came at him Russ kicked Nye in the face, lifting his boot from the deck and catching Nye on the chin. Nye fell face down on the deck. Russ breathed deeply and waited for his neck to stop speaking to him. By that time Zoti was standing over Nye with a length of pipe. He waved her away.

"Now, I'm going to pretend you just slipped and banged your head," Russ said evenly. "Because we got to get out of here fast and I don't want to have to shoot you for insubordination or cowardice in the face of the enemy or any of those other lawyer's reasons. That would take time and we don't have time. So we just go on like you never did anything. Got that?"

Nye opened his mouth and then closed it. Then he nodded.

"Do you . . ." Zoti hesitated. "Do you think we *can* get away?"

"We don't have to," Russ said. "We just have to hide."

"Hide and freeze," Nye said sourly. "How's the carrier gonna—"

"We won't hide long. How much time will it take this truck to reach Hiruko?"

"Three, maybe four hours. It's going to a smelting plant on the rim of the first bubble. I—"

"Close enough for government work," Russ said. He felt infinitely tired and irritable and yet he knew damn well he was going to have to stay awake until all this was done.

Zoti said, "Are you sure you can . . . ?"

He breathed in the stale cabin air. The world veered and whirled.

"No, matter of fact, I'm not."

8

The fusion warhead went off prettily on the far horizon. A brilliant flash, then a bulging yellow-white ball.

Nye had rigged the trigger to go if anybody climbed through the hatch. He further arranged a small vid eye and stuck it into the truck's grille, so they got a good look at the checkpoint which stopped the truck. It was within sight of the rearing, spindly towers of Hiruko Station. The town was really rather striking, Russ thought. Some of the towers used deep blue ice in their outer sheaths, like spouts of water pointing eternally at Jupiter's fat face.

Too bad it all had to go, he thought. The three of them were lying beneath an overhang, facing Hiruko. They ducked their heads when they saw a Fed officer scowl at the truck, walk around it, then pop the forward hatch. He looked like just the officious sort Russ hated, the kind that always gigged him on some little uniform violation just as he was leaving base on a pass.

So he couldn't help grinning mirthlessly when the flash lit the snow around them. The warhead was a full 1.2 megs. Of course it was supposed to be a klick-high air burst, designed to take out the surface structures and Feds and leave the mines. This was a ground-pounder and it sent a wave they watched coming toward them across the next valley. He didn't have time to get to his feet so he just rolled out from under the ledge. The wave slammed into their hill and he felt a soft thump nearby. Then the sound slapped him hard and he squeezed his eyes shut against the pain in his neck.

When he opened them Zoti was looking into his face anxiously. He grinned. She sat in the snow and grinned back saucily.

He looked beyond her. The hill had folded in a little and the ledge wasn't there any more. Neither was Nye.

If it had just been snow that fell on him they might have had some chance. He had gotten partway out from under the ledge, nearly clear. But solid ice and some big rocks had come down on him and there wasn't any hope. They dug him out anyway. It seemed sort of pointless because then all they could think to do was bury him again.

The bomb cloud over Hiruko dispersed quickly, most of the radioactive debris thrown clear off the moon.

Russ recalled their crash of only a few days before. It seemed to lie far back in a curiously constricted past. Now anything was possible.

His memory was still stained by the dislocations he had suffered under sleep-story, though. Sometimes, when he looked out of the corner of his eye, he would seem to see that woman, her tanned face creased by a studious frown. Tina, triumphant engineer. People like her were holding the sad, fat Earth together.

While people like himself fought over the baubles of the outer solar system. Was that what his scrambled memory meant? A foreshadowing of himself, standing on a moon of Saturn? Could the war spread that far, leaving him with a steel skull?

He shook his head. Tina would not leave him.

He had always liked historical sleepstories, the immersion in a simpler time. But maybe no era was simple. They only looked that way from a distance. The way cities looked better at night, because you couldn't see the dirt.

They sat in a protected gully, soaking up what sunlight there was, and waited. As a signal beacon the fusion burst couldn't be beat. Carrier ships came zooming over within an hour.

A survey craft slipped in low on the horizon a little later. Only when it was in sight did Zoti produce the rest of their food. They sat on a big flat orange rock and ate the gluelike bars through their helmet input slots. It tasted no better than usual but nobody cared. They were talking about gravity and its myriad delights.

9

Tina settled into bed, the crisp white sheets caressing her with a velvety touch. The long day was finally over, though crews still worked under floodlights all along the coast. But her job was basically done.

Now the biotech jocks were on the hot plate. The media were making a big deal out of the incident. She had turned down three network interviews already.

She ached for sleep, especially after her long, luxuriant bath. Rachel came in with herbal tea to soothe her further.

But she needed something more. Languidly she reached for the sleep-story module and slipped its pressors to the base of her neck. This would plunge her to the deepest realm of slumber.

Which plotline? Logic said that after the day's events she should choose something soothing. She cocked an eyebrow at the choices. A strong storyline, maybe, with a virile male protagonist. She liked someone she could identify with.

She liked war stories and science fiction. Maybe a combination . . .

She thumbed in her choice and lay back with a sensual sigh.

Music, soft at first, then simmering with dissonant strains of tension.

She was on a bleak, rutted plain. A smashed ship lay behind her and cold bit through her thin skinsuit. Jupiter churned on the rumpled gray horizon. She glanced down at her hands, which already ached from the chill, and found that they were four-fingered clamps.

This is going to be quite an adventure, she thought.

FIRE ZONE EMERALD

Lucius Shepard

"Fire Zone Emerald" was purchased by Gardner Dozois, and appeared in the November 1986 issue of Asimov's *with an illustration by J. K. Potter. It was one of a long string of Shepard stories—more than a dozen sales to* Asimov's *since his debut sale here in 1984—that have made him one of the mainstays of the magazine. You'll see why in the story that follows, a hard-hitting but oddly evocative look at the interplay between faith and survival in the midst of war.*

Lucius Shepard may well have been the most popular and influential new writer of the '80s, rivaled for that title only by William Gibson, Connie Willis, and Kim Stanley Robinson. Shepard won the John W. Campbell Award in 1985 as the year's Best New Writer, and no year since has gone by without him adorning the final ballot for one major award or another, and often for several. In 1987, he won the Nebula Award for his landmark novella "R & R"—an IAsfm story—and in 1988 he picked up a World Fantasy Award for his monumental short-story collection The Jaguar Hunter. *His first novel was the acclaimed* Green Eyes; *his second the bestselling* Life During Wartime; *he is at work on several more. His latest books are a new collection,* The Ends of the Earth, *and a new novel,* Kalimantan. *Born in Lynchberg, Virginia, he now lives in Seattle, Washington.*

"Ain't it weird, soldier boy?" said the voice in Quinn's ear. "There you are, strollin' along in that little ol' green suit of armor, feelin' all cool and killproof . . . and wham! You're down and hurtin' bad. Gotta admit, though, them suits do a job. Can't recall nobody steppin' onna mine and comin' through it as good as you."

Quinn shook his head to clear the cobwebs. His helmet rattled, which was not good news. He doubted any of the connections to the computer in his backpack were still intact. But at least he could move his legs, and that was very good news, indeed. The guy talking had a crazed lilt to his voice, and Quinn thought it would be best to take cover. He tried the computer; nothing worked except for map holography. The visor display showed him to be a blinking red dot in the midst of a contoured green glow: eleven miles inside Guatemala from its border with Belize; in the heart of the Peten Rain Forest; on the eastern edge of Fire Zone Emerald.

"Y'hear me, soldier boy?"

Quinn sat up, wincing as pain shot through his legs. He felt no fear, no panic. Though he had just turned twenty-one, this was his second tour in Guatemala, and he was accustomed to being in tight spots. Besides, there were a lot worse places he might have been stranded. Up until two years before, Emerald had been a staging area for Cuban and guerrilla troops; but following the construction of a string of Allied artillery bases to the west, the enemy had moved their encampments north and—except for recon patrols such as Quinn's—the fire zone had been abandoned.

"No point in playin' possum, man. Me and the boys'll be there in ten-fifteen minutes, and you gonna have to talk to us then."

Ten minutes. Shit! Maybe, Quinn thought, if he talked to the guy, that would slow him down. "Who are you people?" he asked.

"Name's Mathis. Special Forces, formerly attached to the First Infantry." A chuckle. "But you might say we seen the light and opted outta the service. How 'bout you, man? You gotta name?"

"Quinn. Edward Quinn." He flipped up his visor; heat boiled into the combat suit, overwhelming the cooling system. The suit was scorched and shredded from the knees down; plastic armor glinted in the rips. He looked around for his gun. The cable that had connected it to the computer had been severed, probably by shrapnel from the mine, and the gun was not to be seen. "You run across the rest of my patrol?"

A static-filled silence. " 'Fraid I got bad tidin's, Quinn Edward. 'Pears like guerrillas took out your buddies."

Despite the interference, Quinn heard the lie in the voice. He scoped out the terrain. Saw that he was sitting in a cathedral-like glade: vaults of leaves pillared by the tapering trunks of ceibas and giant figs. The ground was carpeted with ferns; a thick green shade seemed to be welling from the tips of the fronds. Here and there, shafts of golden light penetrated the canopy, and these were so complexly figured with dust motes that they appeared to contain flaws and fracture planes, like artifacts of crystal snapped off in mid-air. On three sides, the glade gave out into dense jungle; but to the east lay a body of murky green water, with a forested island standing about a hundred feet out. If he could find his gun, the island might be defensible. Then a few days rest and he'd be ready for a hike.

"Them boys wasn't no friends of yours," said Mathis. "You hit that mine, and they let you lie like meat on the street."

That much Quinn believed. The others had been too wasted on the martial arts ampules to be trustworthy. Chances were they simply hadn't wanted the hassle of carrying him.

"They deserved what they got," Mathis went on. "But you, now . . . boy with your luck. Might just be a place for you in the light."

"What's that mean?" Quinn fumbled a dispenser from his hip pouch and ejected two ampules—a pair of silver bullets—into his palm. Two, he figured, should get him walking.

"The light's holy here, man. You sit under them beams shinin' through the canopy, let 'em soak into you, and they'll stir the truth from your mind." Mathis said all this in dead-earnest, and Quinn, unable to mask his amusement, said, "Oh, yeah?"

"You remind me of my ol' lieutenant," said Mathis. "Man used to tell me I's crazy, and I'd say to him, 'I ain't ordinary crazy, sir. I'm crazy-gone-to-Jesus.' And I'd 'splain to him what I knew from the light, that we's s'posed to build the kingdom here. Place where a man could live pure. No machines, no pollution." He grunted as if tickled by something. "That's how you be livin' if you can cut it. You gonna learn to hunt with knives, track tapir by the smell. Hear what weather's comin' by listenin' to the cry of a bird."

"How 'bout the lieutenant?" Quinn asked. "He learn all that?"

"Y'know how it is with lieutenants, man. Sometimes they just don't work out."

Quinn popped an ampule under his nose and inhaled. Waited for the drugs to kick in. The ampules were the Army's way of insuring that the high incidence of poor battlefield performance during the Vietnam War would not be repeated: each contained a mist of pseudo-endorphins and RNA derivatives that elevated the user's determination and physical potentials to heroic levels for thirty minutes or thereabouts. But Quinn preferred not to rely on them, because of their destructive side-effects. Printed on the dispenser was a warning against abuse, one that Mathis— judging by his rap—had ignored. Quinn had heard similar raps from guys whose personalities had been eroded, replaced in part by the generic mystic-warrior personality supplied by the drugs.

" 'Course," said Mathis, breaking the silence, "it ain't only the light. It's the Queen. She's one with the light."

"The Queen?" Quinn's senses had sharpened. He could see the spidery shapes of monkeys high in the canopy and could hear a hundred new sounds. He spotted the green plastic stock of his gun protruding from beneath a fern not twenty feet away; he came to his feet, refusing to admit to his pain, and went over to it. Both upper and lower barrels were plugged with dirt.

" 'Member them Cuban 'speriments where they was linkin' up animals and psychics with computer implants? Usin' 'em for spies?"

"That was just bullshit!" Quinn set off toward the water. He felt disdain for Mathis and recognized that to be a sign of too many ampules.

"It ain't no bullshit. The Queen was one of them psychics. She's linked up with this little ol' tiger cat. What the Indians call a *tigrillo*. We ain't never seen her, but we seen the cat. And once we got tuned to her, we could feel her mind workin' on us. But at first she can slip them thoughts inside your head without you ever knowin'. Twist you 'round her finger, she can."

"If she's that powerful," said Quinn, smug with the force of his superior logic, "then why's she hidin' from you?"

"She ain't hidin'. We gotta prove ourselves to her. Keep the jungle pure, free of evildoers. Then she'll come to us."

Quinn popped the second ampule. "Evildoers? Like my patrol, huh? That why you wasted my patrol?"

"Whoo-ee!" said Mathis after a pause. "I can't slide nothin' by you, can I, Quinn Edward?"

Quinn's laughter was rich and nutsy: a two-ampule laugh. "Naw," he said, mocking Mathis' cornpone accent. "Don't reckon you can." He flipped down his visor and waded into the water, barely conscious of the pain in his legs.

"Your buddies wasn't shit for soldiers," said Mathis. "Good thing they come along, though. We was runnin' low on ampules." He made a frustrated noise. "Hey, man. This armor ain't nothin' like the old gear . . . all this computer bullshit. I can't get nothin' crankin' 'cept the radio. Tell me how you work these here guns."

"Just aim and pull." Quinn was waist-deep in water, perhaps a quarter of the way to the island, which from that perspective—with its three towering vine-enlaced trees—looked like the overgrown hulk of an old sailing ship anchored in a placid stretch of jade.

"Don't kid a kidder," said Mathis. "I tried that."

"You'll figure it out," Quinn said. "Smart peckerwood like you."

"Man, you gotta attitude problem, don'tcha? But I 'spect the Queen'll straighten you out."

"Right! The Invisible Woman!"

"You'll see her soon enough, man. Ain't gonna be too long 'fore she comes to me."

"To *you*?" Quinn snickered. "That mean you're the king?"

"Maybe." Mathis pitched his voice low and menacing. "Don't go thinkin' I'm just country pie, Quinn Edward. I been up here most of two years, and I got this place down. I can tell when a fly takes a shit! Far as you concerned, I'm lord of the fuckin' jungle."

Quinn bit back a sarcastic response. He should be suckering this guy, determining his strength. Given that Mathis had been on recon prior to deserting, he'd probably started with around fifteen men. "You guys taken many casualties?" he asked after slogging another few steps.

"Why you wanna know that? You a man with a plan? Listen up, Quinn Edward. If you figgerin' on takin' us out, 'member them fancy guns didn't help your buddies, and they ain't gonna help you. Even if you could take us out, you'd still have to deal with the Queen. Just 'cause she lives out on the island don't mean she ain't keepin' her eye on the shore. You might not believe it, man, but right now, right this second, she's all 'round you."

"What island?" The trees ahead suddenly seemed haunted-looking.

"Little island out there on the lake. You can see it if you lift your head."

"Can't move my head," said Quinn. "My neck's fucked up."

"Well, you gonna see it soon enough. And once you healed, you take my advice and stay the hell off it. The Queen don't look kindly on trespassers."

On reaching the island, Quinn located a firing position from which he could survey the shore: a weedy patch behind a fallen tree trunk hemmed in by bushes. If Mathis was as expert in jungle survival as he claimed, he'd have no trouble in discovering where Quinn had gone; and there was no way to tell how strong an influence his imaginary Queen exerted, no way to be sure whether the restriction against trespassing had the severity of a taboo or was merely something frowned on. Not wanting to take chances, Quinn spent a frantic few minutes cleaning the lower barrel of his gun, which fired miniature fragmentation grenades.

"Now where'd you get to, Quinn Edward?" said Mathis with mock concern. "Where *did* you get to?"

Quinn scanned the shore. Dark avenues led away between the trees, and staring along them, his nerves were keyed by every twitching leaf, every shift of light and shadow. Clouds slid across the sun, muting its glare to a shimmering platinum gray; a palpable vibration underscored the stillness. He tried to think of something pleasant to make the waiting easier, but nothing pleasant occurred to him. He wetted his lips and swallowed. His cooling system set up a whine.

Movement at the margin of the jungle, a shadow resolving into a man wearing olive-drab fatigues and carrying a rifle with a skeleton stock . . . likely an old AR-18. He waded into the lake, and as he closed on the island, Quinn trained his scope on him and saw that he had black shoulder-length hair framing a haggard face; a ragged beard bibbed his chest and dangling from a thong below the beard was a triangular piece of mirror. Quinn held his fire, waiting for the rest to emerge. But no one else broke cover, and he realized that Mathis was testing him, was willing to sacrifice a pawn to check out his weaponry.

"Keep back!" he shouted. But the man kept plodding forward, heaving against the drag of the water. Quinn marveled at the hold Mathis must have over him: he *had* to know he was going to die. Maybe he was too whacked out on ampules to give a shit, or maybe Mathis' Queen somehow embodied the promise of a swell afterlife for those who died in battle. Quinn didn't want to kill him, but there was no choice, no point in delaying the inevitable.

He aimed, froze a moment at the sight of the man's fear-widened eyes; then he squeezed the trigger.

The hiss of the round blended into the explosion, and the man vanished inside a fireball and geysering water. Monkeys screamed; birds wheeled up from the shoreline trees. A veil of oily smoke drifted across the lake, and within seconds a pair of legs floated to the surface, leaking red. Quinn felt queasy and sick at heart.

"Man, they doin' wonders with ordinance nowadays," said Mathis.

Infuriated, Quinn fired a spread of three rounds into the jungle.

"Not even close, Quinn Edward."

"You're a real regular army asshole, aren't you?" said Quinn. "Lettin' some poor fucker draw fire."

"You got me wrong, man! I sent that ol' boy out 'cause I loved him. He been with me almost four years, but his mind was goin', reflexes goin'. You done him a favor, Quinn Edward. Reduced his confusion to zero"—Mathis' tone waxed evangelic—"and let him shine forevermore!"

Quinn had a mental image of Mathis, bearded and haggard like the guy he'd shot, but taller, rawboned: a gaunt rack of a man with rotting teeth and blown-away pupils. Being able to fit even an imaginary face to his target turned his rage higher, and he fired again.

"Awright, man!" Mathis' voice was burred with anger; the cadences of his speech built into a rant. "You want bang-bang, you got it. But you stay out there, the Queen'll do the job for me. She don't like nobody creepin' 'round her in the dark. Makes her crazy. You go on, man! Stay there! She peel you down to meat and sauce!"

His laughter went high into a register that Quinn's speakers distorted, translating it as a hiccuping squeal, and he continued to rave. However, Quinn was no longer listening. His attention was fixed on the dead man's legs spinning past on the current. A lace of blood eeled from the severed waist. The separate strands looked to be spelling out characters in some oriental script; but before Quinn could try to decipher them, they lost coherence and were whirled away by the jade green medium into which— staring with fierce concentration, giddy with drugs and fatigue—he, too, felt he was dissolving.

At twilight, when streamers of mist unfurled across the water, Quinn stood down from his watch and went to find a secure place in which to pass the night: considering Mathis' leeriness about his Queen's nocturnal temper, he doubted there would be any trouble before morning. He beat his way through the brush and came to an enormous ceiba tree whose trunk split into two main branchings; the split formed a wide crotch that would support him comfortably. He popped an ampule to stave off pain, climbed up and settled himself.

Darkness fell; the mist closed in, blanketing moon and stars. Quinn stared out into pitch-black nothing, too exhausted to think, too buzzed to sleep. Finally, hoping to stimulate thought, he did another ampule. After it had

taken effect, he could make out some of the surrounding
foliage—vague scrolled shapes that each had their own
special shine—and he could hear a thousand plops and
rustles that blended into a scratchy percussion, its rhythms
providing accents for a pulse that seemed to be coming up
from the roots of the island. But there were no crunchings
in the brush, no footsteps.

No sign of the Queen.

What a strange fantasy, he thought, for Mathis to have
created. He wondered how Mathis saw her. Blond, with
a ragged Tarzan-movie skirt? A black woman with a
necklace of bones? He remembered driving down to see
his old girlfriend at college and being struck by a print
hung on her dorm room wall. It had shown a night jungle,
a tiger prowling through fleshy vegetation, and—off to
the side—a mysterious-looking woman standing naked in
moonshadow. That would be his image of the Queen. It
seemed to him that the woman's eyes had been glowing. . . . But maybe he was remembering it wrong, maybe
it had been the tiger's eyes. He had liked the print, had
peered at the artist's signature and tried to pronounce the
name. "Roo-see-aw," he'd said, and his girl had given a
haughty sniff and said, "Roo-sō. It's Roo-sō." Her attitude
had made clear what he had suspected: that he had lost
her. She had experienced a new world, one that had set its
hooks in her; she had outgrown their little North Dakota
farming town, and she had outgrown him as well. What
the war had done to him was similar, only the world he
had outgrown was a much wider place: he'd learned that
he just wasn't cut out for peace and quiet anymore.

Frogs chirred, crickets sizzled, and he was reminded of
the hollow near his father's house where he had used to go
after chores to be alone, to plan a life of spectacular adven-
tures. Like the island, it had been a diminutive jungle—
secure, yet not insulated from the wild—and recognizing
the kinship between the two places caused him to relax.
Soon he nodded out into a dream, one in which he was

twelve years old again, fiddling with the busted tractor his father had given him to repair. He'd never been able to repair it, but in the dream he worked a gruesome miracle. Wherever he touched the metal, blood beaded on the flaking rust; blood surged rich and dark through the fuel line; and when he laid his hands on the corroded pistons, steam seared forth and he saw that the rust had been transformed into red meat, that his hands had left scorched prints. Then that meat-engine shuddered to life and lumbered off across the fields on wheels of black bone, ploughing raw gashes in the earth, sowing seeds that overnight grew into fiery stalks yielding fruit that exploded on contact with the air.

It was such an odd dream, forged from the materials of his childhood yet embodying an alien sensibility, that he came awake, possessed by the notion that it had been no dream but a sending. For an instant he thought he saw a lithe shadow at the foot of the tree. The harder he stared at it, though, the less substantial it became, and he decided it must have been a hallucination. But after the shadow had melted away, a wave of languor washed over him, sweeping him down into unconsciousness, manifesting so suddenly, so irresistibly, that it seemed no less a sending than the dream.

At first light, Quinn popped an ampule and went to inspect the island, stepping cautiously through the gray mist that still merged jungle and water and sky, pushing through dripping thickets and spiderwebs diamonded with dew. He was certain that Mathis would launch an attack today. Since he had survived a night with the Queen, it might be concluded that she favored him, that he now posed a threat to Mathis' union with her . . . and Mathis wouldn't be able to tolerate that. The best course, Quinn figured, would be to rile Mathis up, to make him react out of anger and to take advantage of that reaction.

The island proved to be about a hundred and twenty

feet long, perhaps a third of that across at the widest, and—except for a rocky point at the north end and a clearing some thirty feet south of the ceiba tree—was choked with vegetation. Vines hung in graceful loops like flourishes depended from illuminated letters; ferns clotted the narrow aisles between the bushes; epiphytes bloomed in the crooks of branches, punctuating the grayness with points of crimson and purple. The far side of the island was banked higher than a man could easily reach; but to be safe, Quinn mined the lowest sections with frags. In places where the brush was relatively sparse, he set flares head-high, connecting them to trip-wires that he rigged with vines. Then he walked back and forth among the traps, memorizing their locations.

By the time he had done, the sun had started to burn off the mist, creating pockets of clarity in the gray, and, as he headed back to his firing position, it was then he saw the tiger cat. Crouched in the weeds, lapping at the water. It wasn't much bigger than a housecat, with the delicate build and wedge-shaped head of an Abyssinian, and fine black stripes patterning its tawny fur. Quinn had seen such animals before while on patrol, but the way this one looked, so bright and articulated in contrast to the dull vegetable greens, framed by the eddying mist, it seemed a gateway had been opened onto a more vital world, and he was for the moment too entranced by the sight to consider what it meant. The cat finished its drink, turned to Quinn and studied him; then it snarled, wheeled about and sprang off into the brush.

The instant it vanished, Quinn became troubled by a number of things. How he'd chosen the island as a fortress; how he'd gone straight to the best firing position; how he'd been anticipating Mathis. All this could be chalked up to common sense and good soldiering . . . yet he had been so assured, so definite. The assurance could be an effect of the ampules; but then Mathis had said the Queen could slip thoughts into your head without you knowing. Until you became attuned to her, that is. Quinn tasted the flavors of his thoughts, searching for evidence of tampering. He knew he was being ridiculous, but panic flared in him nonetheless and he popped an ampule to pull himself together. Okay, he told himself. Let's see what the hell's going on.

For the next half hour he combed the island, prying into thickets, peering at treetops. He found no trace of the Queen, nor did he spot the cat again. But if she could control his mind, she might be guiding him away from her traces. She might be following him, manipulating him like a puppet. He spun around, hoping to catch her unawares. Nothing. Only bushes threaded with mist, trembling in the breeze. He let out a cracked laugh. Christ, he was an idiot! Just because the cat lived on the island didn't mean the Queen was real; in fact, the cat might be the core of Mathis' fantasy. It might have inhabited the lakeshore, and when Mathis and his men had arrived, it had fled out here to be shut of them . . . or maybe even this thought had been slipped into his head. Quinn was amazed by the subtlety of the delusion, at the elusiveness with which it defied both validation and debunking.

Something crunched in the brush.

Convinced that the noise signaled an actual presence, he swung his gun to cover the bushes. His trigger-finger tensed, but after a moment he relaxed. It was the isolation, the general weirdness, that was doing him in. Not some bullshit mystery woman. His job was to kill Mathis, and he'd better get to it. And if the Queen *were* real, well, then she did favor him and he might have help. He popped an ampule and laughed as it kicked in. Oh, yeah! With modern chemistry and the Invisible Woman on his side, he'd go through Mathis like a rat through cheese. Like fire through a slum. The drugs—or perhaps it was the pour of a mind more supple than his own—added a lyric coloration to his thoughts, and he saw himself moving with splendid athleticism into an exotic future wherein he killed the king and wed the shadow and ruled in Hell forever.

Quinn was low on frags, so he sat down behind the fallen tree trunk and cleaned the upper barrel of his gun: it fired caseless .22 caliber ammunition. Set on automatic, it could chew a man in half; but wanting to conserve bullets, he set it to fire single shots. When the sun had cleared the treeline, he began calling to Mathis on his radio. There was no response at first, but finally a gassed, irascible voice answered, saying, "Where the fuck you at, Quinn Edward?"

"The island." Quinn injected a wealth of good cheer into his next words. "Hey, you were right about the Queen!"

"What you talkin' 'bout?"

"She's beautiful! Most beatiful woman I've ever seen."

"You seen her?" Mathis sounded anxious. "Bullshit!"

Quinn thought about the Rousseau print. "She got dark, satiny skin and black hair down to her ass. And the whites of her eyes, it looks like they're glowin' they're so bright. And her tits, man. They ain't too big, but the way they wobble around"—he let out a lewd cackle—"it makes you wanna get down and frolic with them puppies."

"Bullshit!" Mathis repeated, his voice tight.

"Unh-uh," said Quinn. "It's true. See, the Queen's lonely, man. She thought she was gonna have to settle for one of you lovelies, but now she's found somebody who's not so fucked up."

Bullets tore through the bushes on his right.

"Not even close," said Quinn. More fire; splinters flew from the tree trunk. "Tell me, Mathis." He supressed a giggle. "How long's it been since you had any pussy?" Several guns began to chatter, and he caught sight of a muzzle flash; he pinpointed it with his own fire.

"You son of a bitch!" Mathis screamed.

"Did I get one?" Quinn asked blithely. "What's the

matter, man? Wasn't he ripe for the light?"

A hail of fire swept the island. The cap-pistol sounds, the volley of hits on the trunk, the bullets zipping through the leaves, all this enraged Quinn, touched a spark to the violent potential induced by the drugs. But he restrained himself from returning the fire, wanting to keep his position hidden. And then, partly because it was another way of ragging Mathis, but also because he felt a twinge of alarm, he shouted, "Watch out! You'll hit the Queen!"

The firing broke off. "Quinn Edward!" Mathis called.

Quinn kept silent, examining that twinge of alarm, trying to determine if there had been something un-Quinnlike about it.

"Quinn Edward!"

"Yeah, what?"

"It's time," said Mathis, hoarse with anger. "Queen's tellin' me it's time for me to prove myself. I'm comin' at you, man!"

Studying the patterns of blue-green scale flecking the tree trunk, Quinn seemed to see the army of his victims—grim, desanguinated men—and he felt a powerful revulsion at what he had become. But when he answered, his mood swung to the opposite pole. "I'm waitin', asshole!"

"Y'know," said Mathis, suddenly breezy. "I got a feelin' it's gonna come down to you and me, man. 'Cause that's how she wants it. And can't nobody beat me one-on-one in my own backyard." His breath came as a guttural hiss, and Quinn realized that this sort of breathing was typical of someone who had been overdoing the ampules. "I'm gonna overwhelm you, Quinn Edward," Mathis went on. "Gonna be like them ol' Jap movies. Little men with guns actin' all brave and shit 'til they see somethin' big and hairy comin' at 'em, munchin' treetops and spittin' fire. Then off they run, yellin', 'Tokyo is doomed!' "

For thirty or forty minutes, Mathis kept up a line of chatter, holding forth on subjects as varied as the Cuban space station and Miami's chances in the AL East. He launched into a polemic condemning the new statutes protecting the rights of prostitutes ("Part of the kick's bein' able to bounce 'em 'round a little, y'know."), then made a case for Antarctica being the site of the original Garden of Eden, and then proposed the theory that every President of the United States had been a member of a secret homosexual society ("Half them First Ladies wasn't nothin' but guys in dresses."). Quinn didn't let himself be drawn into conversation, knowing that Mathis was trying to distract him; but he listened because he was beginning to have a sense of Mathis' character, to understand how he might attack.

Back in Lardcan, Tennessee or wherever, Mathis had likely been a charismatic figure, glib and expansive, smarter than his friends and willing to lead them from the rear into fights and petty crimes. In some ways he was a lot like the kid Quinn had been, only Quinn's escapades had been pranks, whereas he believed Mathis had been capable of consequential misdeeds. He could picture him lounging around a gas station, sucking down brews and plotting meanness. The hillbilly con-artist out to sucker the Yankee: that would be how he saw himself in relation to Quinn. Sooner or later he would resort to tricks. That was cool with Quinn; he could handle tricks. But he wasn't going to underestimate Mathis. No way. Mathis had to have a lot on the ball to survive the jungle for two years, to rule a troop of crazed Green Berets. Quinn just hoped Mathis would underestimate him.

The sun swelled into an explosive glare that whitened the sky and made the green of the jungle seem a livid, overripe color. Quinn popped ampules and waited. The inside of his head came to feel heavy with violent urges, as if his thoughts were congealing into a lump of mental plastique. Around noon, somebody began to lay down

covering fire, spraying bullets back and forth along the
bank. Quinn found he could time these sweeps, and after
one such had passed him by, he looked out from behind
the tree trunk. Four bearded, long-haired men were crossing the lake from different directions. Plunging through
the water, lifting their knees high. Before ducking back,
Quinn shot the two on the left. Saw them spun around,
their rifles flung away. He timed a second sweep, then
picked off the two on the right; he was certain he had
killed one, but the other might only have been wounded. The gunfire homed in on him, trimming the bushes
overhead. Twigs pinwheeled; cut leaves sailed like paper
planes. A centipede had ridden one of the leaves down and
was still crawling along its fluted edge. Quinn didn't like
its hairy mandibles, its devil's face. Didn't like the fact
that it had survived while men had not. He let it crawl
in front of his gun and blew it up into a fountain of dirt
and grass.

The firing stopped.

Branches ticking the trunk; water slopping against the
bank; drips. Quinn lay motionless, listening. No unnatural
noises. But where were those drips coming from? The
bullets hadn't splashed up much water. Apprehensions
spidered his backbone. He peeked up over the top of the
tree trunk . . . and cried out in shock. A man was standing
in the water about four feet away, blocking the line of
fire from the shore. With the mud freckling his cheeks,
strands of bottomweed ribboning his dripping hair, he
might have been the wild mad king of the lake. Skull-face;
staring eyes; survival knife dangling loosely in his hand.
He blinked at Quinn. Swayed, righted himself, blinked
again. His fatigues were plastered to his ribs, and a big
bloodstain mapped the hollow of his stomach. Fresh blood
pumped from the hole Quinn had punched. The man's
cheeks bulged: it looked as if he wanted to speak but

was afraid more would come out than just words.

"Jesus . . . shit," he said sluggishly. His eyes half-rolled back, his knees buckled. Then he straightened, glancing around as if waking somewhere unfamiliar. He appeared to notice Quinn, frowned and staggered forward, swinging the knife in a lazy arc.

Quinn got off a round before the man reached him. The bullet seemed to paste a red star under the man's eye, stamping his features with a rapt expression. He fell atop Quinn, atop the gun, which—jammed to automatic—kept firing. Lengths of wet hair hung across Quinn's faceplate, striping his view of branches and sky; the body jolted with the bullets tunneling through.

Two explosions nearby.

Quinn pushed the body away, belly-crawled into the brush and popped an ampule. He heard a *thock* followed by a bubbling scream: somebody had tripped a flare. He did a count and came up with nine dead . . . plus the guy laying down covering fire. Mathis, no doubt. It would be nice if that were all of them, but Quinn knew better. Somebody else was out there. He felt him the way a flower feels the sun—autonomic reactions waking, primitive senses coming alert.

He inched deeper into the brush. The drugs burned bright inside him; he had the idea they were forming a manlike shape of glittering particles, an inner man of furious principle. Mattes of blight-dappled leaves pressed against his faceplate, then slid away with underwater slowness. It seemed he was burrowing through a mosaic of muted colors and coarse textures into which even the concept of separateness had been subsumed, and so it was that he almost failed to notice the boot: a rotting brown boot with vines for laces. Visible behind a spray of leaves about six feet off. The boot shifted, and Quinn saw an olive-drab trouserleg tucked into it.

His gun was wedged beneath him, and he was cer-

tain the man would move before he could ease it out.
But apparently the man was playing bird dog, his senses
straining for a clue to Quinn's whereabouts. Quinn lined
the barrel up with the man's calf just above the boottop.
Checked to make sure it was set on automatic. Then he
fired, swinging the barrel back and forth an inch to both
sides of his center mark.

Blood erupted from the calf, and a hoarse yell was
drawn out of Quinn by the terrible hammering of the
gun. The man fell screaming. Quinn tracked fire across
the ground, and the screams were cut short.

The boot was still standing behind the spray of leaves,
now sprouting a tattered stump and a shard of bone.

Quinn lowered his head, resting his faceplate in the dirt.
It was as if all his rectitude had been spat out through the
gun. He lay thoughtless, drained of emotion. Time seemed
to collapse around him, burying him beneath a ton of
decaying seconds. After a while a beetle crawled onto the
faceplate, walking upside-down; it stopped at eye-level,
tapped its mandibles on the plastic and froze. Staring at
its grotesque underparts, Quinn had a glimpse into the
nature of his own monstrosity: a tiny armored creature
chemically programmed to a life of stalking and biting,
and between violences, lapsing into a stunned torpor.

"Quinn Edward?" Mathis whispered.

Quinn lifted his head; the beetle dropped off the faceplate
and scurried for cover.

"You got 'em all, didn'tcha?"

Quinn wormed out from under the bush, got to his feet
and headed back to the fallen tree trunk.

"Tonight, Quinn Edward. You gonna see my knife
flash . . . and then fare-thee-well." Mathis laughed softly.
"It's me she wants, man. She just told me so. Told me I
can't lose tonight."

Late afternoon and Quinn went about disposing of the
dead. It wasn't something he would ordinarily have done,

yet he felt compelled to be rid of them. He was too
weary to puzzle over the compulsion and merely did as
it directed, pushing the corpses into the lake. The man
who had tripped the flare was lying in some ferns, his
face seared down to sinew and laceworks of cartilage;
ants were stitching patterns across the blood-slick bone
of the skull. Having to touch the body made Quinn's flesh
nettle cold, and bile flooded his throat.

That finished, he sat in the clearing south of the ceiba
and popped an ampule. The rays of sunlight slanting
through the canopy were as sharply defined as lasers,
showing greenish-gold against the backdrop of leaves.
Sitting beneath them, he felt guided by no visionary purpose; he was, however, gaining a clearer impression of the
Queen. He couldn't point to a single thought out of the
hundreds that cropped up and say, that one, that's hers.
But as if she were filtering his perceptions, he was coming
to know her from everything he experienced. It seemed the
island had been stepped in her, its mists and midnights
modified by her presence, refined to express her moods;
even its overgrown terrain seemed to reflect her nature:
shy, secretive, yet full of gentle stirrings. Seductive. He
understood now that the process of becoming attuned to
her was a process of seduction, one you couldn't resist
because you, too, were being steeped in her. You were
forced into a lover's involvement with her, and she was
a woman worth loving. Beautiful . . . and strong. She'd
needed that strength in order to survive, and that was
why she couldn't help him against Mathis. The life she
offered was free from the terrors of war, but demanded
vigilance and fortitude. Though she favored him—he was
sure of that—his strength would have to be proved. Of
course Mathis had twisted all this into a bizarre reli-
gion . . .

Christ!

Quinn sat up straight. Jesus fucking Christ! He was

really losing it. Mooning around like some kid fantasizing about a movie star. He'd better get his ass in gear, because Mathis would be coming soon. Tonight. It was interesting how Mathis—knowing his best hope of taking Quinn would be at night—had used his delusion to overcome his fear of the dark, convincing himself that the Queen had told him he would win . . . or maybe she *had* told him.

Fuck that, Quinn told himself. He wasn't that far gone.

A gust of wind roused a chorus of whispery vowels from the leaves. Quinn flipped up his visor. It was hot, cloudless, but he could smell rain and the promise of a chill on the wind. He did an ampule. The drugs withdrew the baffles that had been damping the core of his anger. Confidence was a voltage surging through him, keying new increments of strength. He smiled, thinking about the fight to come, and even that smile was an expression of furious strength, a thing of bulked muscle fibers and trembling nerves. He was at the center of strength, in touch with every rustle, his sensitivity fueled by the light-stained brilliance of the leaves. Gazing at the leaves, at their infinite shades of green, he remembered a line of a poem he'd read once: " . . . *green flesh, green hair, and eyes of coldest silver . . .* " Was that how the Queen would be? If she were real? Transformed into a creature of pure poetry by the unearthly radiance of Fire Zone Emerald. Were they all acting out a mythic drama distilled from the mundane interactions of love and war, performing it in the flawed heart of an immense green jewel whose reality could only be glimpsed by those blind enough to see beyond the chaos of the leaves into its precise facets and fractures? Quinn chuckled at the wasted profundity of his thought and pictured Mathis dead, himself the king of that dead man's illusion, robed in ferns and wearing a leafy crown.

High above, two wild parrots were flying complicated

loops and arcs, avoiding the hanging columns of light as if they were solid.

Just before dusk, a rain squall swept in, lasting only a few minutes but soaking the island. Quinn used it for cover, moving about and rigging more flares. He considered taking a stand on the rocky point at the north end: it commanded a view of both shores, and he might get lucky and spot Mathis as he crossed. But it was risky— Mathis might spot *him*—and he decided his best bet would be to hide, to outwait Mathis. Waiting wasn't Mathis' style. Quinn went back to the ceiba tree and climbed past the crotch to a limb directly beneath an opening in the canopy, shielded by fans of leaves. He switched his gun to its high explosive setting. Popped an ampule. And waited.

The clouds passed away south, and in the half-light the bushes below seemed to assume topiary shapes. After fifteen minutes, Quinn did another ampule. Violet auras faded in around ferns, pools of shadow quivered, and creepers looked to be slithering like snakes along the branches. A mystic star rose in the west, shining alone above the last pink band of sunset. Quinn stared at it until he thought he understood its sparkling message.

The night that descended was similar to the one in the Rousseau print, with a yellow globe moon carving geometries of shadow and light from the foliage. A night for tigers, mysterious ladies, and dark designs. Barnacled to his branch, Quinn felt that the moonlight was lacquering his combat gear, giving it the semblance of ebony armor with gilt filigree, enforcing upon him the image of a knight about to do battle for his lady. He supposed it was possible that such might actually be the case. It was true that his perception of the Queen was growing stronger and more particularized; he even thought he could tell where she was hiding: the rocky point. But he doubted he could trust the perception . . . and besides, the battle itself, not its motive, was the significant thing. To reach that peak moment when perfection drew blood, when you muscled confusion aside and—as large as a constellation with the act, as full of stars and blackness and primitive meaning—you were able to look down onto the world and know you had outperformed the ordinary. Nothing, neither an illusory motive or the illusion of a real motive, could add importance to that.

Shortly after dark, Mathis began to chatter again, regaling Quinn with anecdote and opinion, and by the satisfaction in his voice, Quinn knew he had reached the island. Twenty minutes passed, each of them ebbing away, leaking out of Quinn's store of time like blood dripping from an old wound. Then a burst of white incandescence to the south, throwing vines and bushes into skeletal silhouette . . . and with it a scream. Quinn smiled. The scream had been a dandy imitation of pain, but he wasn't buying it. He eased a flare from his hip pouch. It wouldn't take long for Mathis to give this up.

The white fire died, muffled by the rain-soaked foliage, and finally Mathis said, "You a cautious fella, Quinn Edward."

Quinn popped two ampules.

"I doubt you can keep it up, though," Mathis went on. "I mean, sooner or later you gotta throw caution to the winds."

Quinn barely heard him. He felt he was soaring, that the island was soaring, arrowing through a void whose sole feature it was and approaching the moment for which he had been waiting: a moment of brilliant violence to illuminate the flaws at the heart of the stone, to reveal the shadow play. The first burn of the drugs subsided, and he fixed his eyes on the shadows south of the ceiba tree.

Tension began to creep into Mathis' voice, and Quinn was not surprised when—perhaps five minutes later—he heard the stutter of AR-18: Mathis firing at some movement in the brush. He caught sight of a muzzle flash, lifted his gun. But the next instant he was struck by an overpowering sense of the Queen, one that shocked him with its suddenness.

She was in pain. Wounded by Mathis' fire.

In his mind's eye, Quinn saw a female figure slumped against a boulder, holding her lower leg. The wound wasn't serious, but he could tell she wanted the battle to end before worse could happen.

He was mesmerized by her pervasiveness—it seemed if he were to flip up his visor, he would breathe her in—and by what appeared to be a new specificity of knowledge about her. Bits of memory were surfacing in his thoughts; though he didn't quite believe it, he could have sworn they were hers: a shanty with a tin roof amid fields of tilled red dirt; someone walking on a beach; a shady place overhung by a branch dripping with orchids, with insects scuttling in and out of the blooms, mining some vein of sweetness. That last memory was associated with the idea that it was a place where she went to daydream, and Quinn felt an intimate resonance with her, with the fact that she—like him—relied on that kind of retreat.

Confused, afraid for her yet half-convinced that he had slipped over the edge of sanity, he detonated his flare, aiming it at the opening in the canopy. An umbrella of white light bloomed overhead. He tracked his gun across eerily lit bushes and . . . there! Standing in the clearing to the south, a man wearing combat gear. Before the man could move, Quinn blew him up into marbled smoke and flame. Then, his mind ablaze with victory, he began to shinny down the branch. But as he descended, he realized that something was wrong. The man had just stood there, made no attempt to duck or hide. And his gun. It had been like Quinn's own, not an AR-18.

He had shot a dummy or a man already dead!

Bullets pounded his back, not penetrating but knocking him out of the tree. Arms flailing, he fell into a bush. Branches tore the gun from his grasp. The armor deadened the impact, but he was dazed, his head throbbing. He clawed free of the bush just as Mathis' helmeted shadow—looking huge in the dying light of the flare—crashed through the brush and drove a rifle stock into his faceplate. The plastic didn't shatter, webbing over with cracks; but by the time Quinn had recovered, Mathis was straddling him, knees pinning his shoulders.

"How 'bout that?" said Mathis, breathing hard.

A knife glinted in his hand, arced downward and thudded into Quinn's neck, deflected by the armor. Quinn heaved, but Mathis forced him back and this time punched at the faceplate with the hilt of the knife. Punched again, and again. Bits of plastic sprayed Quinn's face, and the faceplate was now so thoroughly cracked, it was like looking up through a crust of glittering rime. It wouldn't take many more blows. Desperate, Quinn managed to roll Mathis onto his side and they grappled silently. His teeth bit down on a sharp plastic chip and he tasted blood. Still grappling, they struggled to their knees, then to their feet. Their helmets slammed together. The impact came as a hollow click over Quinn's radio, and that click seemed to switch on a part of his mind that was as distant as a flare, calm and observing; he pictured the two of them to be black giants with whirling galaxies for hearts and stars articulating their joints, doing battle over the female half of everything. Seeing it that way gave him renewed strength. He wrangled Mathis off-balance, and they reeled clumsily through the brush. They fetched up against the trunk of the ceiba tree, and for a few seconds they were frozen like wrestlers muscling for an advantage. Sweat poured down Quinn's face; his arms quivered. Then Mathis tried to butt his faceplate, to

finish the job he had begun with the hilt of the knife.
Quinn ducked, slipped his hold, planted a shoulder in
Mathis' stomach and drove him backward. Mathis twisted
as he fell, and Quinn turned him onto his stomach. He
wrenched Mathis' knife-arm behind his back, pried the
knife loose. Probed with the blade, searching for a seam
between the plates of neck armor. Then he pressed it in
just deep enough to prick the skin. Mathis went limp.
Silent.

"Where's all the folksy chit-chat, man?" said Quinn,
excited.

Mathis maintained his silent immobility, and Quinn
wondered if he had snapped, gone catatonic. Maybe he
wouldn't have to kill him. The light from the flare had
faded, and the moon-dappled darkness that had filled in
reminded Quinn of the patterns of blight on the island
leaves: an infection at whose heart they were clamped
together like chitinous bugs.

"Bitch!" said Mathis, suddenly straining against
Quinn's hold. "You lied, goddamn you!"

"Shut up," said Quinn, annoyed.

"Fuckin' bitch!" Mathis bellowed. "You tricked me!"

"I said to shut up!" Quinn gave him a little jab, but
Mathis began to thrash wildly, nearly impaling himself,
shouting, "Bitch!"

"Shut the fuck up!" said Quinn, growing angrier but
also trying to avoid stabbing Mathis, beginning to feel
helpless, to feel that he would have to stab him, that it
was all beyond his control.

"I'll kill you bitch!" screamed Mathis. "I'll . . ."

"Stop it!" Quinn shouted, not sure to whom he was
crying out. Inside his chest, a fuming cell of anger was
ready to explode.

Mathis writhed and kicked. "I'll cut out your
fuckin' . . ."

Poisonous burst of rage. Mandibles snipping shut, Quinn

shoved the knife home. Blood guttered in Mathis' throat. One gauntleted hand scrabbled in the dirt, but that was all reflexes.

Quinn sat up feeling sluggish. There was no glory. It had been a contest essentially decided by a gross stupidity: Mathis' momentary forgetfulness about the armor. But how could he have forgotten? He'd seen what little effects bullets had. Quinn took off his helmet and sucked in hits of the humid air. Watched a slice of moonlight jiggle on Mathis' faceplate. Then a blast of static from his helmet radio, a voice saying, " . . . you copy?"

"Ain't no friendlies in Emerald," said another radio voice. "Musta been beaners sent up that flare. It's a trap."

"Yeah, but I got a reading like infantry gear back there. We should do a sweep over that lake."

Chopper pilots, Quinn realized. But he stared at the helmet with the mute awe of a savage, as if they had been alien voices speaking from a stone. He picked up the helmet, unsure what to say.

Please, no . . .

The words had been audible, and he realized that she had made him hear them in the sighing of the breeze.

Static fizzling. " . . . get the hell outta here."

The first pilot again. "Do you copy? I repeat, do you copy?"

What, Quinn thought, if this had all been the Queen's way of getting rid of Mathis, even down to that last flash of anger, and now, now that he had done the job, wouldn't she get rid of him?

Please, stay . . .

Quinn imagined himself back in Dakota, years spent watching cattle die, reading mail order catalogues, drinking and drinking, comparing the Queen to the dowdy farmgirl he'd have married, and one night getting a little too morbidly weary of that nothing life and driving out onto the flats and riding the forty-five caliber express to nowhere. But at least that was proven, whereas this . . .

Please . . .

A wave of her emotion swept over him, seeding him with her loneliness and longing. He was truly beginning to know her now, to sense the precise configurations of her moods, the stoicism underlying her strength, the . . .

"Fuck it!" said one of the pilots.

The static from Quinn's radio smoothed to a hiss, and the night closed down around him. His feeling of isolation nailed him to the spot. Wind seethed in the massy crown of the ceiba, and he thought he heard again the whispered word *Please*. An icy fluid mounted in his spine. To shore up his confidence, he popped an ampule, and soon the isolation no longer troubled him, but rather seemed to fit about him like a cloak. This was the path he had been meant to take, the way of courage and character. He got to his feet, unsteady on his injured legs, and eased past Mathis, slipping between two bushes. Ahead of him, the night looked to be a floating puzzle of shadow and golden light: no matter how careful he was, he'd never be able to locate all his mines and flares.

But she would guide him.

Or would she? Hadn't she tricked Mathis? Lied to him?

More wind poured through the leaves of the ceiba tree, gusting its word of entreaty, and intimations of pleasure, of sweet green mornings and soft nights, eddied up in the torrent of her thoughts. She surrounded him, undeniable, as real as perfume, as certain as the ground beneath his feet.

For a moment he was assailed by a new doubt. God, he said to himself. Please don't let me be crazy. Not just ordinary crazy.

Please . . .

Then, suffering mutinies of the heart at every step, repelling them with a warrior's conviction, he moved through the darkness at the center of the island toward the rocky point, where—her tiger crouched by her feet, a ripe jungle moon hanging above like the emblem of her mystique—either love or fate might be waiting.

HOME FRONT

James Patrick Kelly

*"Home Front" was purchased by Gardner Dozois,
and appeared in the June 1988 issue of* Asimov's
*with an illustration by J. K. Potter. Kelly has been
one of the mainstays of* Asimov's *for nearly a decade now, under several different editors, and has
enjoyed the unique distinction of having had a story in every June issue of* Asimov's *since 1983.
He made his first sale in 1975, and went on to
become one of the most respected and prominent
new writers of the '80s; indeed, Kelly stories such
as "Solstice," "The Prisoner of Chillon," "Glass
Cloud," and "Mr. Boy" must be ranked among the
most inventive and memorable short works of the
decade. Kelly's novels include* Planet of Whispers,
Freedom Beach *(a novel written in collaboration
with John Kessel), and, most recently,* Look into
the Sun. *Born in Mineola, New York, Kelly now
lives with his family in Portsmouth, New Hampshire,
where he's reported to be at work on a third solo
novel,* Wildlife.*

Here he shows us that not all battles are fought
on the battleground; some are won—or lost—con-
siderably closer to home. . . .*

"Hey, Genius. What are you studying?"

Will hunched his shoulders and pretended not to hear. He had another four pages to review before he could test. If he passed, then he wouldn't have to log onto eighth grade again until Wednesday. He needed a day off.

"What are you, deaf?" Gogolak nudged Will's arm. "Talk to me, Genius."

"Don't call me that."

"Come on, Gogo," said the fat kid, whose name Will had forgotten. He was older: maybe in tenth, more likely a dropout. Old enough to have pimples. "Let's eat."

"Just a minute," said Gogolak. "Seems like every time I come in here, this needle is sitting in this booth with his face stuck to a schoolcomm. It's ruining my appetite. What is it, math? Español?"

"History." Will thought about leaving, going home, but that would only postpone the hassle. Besides, his mom was probably still there. "The Civil War."

"You're still on that? Jeez, you're slow. I finished that weeks ago." Gogolak winked at his friend. "George Washington freed the slaves so they'd close school on his birthday."

The big kid licked his lips and eyed the menu above the vending wall at the rear of the Burger King.

"Lincoln," said Will. "Try logging on sometime, you might learn something."

"What do you mean? I'm logged on right now." Gogolak pulled the comm out of his backpack and thrust it at Will. "Just like you." The indicator was red.

"It doesn't count unless someone looks at it."

"Then you look at it, you're so smart." He tossed the comm onto the table and it slid across, scattering a pile of Will's hardcopy. "Come on, Looper. Get out your plastic."

Will watched Looper push his ration card into the french-fry machine. He and Gogolak were a mismatched pair. Looper was as tall as Will, at least a hundred and ninety centimeters; Looper, however, ran to fat, and Will looked like a sapling. Looper was wearing official Johnny America camouflage and ripped jeans. He didn't seem to be carrying a schoolcomm, which meant he probably was warbait. Gogolak was the smallest boy and the fastest mouth in Will's class. He dressed in skintight style; everyone knew that girls thought he was cute. Gogolak didn't have to worry about draft sweeps; he was under age and looked it, and his dad worked for the Selective Service.

Will realized that they would probably be back to bother him. He hit save so that Gogolak couldn't spoil his afternoon's work. When they returned to Will's booth, Looper put his large fries down on the table and immediately slid across the bench to the terminal on the wall. He stuck his fat finger into the coin return. Will already knew it was empty. Then Looper pressed select, and the tiny screen above the terminal lit up.

"Hey," he said to Will, "you still got time here."

"So?" But Will was surprised; he hadn't thought to try the selector. "I was logged on." He nodded at his comm.

"What did I tell you, Loop?" Gogolak stuffed Looper's fries into his mouth. "Kid's a genius."

Looper flipped channels past cartoons, plug shows, catalogs, freebies, music vids, and finally settled on the war. Johnny America was on patrol.

"Gervais buy it yet?" said Gogolak.

"Nah." Looper acted like a real fan. "He's not going to either; he's getting short. Besides, he's wicked smart."

The patrol trotted across a defoliated clearing toward a line of trees. With the sun gleaming off their helmets, they looked to Will like football players running a screen, except that Johnny was carrying a minimissile instead of a ball. Without warning, Johnny dropped to one knee and brought the launcher to his shoulder. His two range-finders fanned out smartly and trained their lasers on the

far side of the clearing. There was a flash; the jungle
exploded.

"Foom!" Looper provided the sound effects. "Yah,
you're barbecue, Pedro!" As a sapodilla tree toppled into
the clearing, the time on the terminal ran out.

"Too bad," Gogolak poured salt on the table and smeared
a fry in it. "I wanted to see the meat."

"Hey, you scum! That's my dinner." Looper snatched
the fries pouch from Gogolak. "You hardly left me any."

He shrugged. "Didn't want them to get cold."

"Stand-ins." A girl in baggy blue disposables stood at
the door and surveyed the booths. "Any stand-ins here?"
she called.

It was oldie Warner's granddaughter, Denise, who had
been evacuated from Texas and was now staying with
him. She was in tenth and absolutely beautiful. Her accent
alone could melt snow. Will had stood in for her before.
Looper waved his hand hungrily until she spotted them.

"Martin's just got the monthly ration of toilet paper,"
she said. "They're limiting sales to three per customer.
Looks like about a half-hour line. My grandpa will come
by at four-thirty."

"How much?" said Looper.

"We want nine rolls." She took a five out of her purse.
"A quarter for each of you."

Will was torn. He could always use a quarter and he
wanted to help her. He wanted her to ask his name. But
he didn't want to stand in line for half an hour with these
stupid jacks.

Gogolak was staring at her breasts. "Do I know you?"

"I may be new in town, sonny—" she put the five on
the table "—but you don't want to rip me off."

"Four-thirty." Gogolak let Looper take charge of the
money. Will didn't object.

Martin's was just next door to the Burger King. The line
wasn't bad, less than two aisles long when they got on.

There were lots of kids from school standing in, none of them close enough to talk to.

"Maybe she got tired of using leaves," said Gogolak.

Looper chuckled. "Who is she?"

"Seth Warner's granddaughter," said Will.

"Bet she's hot." Gogolak leered.

"Warner's a jack," said Looper. "Pig-faced oldie still drives a car."

Most of the shelves in aisle 2 were bare. There was a big display of government surplus powdered milk, the kind they loaded up with all those proteins and vitamins and tasted like chalk. It had been there for a week and only three boxes were gone. Then more empty space, and then a stack of buckets with no labels. Someone had scrawled "Korn Oil" on them: black marker on bare metal. At the end of the aisle was the freezer section, which was mostly jammed with packages of fries. Farther down were microwave dinners for the rich people. They wound past the fries and up aisle 3, at the end of which Will could see Mr. Rodenets, the stock boy, dispensing loose rolls of toilet paper from a big cardboard box.

"How hard you think it is to get chosen Johnny America?" Looper said. "I mean really."

"What do you mean, really?" said Gogolak. "You think J. A. is real?"

"People die. They couldn't fake that kind of stuff." Looper's face got red. "You watch enough, you got to believe."

"Maybe," Gogolak said. "But I bet you have to know someone."

Will knew it wasn't true. Gogolak just liked to pop other people's dreams. "Mr. Dunnell swears they pick the team at random," he said.

"Right," Gogolak said. "Whenever somebody gets dead."

"Who's Dunnell?" said Looper.

"Socialization teacher." Will wasn't going to let Gogolak run down Johnny America's team, no matter who his father was. "Most of them make it. I'll bet seventy percent at least."

"You think that many?" Looper nodded eagerly. "What I heard is they get discharged with a full boat. Whatever they want, for the rest of their lives."

"Yeah, and Santa is their best friend," Gogolak said. "You sound like recruiters."

"It's not like I'd have to be J. A. himself. I just want to get on his team, you know? Like maybe in body armor." Looper swept his arm down the aisle with robotic precision, exterminating bacon bits.

"If only you didn't have to join the army," said Will. Silence.

"You know," said Looper, "they haven't swept the Seacoast since last July."

A longer silence. Will figured out why Looper was hanging around Gogolak, why he had not complained more about the fries. He was hoping for a tip about the draft. Up ahead, Mr. Rodenets opened the last carton.

"I mean, you guys are still in school." Looper was whining now. "They catch me, and I'm southern front for sure. At least if I volunteer, I get to pick where I fight. And I get my chance to be Johnny."

"So enlist already." Gogolak was daring him. "The war won't last forever. We've got Pedro on the run."

"Maybe I will. Maybe I'm just waiting for an opening on the J. A. team."

"You ever see a fat Johnny with pimples?" said Gogolak. "You're too ugly to be a vid. Isn't that right, Mr. Rodenets?"

Mr. Rodenets fixed his good eye on Gogolak. "Sure, kid." He was something of a local character—Durham, New Hampshire's only living veteran of the southern front. "Whatever you say." He handed Gogolak three rolls of toilet paper.

• • •

Will's mom was watching cartoons when Will got home. She watched a lot of cartoons, mostly the stupid ones from when she was a girl. She liked the Smurfs and the Flintstones and Roadrunner. There was an inhaler on the couch beside her.

"Mom, what are you doing?" Will couldn't believe she was still home. "Mom, it's quarter to five! You promised."

She stuck out her tongue and blew him a raspberry.

Will picked up the inhaler and took a whiff. Empty. "You're already late."

She held up five fingers. "Not 'til five." Her eyes were bright.

Will wanted to hit her. Instead he held out his hands to help her up. "Come on."

She pouted. "My shows."

He grabbed her hands and pulled her off the couch. She stood, tottered, and fell into his arms. He took her weight easily; she weighed less than he did. She didn't eat much.

"You've got to hurry," he said.

She leaned on him as they struggled down the hall to the bathroom; Will imagined he looked like Johnny America carrying a wounded buddy to the medics. Luckily, there was no one in the shower. He turned it on, undressed her, and helped her in.

"Will! It's cold, Will." She fumbled at the curtain and tried to come out.

He forced her back into the water. "Good," he muttered. His sleeves got wet.

"Why are you so mean to me, Will? I'm your mother."

He gave her five minutes. It was all that he could afford. Then he toweled her off and dressed her. He combed her hair out as best he could; there was no time to dry it. The water had washed all her brightness away,

and now she looked dim and disappointed. More like
herself.

By the time they got to Mr. Dunnell's house, she was
ten minutes late. At night, Mr. Dunnell ran a freelance
word-processing business out of his kitchen. Will knocked;
Mr. Dunnell opened the back door, frowning. Will wished
he'd had more time to get his mom ready. Strands of wet
stringy hair stuck to the side of her face. He knew Mr.
Dunnell had given his mom the job only because
of him.

"Evening, Marie," Mr. Dunnell said. His printer was
screeching like a cat.

"What so good about it?" She was always rude to him.
Will knew it was hard for her, but she wouldn't even give
Mr. Dunnell a chance. She went straight to the old Apple
that Mr. Dunnell had rewired into a dumb terminal and
started typing.

Mr. Dunnell came out onto the back steps. "Christ,
Will. She's only been working for me three weeks and
she's already missed twice and been late I don't know
how many times. Doesn't she want this job?"

Will couldn't answer. He didn't say that she wanted
her old job at the school back, that she wanted his father
back, that all she really wanted was the shiny world she
had been born into. He said nothing.

"This can't go on, Will. Do you understand?"

Will nodded.

"I'm sorry about last night."

Will shrugged and bit into a frozen fry. He was not sure
what she meant. Was she sorry about being late for work
or about coming home singing at three-twenty-four in the
morning and turning on all the lights? He slicked a pan
with oil and set it on the hot plate. He couldn't turn the
burner to high without blowing a fuse but his mom didn't
mind mushy fries. Will did; he usually ate right out of the
bag when he was at home. He'd been saving quarters for

a french fryer for her birthday. If he unplugged the hot plate, there'd be room for it on top of the dresser. He wanted a microwave, too—but then they couldn't afford real microwave food. Someday.

His mom sat up in bed and ate breakfast without looking at it. The new tenants in the next bedroom were watching the war. Will could hear gunfire through the wall.

Normally this was the best time of day, because they talked. She would ask him about school. He told her the truth, mostly. He was the smartest kid in eighth, but she wasn't satisfied. She always wanted to know why he was not making friends. Will couldn't help it; he didn't trust rich kids. And then she would talk about . . . what she always talked about.

Today, however, Will didn't feel much like conversation. He complained half-heartedly that Gogolak was still bothering him.

"I'll bet you have him all wrong, Will."

"No way."

"Maybe he just wants to be your friend."

"The guy's a jack."

"It's hard on him, you know. Kids try to use him to get to his father. They're always pumping him for draft information."

"Well, I don't." Will thought about it. "How do you know so much anyway?"

"Mothers have their little secrets," she said with a sparkle. He hated it when she did that; she looked like some kind of starchy sitcom mom.

"You've never even met him."

She leaned over the edge of the bed and set her empty plate on the floor. "I ran into his father." She straightened up and began to sort through her covers. "He's worried about the boy."

"Was that who you were with last night?" Will threw a half-eaten fry back into the bag. "Gogolak's dad?"

"What I do after work is none of your business." She found her remote and aimed it at the screen. "We knew him before—your father and I. He's an old friend." A cartoon robot brought George Jetson a drink. "And he does work for Selective Service. He knows things."

"Don't try to help me, Mom."

"Look at that," she said, pointing to the screen. "He spills something and a robot cleans it up. You know, that's the way I always thought it would be when I was a kid. I always thought it would be clean."

"Mom—"

"I remember going to Disney World. It was so clean. It was like a garden filled with beautiful flowers. When they used to talk about heaven, I always thought of Disney World."

Will threw the bag at the screen and fries scattered across the room.

"Will!" She swung her legs out of bed. "What's wrong with you today? You all right, honey?"

He was through with her dumb questions. He didn't want to talk to her anymore. He opened the door.

"I said I was sorry."

He slammed it behind him.

It wasn't so much that it was Gogolak's dad this time. Will wasn't going to judge his mom; it was a free country. He wanted to live life, too—except that he wasn't going to make the same mistakes that she had. She was right in a way: it was none of his business who she made it with or what she sniffed. He just wanted her to be responsible about the things that mattered. He didn't think it was fair that he was the only grown-up in his family.

Because he had earned a day off from school, Will decided to skip socialization, too. It was a beautiful day and volleyball was a dumb game anyway, even if there were girls in shorts playing it. Instead he slipped into the socialization center, got his dad's old basketball out of his locker, and went down to the court behind the abandoned high school. It helped to shoot when he was angry. Besides, if he could work up any kind of jumper, he might make the ninth basketball team. He was already the tallest kid in eighth, but his hands were too small, and he kept bouncing the ball off his left foot. He was practicing reverse lay-ups when Looper came out of the thicket that had once been the baseball field.

"Hey, Will." He was flushed and breathing hard, as if he had been running. "How you doing?"

Will was surprised that Looper knew his name. "I'm alive."

Looper stood under the basket, waiting for a rebound. Will put up a shot that clanged off the rim.

"Hear about Johnny America?" Looper took the ball out to the foul line. "Old Gervais got his foot blown off. Stepped on a mine." He shot: swish. "Some one-on-one?"

They played two games and Looper won them both. He was the most graceful fat kid Will had ever seen. After the first game, Looper walked Will through some of his best post-up moves. He was a good teacher. By the end of the second game, sweat had darkened Looper's T-shirt. Will said he wouldn't mind taking a break. They collapsed in the shade.

"So they're recruiting for a new Johnny?" Will tried in vain to palm his basketball. "You ready to take your chance?"

"Who, me?" Looper wiped his forehead with the back of his hand. "I don't know."

"You keep bringing it up."

"Someday I've got to do something."

"Johnny Looper." Will made an imaginary headline with his hands.

"Yeah, right. How about you—ever think of joining? You could, you're tall enough. You could join up today.

As long as you swear that you're fifteen, they'll take you. They'll take anyone. Remember Johnny Stanczyk? He was supposed to have been thirteen."

"I heard he was fourteen."

"Well, he looked thirteen." Looper let a caterpillar crawl up his finger. "You know what I'd like about the war?" he said. "The combat drugs. They make you into some kind of superhero, you know?"

"Superheroes don't blow up."

Looper fired the caterpillar at him.

Will's conscience bothered him for saying that; he was starting to sound like Gogolak. "Still, it is our country. Someone has to fight for it, right?" Will shrugged. "How come you dropped out, anyway?"

"Bored." Looper shrugged. "I might go back, though. Or I might go to the war. I don't know." He swiped the basketball from Will. "I don't see you carrying a comm today."

"Needed to think." Will stood and gestured for his ball.

"Hey, you hear about the lottery?" Looper fired a pass. Will shook his head.

"They were going to announce it over the school channels this morning; Gogo tipped me yesterday. Town's going to hire twenty kids this summer. Fix stuff, mow grass, pick up trash, you know. Buck an hour—good money. You got to go register at the post office this afternoon, then next month they pick the lucky ones."

"Kind of early to think about the summer." Will frowned. "Bet you that jack Gogolak gets a job."

Looper glanced at him. "He's not that bad."

"A jack. You think he worries about sweeps?" Will didn't know why he was so angry at Looper. He was beginning to like Looper. "He's probably rich enough to buy out of the draft if he wants. He gets everything his way."

"Not everything." Looper laughed. "He's short."

Will had to laugh too. "You want to check this lottery out?"

"Sure." Looper heaved himself up. "Show you something on the way over."

There was blood on the sidewalk. A crowd of about a dozen had gathered by the abandoned condos on Coe Drive to watch the EMTs load Seth Warner into the ambulance which was parked right behind his Peugeot. Will looked for Denise but didn't see her. A cop was recording statements.

"I got here just after Jeff Roeder." Mrs. O'Malley preened as she spoke into the camera; it had been a long time since anyone paid attention to her. "He was lying on the sidewalk there, all bashed up. The car door was open and his disk was playing. Jeff stayed with him. I ran for help."

The driver shut the rear doors of the ambulance. Somebody in the crowd called out, "How is he?"

The driver grunted. "Wants his lawyer." Everyone laughed.

"Must've been a fight," Jeff Roeder said. "We found this next to him." He handed the cop a bloody dental plate.

"Did anyone else here see anything?" The cop raised her voice.

"I would've liked to've seen it," whispered the woman in front of Will. "He's one oldie who had it coming." People around her laughed uneasily. "Shit. They all do."

Even the cop heard that. She panned the crowd and then slammed the Peugeot's door.

Looper grinned at Will. "Let's go." They headed for Madbury Road.

"He wanted me to get in the car with him," Looper said as they approached the post office. "He offered me a buck. Didn't say anything else, just waved it at me."

Will wished he were somewhere else.

"A stinking buck," said Looper. "The pervert."

"But if he didn't say what he wanted . . . maybe it was for a stand-in someplace."

"Yeah, sure." Looper snorted. "Wake up and look around you." He waved at downtown Durham. "The oldies screwed us. They wiped their asses on the world. And they're still at it."

"You're in deep trouble, Looper." No question Looper had done a dumb thing, yet Will knew exactly how the kid felt.

"Nah. What are they going to do? Pull me in and say 'You're fighting on the wrong front, Johnny. Better enlist for your own good.' No problem. Maybe I'm ready to enlist now, anyway." Looper nodded; he looked satisfied with himself. "It was the disk, you know. He was playing it real loud and tapping his fingers on the wheel like he was having a great time." He spat into the road. "Boomer music. I hate the damn Beatles, so I hit him. He was real easy to hit."

There was already a ten-minute line at the post office and the doors hadn't even opened yet. Mostly it was kids from school who were standing in, a few dropouts like Looper and one grown-up, weird Miss Fisher. Almost all of the kids with comms were logged on, except that no one paid much attention to the screens. They were too busy chatting with the people around them. Will had never mastered the art of talking and studying at the same time.

They got on line right behind Sharon Riolli and Megan Brown. Sharon was in Will's class, and had asked him to a dance once when they were in seventh. Over the summer he had grown thirteen centimeters. Since then she'd made a point of ignoring him; he looked older than he was. Old enough to fight.

"When are they going to open up?" said Looper.

"Supposed to be one-thirty," said Megan. "Hi, Will. We missed you at socialization."

"Hi, Megan. Hi, Sharon."

Sharon developed a sudden interest in fractions.

"Have you seen Denise Warner?" said Will.

"The new kid?" Megan snickered. "Why? You want to ask her out or something?"

"Her grandpa got into an accident up on Coe Drive."

"Hurt?"

"He'll live." Looper kept shifting from foot to foot as if the sidewalk was too hot for him.

"Too bad." Sharon didn't look up.

"Hey, Genius. Loop." Gogolak cut in front of the little kid behind Looper, some stiff from sixth who probably wasn't old enough for summer work anyway. "Hear about Gervais?"

"What happened?" said Sharon. Will noticed that she paid attention to Gogolak.

"Got his foot turned into burger. They're looking for a new Johnny."

"Oh, war stuff." Megan sniffed. "That's all you guys ever talk about."

"I think a girl should get a chance," said Sharon.

"Yeah, sure," said Looper. "Just try toting a launcher through the jungle in the heat."

"I could run body armor." She gave Looper a pointed stare. "Something that takes brains."

The line behind them stretched. It was almost one-thirty when Mr. Gogolak came running out of the side door of the post office. The Selective Service office was on the second floor. He raced down the line and grabbed his kid.

"What are you doing here? Go home." He grabbed Gogolak's wrist and turned him around.

"Let go of me!" Gogolak struggled. It had to be embarrassing to be hauled out of a job line like some stupid elementary school kid.

His dad bent over and whispered something. Gogolak's eyes got big. A flutter went down the line; everyone was quiet, watching. Mr. Gogolak was wearing his Selective Service uniform. He pulled his kid into the street.

Mr. Gogolak had gone to the western front with Will's dad. Mr. Gogolak had come back. And last night he had been screwing Will's mom. Will wished she were here to see this. They were supposed to be old friends, maybe he owed her a favor after last night. But the only one Mr. Gogolak whispered to was *his* kid. It wasn't hard to figure out what he had said.

Gogolak gazed at Looper and Will in horror. "It's a scam!" he shouted. "Recruiters!"

His old man slapped him hard and Gogolak went to his knees. But he kept shouting even as his father hit him again. "Draft scam!" They said a top recruiter could talk a prospect into anything.

Will could not bear to watch Mr. Gogolak beat his kid. Will's anger finally boiled over; he hurled his father's basketball and it caromed off Mr. Gogolak's shoulder. The man turned, more surprised than angry. Will was one hundred and ninety centimeters tall and even if he was built like a stick, he was bigger than this little grown-up. Lucky Mr. Gogolak, the hero of the western front, looked shocked when Will punched him. It wasn't a very smart thing to do but Will was sick of being smart. Being smart was too hard.

"My mom says hi." Will lashed out again and missed this time. Mr. Gogolak dragged his crybaby kid away from the post office. Will pumped his fist in triumph.

"Run! Run!" The line broke. Some dumb kid screamed, "It's a sweep!" but Will knew it wasn't. Selective Service had run this scam before: summer job, fall enlistment. Still, kids scattered in all directions.

But not everyone. Weird Miss Fisher just walked to the door to the post office like she was in line for ketchup. Bobby Mangann and Eric Orr and Danny Jarek linked arms and marched up behind her; their country needed them. Will didn't have anywhere to run to.

"Nice work." Looper slapped him on the back and grinned. "Going in?"

Will was excited; he had lost control and it had felt *great*. "Guess maybe I have to now." It made sense, actually. What was the point in studying history if you didn't believe in America? "After you, Johnny."

TAGS

Robert Frazier

"Tags" was purchased by Gardner Dozois, and appeared in the April 1988 issue of Asimov's *with an illustration by J. K. Potter. An elegant and powerful little snapper, it packs a punch way out of proportion to its size, a punch that cuts like a razor. . . .*

Robert Frazier published dozens of poems in Asimov's *and elsewhere throughout the '80s—he is, in fact, one of the genre's best known and most respected poets, and has probably published more poetry in* Asimov's *over the years, by a considerable margin, than any other contributor. Several collections of his poetry have been published, including* Peregrine, Perception Barriers, Co-Orbital Moons, Chronicles of the Mutant Rain Forest *(with Bruce Boston), and* A Measure of Calm *(with Andrew Joron), and he has also edited the poetry anthology* Burning With a Vision: Poetry of Science and the Fantastic. *In 1980, he won the Rhysling Award for his poem "Encased in the Amber of Eternity." Toward the end of the decade, however, he began writing prose stories as well. He made his first prose sale to* Asimov's *in 1988, and has since sold several more to us, as well as to markets like* Amazing, The Twilight Zone Magazine, New Pathways, *and elsewhere.*

Looking crisp and spit-shined in a new green uniform, Corporal Sun Rollins slapped a handful of credits on the bar for two drinks and wove his way through the noisy crowd to Prouse's table. Rollins was peeved at the journalist for boasting that he'd seen more than his share of worlds like Merwin Three, more than a mere soldier ever saw. What did this smart boy *really* know? Rollins decided to turn Prouse on his ear.

"Care for a sundowner, on me?" Rollins asked with a poorly disguised sneer. "They taste like yesterday's piss."

Prouse looked unruffled, though Rollins noted how he fidgeted at the collar of his silk suitcoat and brushed at the fine black curls on the back of his black neck.

"Too bad," Prouse said casually, with an accepting nod. "You'd expect better in an exclusive officers' club."

"Son, we're *all* officers here. 'Cause there's only a thousand tags all total fightin' on Merwin Three."

Prouse swallowed his drink with a sputter. "A *thousand*?"

Rollins grinned. Sweet Jesus, the official contacts had probably told Prouse twenty thousand soldiers, maybe thirty.

"Can ya believe it?" Rollins said slowly in his Louisiana drawl. "Credit it to all this here *high*tech."

Rollins's face lit up, and he pushed the empty glasses away from him so that he could lean forward. His white-rimmed eyes and greasy blond hair reflected brightly on the tabletop.

"Picture *this*, Prouse." Rollins lowered his voice. "It's a hot night like tonight. Everythin' real quiet-like. I'm in my stiff. A good one. All hard-wired reflexes. Armored but light. Infrared eyes with blindfire for my heat-seekin' wrist rockets.

"Anyways, I'm leapin' through the muck, retros keepin' me dry, when I dump down in a nest of Proties. A few brave slugs fire wildly at me. The few that are left, that is. Within seconds, I've lofted in a couple rockets and started slingin' chucks, the napalm disks that make the Prots scream as they burn blue."

Rollins waited for that to sink in.

"Now, these aliens *get* me sometimes. KIA. Killed In Fuckin' Action, you better believe it. But it doesn't matter." Rollins cocked his head. "Ever see a tag, Prouse?"

"Sure," Prouse said. "It's the interface wafer they use to boot you into the android warrior."

"The stiff!" Rollins slammed his fist on the table. He was sloppy drunk now. "Get the term *right*, boy. It's *stiff*, not fuckin' 'android.' Besides, that ain't what tag hardware's really *for*. Nosir. It's for recoverin' us when we're dead meat."

"The persona is preserved as an electrical thumbprint."

"The *juice*, damn it! Get it right!"

Prouse wrote it down in big letters on his pad. J-U-I-C-E.

Rollins smirked. "Yeah! Ya see, the tag's a lesson that goes back to 'Nam. The public don't care what war *costs*. Shit no. They just don't like their boys *snuffed*." His eyes suddenly glazed over. "So they recover our tags and rejuice us to fight again."

A bomb flash lit the smoky depths of the club from outside, and a tremor shook the building. Rollins didn't care. He didn't move or flinch. He was intent on Prouse's rigid, emotionless face.

"And we go back, again and again. . . ."

He was tiring now. Too many drinks were dulling his senses.

"Only, ya know what? There's a difference between feelin' immortal and not bein' able to *die*. Big fraggin' difference. We gotta wear tags now when we're back in our real bodies too." Rollins wobbled his neck around to let Prouse see the tag wafer on the occipital ridge at the base of his skull. "Too many of us have twigged out and had 'ac-*ci*-dents.' Too goddamn many."

Rollins collapsed suddenly. His face smeared the table with sweat and his hairy arms knocked several glasses to the floor.

"They won't let us die, boy," he blubbered. "They won't let us *die*."

Prouse stared blankly at Rollins and shrugged. Another bomb flash lit the club. Prouse fingered the back of his hair and wondered if there was anything that Rollins could have told him that he didn't already know. He knew the *real* situation, better than Rollins could. Rollins had been stuck out here on Merwin Three for two years. In that time, the government had applied the lessons learned here to running things back home, a fresh approach, with war-tested innovations. The air filled with a thunderous whistle.

"Incoming!" someone shouted, but it didn't matter.

By this time tomorrow, Prouse thought, they'd have him interviewing another white-god hero like Rollins—or maybe even *this* Rollins—in an identical club, on an identical assignment. Then he went rigid, his last thoughts blanked and forever lost, and as the room flared white and the heat wave cooked him in his seat, Prouse drained back into his tag like the shrinking phospor dot at the center of a fading picture tube.

PERSONAL SILENCE

Molly Gloss

"Personal Silence" was purchased by Gardner Dozois, and appeared in the January 1990 issue of Asimov's *with an illustration by A. C. Farley. It's one of only a handful of sales that Gloss has made to* Asimov's *over the past few years, but each of them has been a strong and highly individual work. Molly Gloss was born in Portland, Oregon, and lives there still with her family. She made her first sale in 1984, and since, in addition to several sales to* Asimov's, *has sold several stories to* The Magazine of Fantasy and Science Fiction, Universe, *and elsewhere. She published a fantasy novel,* Outside the Gates, *in 1986, and another novel,* The Jump-Off Creek, *a non-SF "woman's western," was released in 1990. She is currently at work on a new novel, this one science fiction.*

Here she gives us a thoughtful and thought-provoking study of one man's personal commitment to his ideals, in the face of overwhelming odds, and how that commitment, without a word being spoken, can reach out to touch other lives and alter them forever. . . .

There was a little finger of land, a peninsula, that stuck up from the corner of Washington State pointing straight north at Vancouver Island. On the state map it was small

enough it had no name. Jay found an old Clallam County
map in a used bookstore in Olympia and on the county map the name was printed the long way, marching
northward up the finger's reach: Naniamuk. There was
a clear bubble near the tip, like a fingernail, and that was
named too: Mizzle. He liked the way the finger pointed at
Vancouver Island. Now he liked the name the town had.
He bought a chart of the strait between Mizzle and Port
Renfrew and a used book on small boat building and when
he left Olympia he went up the county roads to Naniamuk
and followed the peninsula's one paved road all the way
out to its dead end at Mizzle.

It was a three-week walk. His leg had been broken and
badly healed a couple of years ago when he had been
arrested in Colombia. He could walk long-strided, leaning
into the straps of the pack, arms pumping loosely, hands
unfisted, and he imagined anyone watching him would
have had a hard time telling, but if he did more than
eight or ten miles in a day he got gimpy and that led
to blisters. So he had learned not to push it. He camped
in a logged-over state park one night, bummed a couple
of nights in barns and garages, slept other nights just off
the road, in whatever grass and stunted trees grew at the
edge of the right-of-way.

The last day, halfway along the Naniamuk peninsula,
he left the road and hiked west to the beach, through the
low pines and grassy dunes and coils of rusted razorwire,
and set his tent on the sand at the edge of the grass. It
was a featureless beach, wide and flat, stretching toward
no visible headlands. There were few driftlogs, and at
the tide line just broken clamshells, dead kelp, garbage,
wreckage. No tidepools, no off-shore stacks, no agates.
The surf broke far out and got muddy as it rolled in.
When the sun went down behind the overcast, the brown
combers blackened and vanished without luminescence.

The daylight that rose up slowly the next morning was
gray and damp, standing at the edge of rain. He wore his

rubber-bottom shoes tramping in the wet grass along the edge of the road to Mizzle. The peninsula put him in mind of the mid-coast of Chile, the valleys between Talca and Puerto Montt—flat and low-lying, the rain-beaten grass pocked with little lakes and bogs. There was not the great poverty of the Chilean valleys, but if there had been prosperity up here once, it was gone. The big beachfront houses were boarded up, empty. The rich had moved in from the coasts. Houses still lived in were dwarfish, clinker-built, with small windows oddly placed. People were growing cranberries in the bogs and raising bunches of blond, stupid-faced cattle on the wet pasturage.

At the town limit of Mizzle a big, quaintly painted signboard stood up beside the road. WELCOME TO MIZZLE! MOST WESTERLY TOWN IN THE CONTIGUOUS UNITED STATES OF AMERICA! Jay stood at the shoulder of the road and sketched the sign in his notebook for its odd phrasing, its fanciful enthusiasm.

The town was more than he had thought, and less. There had been three or four motels—one still ran a neon vacancy sign. An RV park had a couple of trailers standing in it. The downtown was a short row of gift shops and ice cream stores, mostly boarded shut. There was a town park—a square of unmown lawn with an unpainted gazebo set on it. Tourists had got here ahead of him and had gone again.

He walked out to where the road dead-ended at the tip of the peninsula. It was unmarked, unexceptional. The paving petered out and a graveled road kept on a little way through weeds and hillocks of dirt. Where the graveled road ended, people had been dumping garbage. He stood up on one of the hillocks and looked to the land's end across the dump. There was no beach, just a strip of tidal mud. The salt water of the strait lay flat and gray as sheet metal. The crossing was forty-three nautical miles—there was no seeing Vancouver Island.

He went back along the road through the downtown,

looking up the short cross-streets for the truer town: the hardware store, the grocery, the lumber yard. An AG market had a computerized checkout that was broken, perhaps had been broken for months or years—a clunky mechanical cash register sat on top of the scanner, and a long list of out-of-stock goods was taped across the LED display.

Jay bought a carton of cottage cheese and stood outside eating it with the spoon that folded out of his Swiss army knife. He read from a free tourist leaflet that had been stacked up in a wire rack at the front of the store. The paper of the top copy was yellowed, puckered. On the first inside page was a peninsula map of grand scale naming all the shallow lakes, the graveled roads, the minor capes and inlets. There was a key of symbols: bird scratchings were the nesting grounds of the snowy plover, squiggly ovoids were privately held oyster beds, a stylized anchor marked a public boat launch and a private anchorage on the eastern, the protected shoreline. Offshore there, on the white paper of the strait, stood a nonspecific fish, a crab, a gaffrigged daysailer, and off the oceanside, a longnecked razor clam and a kite. He could guess the boat launch was shut down: recreational boating and fishing had been banned in the strait and in Puget Sound for years. There was little likelihood any oysters had been grown in a while, nor kites flown, clams dug.

Bud's Country Store sold bathtubs and plastic pipe, clamming guns, Coleman lanterns, two-by-fours and plywood, marine supplies, tea pots, towels, rubber boots. What they didn't have they would order, though it was understood delivery might be uncertain. He bought a weekly paper printed seventy miles away in Port Angeles, a day-old copy of the Seattle daily, and a canister of butane, and walked up the road again to the trailer park. *Four Pines RV Village* was painted on a driftwood log mounted high on posts to make a gateway. If there had been pines, they'd been cut down. Behind the arch was a weedy lawn striped with whitish oyster-shell driveways. Stubby posts held out electrical outlets, water couplings, waste water hoses. Some of them were dismantled. There was a gunite building with two steamed-up windows: a shower house, maybe, or a laundromat, or both. The trailer next to the building was a single-wide with a tip-out and a roofed wooden porch. *Office* was painted on the front of it in a black childish print across the fiberglass. There was one other trailer parked along the fence, somebody's permanent home, an old round-back with its tires hidden behind rusted aluminum skirting.

Jay dug out a form letter and held it against his notebook while he wrote across the bottom, "I'd just like to pitch a tent, stay out of your way, and pay when I use the shower. Thanks." He looked at what he had written, added exclamation points, went up to the porch and knocked, waiting awkwardly with the letter in his hand. The girl who opened the door was thin and pale; she had a small face, small features. She looked at him without looking in his eyes. Maybe she was eleven or twelve years old.

He smiled. This was always a moment he hated, doubly so if it was a child—he would need to do it twice. He held out the letter, held out his smile with it. Her eyes jumped to his face and then back to the letter with a look that was difficult to pin down—confusion or astonishment, and then something like preoccupation, as if she had lost sight of him standing there. It was common to get a quick shake of the head, a closed door. He didn't know what the girl's look meant. He kept smiling gently. Several women at different times had told him he had a sweet smile. That was the word they all had used—"sweet." He usually tried to imagine they meant peaceable, without threat.

After a difficult silence, the girl may have remembered him standing there. She finally put out her hand for the letter. He hated waiting while she read it. He looked across the trailer park to a straggly line of scotch broom on the other side of the fence. In a minute she held out the paper to him again without looking in his face. "You have to ask my dad." Her voice was small, low.

He didn't take the letter back yet. He raised his eyebrows in a questioning way. Often it was easier from this point. She would be watching him for those kinds of nonverbal language. He was "keeping a personal silence," he had written in the letter.

"Over in the shower house," she said. She had fine brown hair that hung straight down to her shoulders, and straight bangs she hid behind. Jay glanced toward the gunite building with deliberate, self-conscious hesitation, then made a helpless gesture. The girl may have looked at him from behind her scrim of bangs. "I can ask him," she said, murmuring.

Her little rump was flat, in corduroy pants too big for her. She had kept his letter, and she swung it fluttering in her hand as he followed her to the shower house. A man knelt on the concrete floor, hunched up at the foot of the hot water tank. His pants rode low, baring some of the shallow crack of his buttocks. He looked tall, heavy-boned, though there wasn't much weight on him now, if there ever had been.

"Dad," the girl said.

He had pulled apart the thick fiberglass blanket around the heater to get at the thermostat. His head was shoved inside big loose wings of the blanketing. "What," he said, without bringing his head out.

"He wants to put up a tent," she said. "Here, read this." She shook Jay's letter.

He rocked back on his hips and his heels and rubbed his scalp with a big hand. There were bits of fiberglass, like mica chips, in his hair. "Shit," he said loudly, addressing the hot water heater. Then he stood slowly, hitching up his pants above the crack. He was very tall, six and a half feet or better, bony-faced. He looked at the girl. "What," he said.

She pushed the letter at him silently. Jay smiled, made

a slight, apologetic grimace when the man's eyes finally came around to him. It was always a hard thing trying to tell by people's faces whether they'd help him out or not. This one looked him over briefly, silently, then took the letter and looked at it without much attention. He kept picking fiberglass out of his hair and his skin, and afterward looking under his fingernails for traces of it. "I read about this in *Time*," he said at one point, but it was just recognition, not approval, and he didn't look at Jay when he said it. He kept reading the letter and scrubbing at the bits of fiberglass. It wasn't clear if he had spoken to Jay or to the girl.

Finally he looked at Jay. "You're walking around the world, huh." It evidently wasn't a question, so Jay stood there and waited. "I don't see what good will come of it—except after you're killed you might get on the night news." He had a look at his mouth, smugness, or bitterness. Jay smiled again, shrugging.

The man looked at him. Finally he said, "You know anything about water heaters? If you can fix it, I'd let you have a couple of dollars for the shower meter. Yes? No?"

Jay looked at the heater. It was propane-fired. He shook his head, tried to look apologetic. It wasn't quite a lie. He didn't want to spend the rest of the day fiddling with it for one hot shower.

"Shit," the man said mildly. He hitched at his pants with the knuckles of both hands. Jay's letter was still in one fist and he looked down at it inattentively when the paper made a faint crackly noise against his hip. "Here," he said, holding the sheet out. Jay had fifty or sixty clean copies of it in a plastic ziplock in his backpack. He went through a lot of them when he was on the move. He took the rumpled piece of paper, folded it, pushed it down in a front pocket.

"I had bums come in after dark and use my water," the man said. He waited as if that was something Jay might want to respond to. Jay waited too.

"Well, keep off to the edge by the fence," the man warned him. "You can put up a tent for free, I guess, it's not like we're crowded, but leave the trailer spaces clear anyway. I got locks on the utilities now, so you pay me if you want water, or need to take a crap, and don't take one in the bushes or I'll have to kick you out of here."

Jay nodded. He stuck out his hand and after a very brief moment the man shook it. The man's hand was prickly, damp.

"You show him, Mare," he said to the girl. He tapped her shoulder with his fingertips lightly, but his eyes were on Jay.

Jay followed the young girl, Mare, across the trailer park, across the wet grass and broken-shell driveways to a low fence of two-by-fours and wire that marked the property line. The grass was mowed beside the fence but left to sprout in clumps along the wire and around the wooden uprights. There was not much space between the fence and the last row of driveways. If anybody ever parked a motor home in the driveway behind him, he'd have the exhaust pipe in his vestibule. The girl put her hands in her corduroy pockets and stubbed the grass with the toe of her shoe. "Here?" she asked him. He nodded and swung his pack down onto the grass.

Mare watched him make his camp. She didn't try to help him. She was comfortably silent. When he had every-thing ordered, he looked at her and smiled briefly and sat down on his little sitz pad on the grass. He took out his notebook but he didn't work on the journal. He pulled around a clean page and began a list of the materials he would need for beginning the boat. He wrote down substitutes when he could think of them, in case he had trouble getting his first choice. He planned to cross the strait to Vancouver Island and then sail east and north through the Gulf Islands and the Strait of Georgia, across the Queen Charlotte Strait and then up through the inland passage to Alaska. He hadn't figured out yet how he would get across the Bering Strait to Siberia—whether he would try to sail across in this boat he would build, or if he'd barter it up there to get some other craft, or a ride. It might take him all winter to build the skipjack, all summer to sail it stop and go up the west coast of Canada and Alaska, and then he would need to wait for summer again before crossing the Bering Strait. He'd have time to find out what he wanted to do before he got to it.

The girl after a while approached him silently and squatted down on her heels so she could see what he was writing. She didn't ask him about the list. She read it over and then looked off toward her family's trailer. She kept crouching there beside him, balancing lightly.

"Do you think it's helping yet?" she asked in a minute. She whispered it, looking at him sideward through her long bangs.

He raised his eyebrows questioningly.

"They're still fighting," she murmured. "Aren't they?"

His mother had written to the Oklahoma draft board pleading Jay's only-child status, but by then the so-called Third-World's War was taking a few thousand American lives a day and they weren't exempting anyone. Within a few weeks of his eighteenth birthday, they sent him to the Israeli front.

The tour of duty was four years at first, then extended to six. He thought they would extend it again, but after six years few of them were alive anyway, and they sent him home on a C31 full of cremation canisters. He sat on the toilet in the tail of the plane and swallowed all the pills he had, three at a time, until they were gone. The illegal-drug infrastructure had come overseas with the war and eventually he had learned he could sleep and not dream if he took Nembutal, which was easy to get. Gradually after that he had begun to take Dexamyl to wake up from the Nembutal, Librium to smooth the jitters out of the Dexamyl, Percodan to get high, Demerol when he needed to come down quickly from the high, Dexamyl again if the Demerol took him down too far. He thought he would be dead by the time the plane landed but his body remained inexplicably, persistently, resistant to death. He wound up in a Delayed Stress Syndrome Inpatient Rehab Center which was housed in a prison. He was thirty years old when the funding for the DSS Centers was dropped in favor of research that might lead to a Stealth aircraft carrier. Jay was freed to walk and hitchhike from the prison in Idaho to his mother's house in Tulsa. She had been dead for years but he stood in the street in front of the house and waited for something to happen, a memory or a sentiment, to connect him to his childhood and adolescence. Nothing came. He had been someone else for a long time.

He was still standing on the curb there after dark when a man came out of the house behind him. The man had a flashlight but he didn't click it on. He came over to where Jay stood.

"You should get inside," he said to Jay. "They'll be coming around pretty soon, checking." He spoke quietly. He might have meant a curfew. Tulsa had been fired on a few times by planes flying up to or back from the Kansas missile silos, out of bases in Haiti—crazy terrorists of the crazy Jorge Ruiz government. Probably there was a permanent brownout and a curfew here.

Jay said, "Okay," but he didn't move. He didn't know where he would go anyway. He was cold and needing sleep. There was an appeal in the possibility of arrest.

The man looked at him in the darkness. "You can come inside my house," he said, after he had looked at Jay.

He had a couch in a small room at the front of his house, and Jay slept on it without taking off his clothes. In the daylight the next morning he lay on the couch and looked out the window to his mother's house across the street.

The man who had taken him in was a Quaker named Bob Settleman. He had a son who was on an aircraft carrier in the Indian Ocean, and a daughter who was in a federal prison serving a ten year sentence for failure to report. Jay went with him to a First Day Meeting. There was nothing much to it. People sat silently. After a while an old woman stood and said something about the droughts and cold weather perhaps reflecting God's unhappiness with the state of the world. But that was the only time anyone mentioned God. Three other people rose to speak. One said he was tired of being the only person who remembered to shut the blackout screens in the Meeting Room before they locked up. Then, after a long silence, a woman stood and expressed her fear that an entire generation had been desensitized to violence, by decades of daily video coverage of the war. She spoke gently, in a trembling voice, just a few plain sentences. It didn't seem to matter a great deal, the words she spoke. While she was speaking, Jay felt something come into the room. The woman's voice, some quality in it, seemed to charge the air with its manifest, exquisitely painful truth. After she had finished, there was another long silence. Then Bob Settleman stood slowly and told about watching Jay standing on the curb after dark. He seemed to be relating it intangibly to what had been said about the war. "I could see he was in some need," Bob said, gesturing urgently. Jay looked at his hands. He thought he should be embarrassed, but nothing like that arose in him. He could still feel the palpable trembling of the woman's voice—in the air, in his bones.

Afterward, walking away from the Meeting house, Bob looked at his feet and said, as if it was an apology, "It's been a long time since I've been at a Meeting that was Gathered into the Light like that. I guess I got swept up in it."

Jay didn't look at him. After a while he said, "It's okay." He didn't ask anything. He felt he knew, without asking, what Gathered into the Light meant.

He stayed in Tulsa, warehousing for a laundry products distributor. He kept going to the First Day Meetings with Bob. He found it was true, Meetings were rarely Gathered. But he liked the long silences anyway, and the unpredictability of the messages people felt compelled to share. For a long time, he didn't speak himself. He listened without hearing any voice whispering inside him. But finally he did hear one. When he stood, he felt the long silence Gathering, until the trembling words he spoke came out on the air as Truth.

"If somebody could walk far enough, they'd have to come to the end of the war, eventually."

He had, by now, an established web of support: a New York Catholic priest who banked his receipts from the journal subscriptions, kept his accounts, filed his taxes, wired him expense money when he asked for it; a Canadian rare-seeds collective willing to receive his mail, sort it, bundle it up and send it to him whenever he supplied them with an address; a Massachusetts Monthly Meeting of Friends whose members had the work of typing from the handwritten pages he sent them, printing, collating, stapling, mailing the 10,000 copies of his sometimes-monthly writings. He had a paid subscription list of 1,651, a non-paid "mailing list" of 8,274. Some of those were churches, environmental groups, cooperatives, many were couples, so the real count of persons who supported him was greater by a factor of three or four, maybe. Many of them were people he had met, walking. He hadn't walked, yet, in the Eastern Hemisphere. If he lived long enough to finish what he had started, he thought he could hope for a total list as high as fifty or sixty thousand names. A Chilean who had been a delegate at the failed peace conferences in Surinam had kept a year-long public silence as a protest of Jay's arrest and bad treatment in Colombia. And he knew of one other world-peace-walker he had inspired, a Cuban Nobel chemist who had been the one primarily featured in

Time. He wasn't fooled into believing it was an important circle of influence. He had to view it in the context of the world. Casualties were notoriously underreported, but at least as many people were killed in a given day, directly and indirectly by the war, as made up his optimistic future list of subscribers. It may have been he kept at it because he had been doing it too long now to stop. It was what he did, who he was. It had been a long time since he had felt the certainty and clarity of a Meeting that was Gathered into the Light.

On the Naniamuk peninsula, he scouted out a few broken-down sheds, and garages with overgrown driveways, and passed entreating notes to the owners. He needed a roof. He expected rain in this part of the world about every day.

One woman had a son dead in India and another son who had been listed AWOL or MIA in the interior of Brazil for two years. She asked Jay if he had walked across Brazil yet. *Yes*, he wrote quickly, *eight months there*. She didn't ask him anything else—nothing about the land or the weather or the fighting. She showed him old photos of both her sons without asking if he had seen the lost one among the refugees in the cities and villages he had walked through. She lent him the use of her dilapidated garage, and the few cheap tools he found in disarray inside it.

The girl, Mare, came unexpectedly after a couple of days and watched him lofting the deck and hull bottom panels onto plywood. It had been raining a little. She stood under her own umbrella a while, without coming in close enough to shelter under the garage roof. But gradually she came in near him and studied what he was doing. A look rose in her face—distractedness, as before on the porch of her trailer, and then fear, or something like grief. He didn't know what to make of these looks of hers.

"You're building a boat," she said, low voiced.

He stopped working a minute and looked at the two
pieces of plywood he had laid end to end. He was mark-
ing and lining them with a straight edge and a piece of
curving batten. He had gone across the Florida Strait in
a homemade plywood skipjack, had sailed it around the
coast of Cuba to Haiti, Puerto Rico, Jamaica, and then
across the channel to Yucatan. And later he had built a
punt to cross the mouths of the Amazon. A Cuban refugee,
a fisherman, had helped him build the Caribbean boat, and
the punt had been a simple thing, hardly more than a raft.
This was the first time he had tried to build a skipjack
without help, but he had learned he could do about anything if he had time enough to make mistakes, undo them,
set them right. He nodded, yes, he was building a boat.

"There are mines in the strait," Mare said, dropping her
low voice down.

He smiled slightly, giving her a face that belittled the
problem. He had seen mines in the Yucatan channel too,
and in the strait off Florida. His boat had slid by them,
ridden over them. They were triggered for the heavy war
ships and the armored oil tankers.

He went on working. Mare watched him seriously,
without saying anything else. He thought she would leave
when she saw how slow the boat-making went, but she
stayed on in the garage, handing him tools, and helping
him to brace the batten against the nails when he lofted the
deck piece. At dusk she walked with him up the streets to
the Four Pines. There was a fine rain falling still, and she
held her umbrella high up so he could get under it if he
hunched a little.

In the morning she was waiting for him, sitting on the
porch of her trailer when he tramped across the wet grass
toward the street. Since Colombia, he had had a difficulty
with waking early. He had to depend on his bladder, usually, to force him out of the sleeping bag, then he was slow
to feel really awake, his mouth and eyes thick, heavy, until
he had washed his face, eaten something, walked a while.

He saw it was something like that with the girl. She sat hunkered up on the top step, resting her chin on her knees, clasping her arms about her thin legs. Under her eyes, the tender skin was puffy, dark. Her hair stuck out uncombed. She didn't speak to him. She came stiffly down from the porch and fell in beside him, with her eyes fixed on the rubber toe caps of her shoes. She had a brown lunch sack clutched in one hand and the other hand sunk in the pocket of her corduroys.

They walked down the paved road and then the graveled streets to where the boat garage was. Their walking made a quiet scratching sound. There was no one else out. Jay thought he could hear the surf beating on the ocean side of the peninsula, but maybe not. He heard a dim, continuous susurration. They were half a mile from the beach. Maybe what he heard was wind moving in the trees and the grass, or the whisperings of the snowy plover, nesting in the brush above the tidal flats, on the strait side of the peninsula.

He had not padlocked the garage—a pry-bar would have got anybody in through the small side door in a couple of minutes. He pulled up the rollaway front door, let the light in on the tools, the sheets of plywood. Mare put her lunch down on a sawhorse and stood looking at the lofted pieces, the hull bottom and deck panels drawn on the plywood. He would make those cuts today. He manhandled one of the sheets up off the floor onto the sawhorses. Mare took hold of one end silently. It occurred to him that he could have gotten the panels cut out without her, but it would be easier with her there to hold the big sheets of wood steady under the saw.

He cut the deck panel slowly with hand tools—a brace and bit to make an entry for the keyhole saw, a ripsaw for the long outer cuts. When he was most of the way along the straight finish of the starboard side, on an impulse he gave the saw over to Mare and came around to the other side to hold the sheet down for her. She looked at him once shyly from behind her long bangs and then stood at his place before the wood, holding the saw in both hands. She hadn't drawn a saw in her life, he could tell that, but she'd been watching him. She pushed the saw into the cut he had started and drew it up slow and wobbly. She was holding her mouth out in a tight, flat line, all concentration. He had to smile, watching her.

They ate lunch sitting on the sawhorses at the front of the garage. Jay had carried a carton of yogurt in the pocket of his coat and he ate that slowly with his spoon. Mare offered him part of her peanut butter sandwich, and quartered pieces of a yellow apple. He shook his head, shrugging, smiling thinly. She considered his face, and then looked away.

"I get these little dreams," she said in a minute, low voiced, with apple in her mouth.

He had a facial expression he relied on a good deal, a questioning look. *What? Say again? Explain.* She glanced swiftly sideward at his look and then down at her fingers gathered in her lap. "They're not dreams, I guess. I'm not asleep. I just get them all of a sudden. I see something that's happened, or something that hasn't happened yet. Things remind me." She looked at him again cautiously through her bangs. "When I saw you on the porch, when you gave me the letter, I remembered somebody else who gave me a letter before. I think it was a long time ago."

He shook his head, took the notepad from his shirt pocket and wrote a couple of lines about *déjà vu*. He would have written more but she was reading while he wrote and he felt her stiffening, looking away.

"I know what that is," she said, lowering her face. "It isn't that. Everybody gets that."

He waited silently. There wouldn't have been anything to say anyway. She picked at the corduroy on the front of her pant legs. After a while she said, whispering, "I remember things that happened to other people, but they were me. I think I might be dreaming other people's lives, or the dreams are what I did before, when I was alive a different time, or when I'll be somebody else, later on." Her fingernails kept picking at the cord. "I guess you don't get dreams like that." Her eyes came up to him. "Nobody else does, I guess." She looked away. "I do though. I get them a lot. I just don't tell anymore." Her mouth was small, drawn up. She looked toward him again. "I can tell you, though."

Before she had finished telling him, he had thought of an epilepsy, *Le Petit Absentia*, maybe it was called. He had seen it once in a witch-child in Haiti, a girl who fell into a brief, staring trance a hundred times a day. A neurologist had written to him, naming it from the description he had read in Jay's journal. He could write to the neurologist, ask if this was *Le Petit* again. Maybe there was a simple way to tell, a test, or a couple of things to look for. Of course, maybe it wasn't that. It might only be a fancy, something she'd invented, an attention-getter. But her look made him sympathetic. He pushed her bangs back, kissed her smooth brow solemnly. *It's okay*, he said by his kiss, by his hand lightly on her bangs. *I won't tell*.

There hadn't been a long Labor Day weekend for years. It was one of the minor observances scratched from the calendar by the exigencies of war. But people who were tied in with the school calendar still observed the first weekend of September as a sort of holiday, a last hurrah before the opening Monday of the school year. Some of them still came to the beach.

The weather by good luck was fair, the abiding peninsula winds balmy, sunlit, so there were a couple of small trailers and a few tents in the RV park, and a no-vacancy sign at the motel Saturday morning by the time the fog was burned off.

Jay spent both days on the lawn in front of the town's gazebo, behind a stack of old journals and a big posterboard display he had pasted up, with an outsized rewording of his form letter, and clippings from newspapers and from *Time*. He put out a hat on the grass in front of him, with a couple of seed dollars in it. His personal style of buskering was diffident, self-conscious. He kept his attention mostly on his notebook, in his lap. He sketched from memory the archway at the front of the RV Park, the humpbacked old trailer, the girl, Mare's, thin face. He made notes to do with the boat, and fiddled with an op-ed piece he would send to *Time*, trying to follow up on the little publicity they'd given the Cuban chemist. The op-ed would go in his October journal, whether *Time* took it or not, and the sketches would show up there too, in the margins of his daybook entries, or on the cover. He printed other people's writings too, things that came in his mail—poetry, letters, meeting notices, back page news items pertaining to peace issues, casualty and armament statistics sent at rare intervals by an anonymous letter writer with a Washington, D.C. postmark—but most of the pages were his own work. On bureaucratic forms he entered *Journalist* as his occupation without feeling he was misrepresenting anything. He liked to write. His writing had gotten gradually better since he had been doing the journal—sometimes he thought it was not from the practice at writing, but the practice at silence.

Rarely somebody stooped to pick up a journal, or put money in his hat, or both. Those people he tried to make eye contact with, smiling gently by way of inviting them in. He wouldn't get any serious readers, serious talkers, probably, on a holiday weekend in a beach town, but you never knew. He was careful not to look at the others, the bypassers, but he kept track of them peripherally. He had been arrested quite a few times, assaulted a few. And since Colombia, he suffered from a chronic fear.

Mare came and sat with him on Sunday. He didn't mind having her there. She was comfortable with his silence; she seemed naturally silent herself, much of the time. She read from old copies of his journal and shared the best parts with him as if he hadn't been the writer, the editor, holding a page out for him silently and waiting, watching, while he read to the end. Then her marginalia were terse, absolute: "Ick." "I'm glad." "She shouldn't have gone." "I'd never do that."

After quite a while, she had him read what he had written about a town in the Guatemala highlands where he had spent a couple of months, and then she said, in a changed way, timid, earnest, "I lived there before. But I was a different person."

He had not got around to writing anyone about the epilepsy after he'd lost that first strong feeling of its possibility. His silence invited squirrels, he knew that, though it made him tired, unhappy, thinking of it. He was tired now, suddenly, and annoyed with her. He shook his head, let her see a flat, skeptical smile.

"Mare!"

The father came across the shaggy grass moving swiftly, his arms swinging in a stiff way, elbows akimbo. Jay stood up warily.

"I'm locked out of the damn house," the man said, not looking at Jay. "Where's your key?"

Mare got up from the grass, dug around in her pockets and brought out a key with a fluorescent pink plastic keeper. He closed his fingers on it, made a vague gesture with the fist. "I about made up my mind to bust a window," he said. "I was looking for you." He was annoyed.

Mare put her hands in her pockets, looked at her feet. "I'm helping him stop the war," she said, murmuring.

The man's eyes went to Jay and then the posterboard sign, the hat, the stacked-up journals. His face kept hold of that look of annoyance, but took on something else too, maybe it was just surprise. "He's putting up signs and hustling for money, is what it looks like he's doing," he said, big and arrogant. For a while longer he stood there looking at the sign as if he were reading it. Maybe he was. He had a manner of standing—shifting his weight from foot to foot and hitching at his pants every so often with the knuckles of his hands.

"I got a kidney shot out, in North Africa," he said suddenly. "But there's not much fighting there anymore, that front's moved south or somewhere. I don't know who's got that ground now. They can keep it, whoever." He had a long hooked nose, bony ridges below his eyes, a wide, lipless mouth. Strong features. Jay could see nothing of him in Mare's small pale face. It wasn't evident, how they were with each other. Jay saw her now watching her dad through her bangs, with something like the shyness she had with everyone else.

"Don't be down here all day," her dad said to her, gesturing again with the fist he had closed around the housekey. He looked at Jay but he didn't say anything else. He shifted his weight one more time and then walked off long-strided, swinging his long arms. He was tall enough some of the tourists looked at him covertly after he'd passed them. Mare watched him too. Then she looked at Jay, a ducking, sideward look. He thought she was embarrassed by her dad. He shrugged. *It's okay.* But that wasn't it. She said, pulling in her thin shoulders timidly, "There is a lake there named Negro because the water is so dark." She had remained focused on his disbelief, waiting to say this small proving thing about Guatemala. And it was true enough to shake him a little. There was a Lago Negro in about every country below the U.S. border, he remembered that in a minute. But there was a long startled moment before that, when he only saw the little black lake in the highlands, in Guatemala, and Mare, dark faced, in a dugout boat paddling away from the weedy shore.

He had the store rip four long stringers out of a clear fir board and then he kerfed the stringers every three inches along their lengths. With the school year started he didn't have Mare to hold the long pieces across the saw horses. He got the cuts done slowly, single-handed, bracing the bouncy long wood with his knee.

Mare's dad came up the road early in the day. Jay thought he wasn't looking for the garage. There was a flooded cranberry field on the other side of the road and he was watching the people getting in the crop from it. There were two men and three women wading slowly up and down in green rubber hip waders, stripping off the berries by hand into big plastic buckets. Mare's dad, walking along the road, watched them. But when he came even with the garage he turned suddenly and walked up the driveway. Jay stopped what he was doing and waited, holding the saw. Mare's dad stood just inside the rollaway door, shifting his weight, knuckling his hips.

"I heard you were building a boat," he said, looking at the wood, not at Jay. "You never said how long you wanted to camp, but I didn't figure it would be long enough to build a boat." Jay thought he knew where this was headed. He'd been hustled along plenty of times before this. But it didn't go that way. The man looked at him. "In that letter you showed, I figured you meant you could talk if you wanted to." He sounded annoyed, as he had been on Labor Day weekend with Mare. "Now I heard your tongue was cut off," he said, lifting his chin, reproachful.

Jay kept standing there holding the saw, waiting. He hadn't been asked anything. The man dropped his eyes. He turned partway from Jay and looked over his shoulder toward the cranberry bog, the people working there. There was a long stiff silence.

"She's a weird kid," he said suddenly. "You figured that out by now, I guess." His voice was loud; he may not have had soft speaking in him anywhere. "I'd have her to a psychiatrist, but I can't afford it." He hitched at his pants with the backs of both hands. "I guess she likes you because you don't say anything. She can tell you whatever she wants and you're not gonna tell her she's nuts." He looked at Jay. "You think she's nuts?"

His face had a sorrowful aspect now, his brows drawn up in a heavy pleat above the bridge of his nose.

Jay looked at the saw. He tested the row of teeth against the tips of his fingers and kept from looking at the man. He realized he didn't know his name, first or last, or if he had a wife. Where was Mare's mother?

The man blew out a puffing breath through his lips. "I guess she is," he said unhappily. Jay ducked his head, shrugged. *I don't know.* He had been writing about Mare lately—pages that would probably show up in the journal, in the October mailing. He had spent a lot of time wondering about her, and then writing it down. This was something new to wonder about. He had thought her dad was someone else, not this big sorrowful man looking for reassurance from a stranger who camped in his park.

A figure of jets passed over them suddenly, flying inland from the ocean. There were six. They flew low, dragging a screaming roar, a shudder, through the air. Mare's dad didn't look up.

"She used to tell people these damn dreams of hers all the time," the man said, after the noise was past. "I know I never broke her of it, she just got sly who she tells them to. She never tells me anymore." He stood there silently looking at the cranberry pickers. "The last one she told me," he said, in his heavy, unquiet voice, "was how she'd be killed dead when she was twelve years old." He looked over at Jay. "She didn't tell you that yet," he said, when he saw Jay's face. He smiled in a bitter way. "She was about eight, I guess, when she told me that one." He thought about it and then he added, "She's twelve now. She was twelve in June." He made a vague gesture with both hands, a sort of open-palms shrugging. Then he pushed his hands down in his back pockets. He kept them there while he shifted his weight in that manner he had, almost a rocking back and forth.

Watching him, Jay wondered suddenly if Mare might not put herself in the path of something deadly, to make

sure this dream was a true one—a proof for her dad. He
wondered if her dad had thought of that.

"I don't know where she gets her ideas," the man said,
making a pained face, "if it's from TV or books or what,
but she told me when she got killed it'd be written up,
and in the long run it'd help get the war ended. Before
that, she never had noticed we were even in a war." He
looked at Jay wildly. "Maybe I'm nuts too, but here you
are, peace-peddling in our backyard, and when I saw you
with those magazines you write, I started to wonder what
was going on. I started to wonder if this is a damn different
world than I've been believing all my life." His voice had
begun to rise so by the last few words he sounded plain-
tive, teary. Jay had given up believing in God the year he
was eighteen. He didn't know what it was that Gathered a
Meeting into the Light, but he didn't think it was God. It
occurred to him, he couldn't have told Mare's dad where
the borders were of the world he, Jay, believed in.

"I don't have a reason for telling you this," the man
said after a silence. He had brought his voice down again
so he sounded just agitated, defensive. "Except I guess I
wondered if I was nuts, and I figured I'd ask somebody
who couldn't answer." His mouth spread out flat in a
humorless grin. He took his hands out of his pockets,
hitched up his pants. "I thought about kicking you on
down the road, but I guess it wouldn't matter. If it isn't
you, it'll be somebody else. And"—his eyes jumped away
from Jay—"I was afraid she might quick do something to
get herself killed, if she knew you were packing up." He
waited, looking off across the road. Then he looked at Jay
"I've been worrying, lately, that she'll get killed all right,
one way or the other, either it'll come true on its own or
she'll make it."

They stood together in silence in the dim garage, looking at the cut out pieces of Jay's boat. He had the deck
and hull bottom pieces, the bulkheads, the transom, the
knee braces cut out. You could see the shape of the boat

in some of them, in the curving lines of the cuts.

"I guess you couldn't taste anything without a tongue," the man said after a while. He looked at Jay "I'd miss that more than the talking." He knuckled his hips and walked off toward the road. All his height was in his legs. He walked fast with a loose, sloping gait on those long legs.

In the afternoon Jay took a clam shovel out of the garage and walked down to the beach. The sand was black and oily from an offshore spill or a sinking. There wasn't any debris on the low tide, just the oil. Maybe on the high tide there would be wreckage, or oil-fouled birds. He walked along the edge of the surf on the wet black sand looking for clam sign. There wasn't much. He dug a few holes without finding anything. He hadn't expected to. Almost at dusk he saw somebody walking toward him from way down the beach. Gradually it became Mare. She didn't greet him. She turned alongside him silently and walked with him, studying the sand. She carried a denim knapsack that pulled her shoulders down: blocky shapes of books, a lunch box. She hadn't been home yet. If she had gone to the garage and not found him there, she didn't say so.

He touched the blade of the shovel to the sand every little while, looking in the pressure circle for the stipple of clams. He didn't look at Mare. Something, maybe it was a clam sign, irised in the black sheen on the sand. He dug a fast hole straight down, slinging the wet mud sideways. Mare crouched out of the way, watching the hole. "I see it!" She dropped on the sand and pushed her arm in the muddy hole, brought it out again reflexively. Blood sprang along the cut of the razor-shell, bright red. She held her hands together in her lap while her face brought up a look, a slow unfolding of surprise and fear. Jay reached for her, clasping both her hands between his palms, and in a moment she saw him again. "It cut me," she said, and started to cry. The tears maybe weren't about her hand.

He washed out the cut in a puddle of salt water. He didn't have anything to wrap around it. He picked up the clam shovel in one hand and held onto her cut hand with the other. They started back along the beach. He could feel her pulse in the tips of his fingers. *What did you dream*, he wanted to say.

It had begun to be dark. There was no line dividing the sky from the sea, just a griseous smear and below it the cream-colored lines of surf. Ahead of them Jay watched something rolling in the shallow water. It came up on the beach and then rode out again. The tide was rising. Every little while the surf brought the thing in again. It was pale, a driftlog, it rolled heavily in the shallow combers. Then it wasn't a log. Jay let down the shovel and Mare's hand and waded out to it. The water was cold, dark. He took the body by its wrist and dragged it up on the sand. It had been chewed on, or shattered. The legs were gone, and the eyes, the nose. He couldn't tell if it was a man or a woman. He dragged it way up on the beach, on the dry sand, above the high tide line. Mare stood where she was and watched him.

He got the clam shovel and went back to the body and began to dig a hole beside it. The sand was silky, some of it slipped down and tried to fill the grave as he dug. In the darkness, maybe he was shoveling out the same hole over and over. The shovel handle was sticky, from Mare's blood on his palms. When he looked behind him, he saw Mare sitting on the sand, huddled with her thin knees pulled up, waiting. She held her hurt hand with the other one, cradled.

When he had buried the legless body, he walked back to her and she stood up and he took her hand again and they went on along the beach in the darkness. He was cold. His wet shoes and his jeans grated with sand. The cut on Mare's hand felt sticky, hot, where he clasped his palm against it. She said, in a whisper, "I dreamed this, once." He couldn't see her face. He looked out but he couldn't see the water, only hear it in the black air, a ceaseless, numbing murmur. He remembered the look that had come in her face when she had first seen his boat-building. *There are mines in the strait.* He wondered if that was when she had dreamed this moment, this white body rolling up on the sand.

He imagined Mare dead. It wasn't hard. He didn't know what kind of a death she could have that would end the war, but he didn't have any trouble seeing her dead. He had seen a lot of dead or dying children, written about them. He didn't know why imagining Mare's thin body, legless, buried in sand, brought up in his mouth the remembered salt taste of tears, or blood, or the sea.

"I know," he said, though what came out was shapeless, ill-made, a sound like *Ah woe*. Mare didn't look at him. But in a while she leaned in to him in the darkness and whispered against his cheek. "It's okay," she said, holding on to his hand. "I won't tell."

He had sent off the pages of his October journal already, and Mare was in them, and Lago Negro, and the father standing shifting his feet, not looking up as the jets screamed over him. It occurred to Jay suddenly, it would not matter much, the manner of her dying. She had dreamed her own death and he had written it down, and when she was dead he would write that, and her death would charge the air with its manifest, exquisitely painful truth.

MADNESS HAS ITS PLACE

Larry Niven

"Madness Has Its Place" was purchased by Gardner Dozois, and appeared in the June 1990 issue of Asimov's, *with an interior illustration by Bob Walters. Niven doesn't appear all that often in* Asimov's, *but his appearances have been memorable, including the well-known "Draco Tavern" stories, which were published in the magazine under the editorship of George Scithers. Here he gives us a taut, hard-edged, and suspenseful look at a high-tech conspiracy that must somehow spread itself unnoticed across the solar system if the human race is to have any chance to survive. . . .*

Larry Niven made his first sale to Worlds of If *magazine in 1964, and soon established himself as one of the best new writers of "hard" science fiction since Robert Heinlein. By the end of the '70s, Niven had won several Hugo and Nebula awards, published* Ringworld, *one of the most acclaimed technological novels of the decade, and had written several best-selling novels in collaboration with Jerry Pournelle. Niven's books include the novels* Protector, World of Ptavvs, A Gift From Earth, Ringworld Engineers, *and* Smoke Ring, *and the collections* Tales of Known Space, Inconstant Moon, Neutron Star, *and* N-Space. *His most recent book is a new collection,* Playground of the Mind.

I

A lucky few of us know the good days before they're gone.

I remember my eighties. My job kept me in shape, and gave me enough variety to keep my mind occupied. My love life was imperfect but interesting. Modern medicine makes the old fairy tales look insipid; I almost never worried about my health.

Those were the good days, and I knew them. I could remember worse.

I can remember when my memory was better, too. That's what this file is for. I keep it updated for that reason, and also to maintain my sense of purpose.

The Monobloc had been a singles bar since the 2320s.

In the '30s I'd been a regular. I'd found Charlotte there. We held our wedding reception at the Monobloc, then dropped out for twenty-eight years. My first marriage, hers too, both in our forties. After the children grew up and moved away, after Charlotte left me too, I came back.

The place was much changed.

I remembered a couple of hundred bottles in the hologram bar display. Now the display was twice as large and seemed more realistic—better equipment maybe— but only a score of bottles in the middle were liquors. The rest were flavored or carbonated water, high-energy drinks, electrolytes, a thousand kinds of tea; food to match, raw vegetables and fruits kept fresh by high-tech means, arrayed with low-cholesterol dips; bran in every conceivable form short of injections.

The Monobloc had swallowed its neighbors. It was bigger, with curtained alcoves, and a small gym upstairs for working out or for dating.

Herbert and Tina Schroeder still owned the place. Their marriage had been open in the '30s. They'd aged since. So

had their clientele. Some of us had married or drifted away
or died of alcoholism; but word of mouth and the Velvet
Net had maintained a continuous tradition. Twenty-eight
years later they looked better than ever . . . wrinkled, of
course, but lean and muscular, both ready for the Gray
Olympics. Tina let me know before I could ask: she and
Herb were lockstepped now.

To me it was like coming home.

For the next twelve years the Monobloc was an intermit-
tent part of my life.

I would find a lady, or she would find me, and we'd
drop out. Or we'd visit the Monobloc and sometimes trade
partners; and one evening we'd go together and leave
separately. I was not evading marriage. Every woman I
found worth knowing, ultimately seemed to want to know
someone else.

I was nearly bald even then. Thick white hair covered
my arms and legs and torso, as if my head hairs had
migrated. Twelve years of running construction robots
had turned me burly. From time to time some muscular
lady would look me over and claim me. I had no trouble
finding company.

But company never stayed. Had I become dull? The
notion struck me as funny.

I had settled myself alone at a table for two, early on a
Thursday evening in 2375. The Monobloc was half empty.
The earlies were all keeping one eye on the door when
Anton Brillov came in.

Anton was shorter than me, and much narrower, with a
face like an axe. I hadn't seen him in thirteen years. Still,
I'd mentioned the Monobloc; he must have remembered.

I semaphored my arms. Anton squinted, then came
over, exaggeratedly cautious until he saw who it was.

"Jack Strather!"

"Hi, Anton. So you decided to try the place?"

"Yah." He sat. "You look good." He looked a moment longer and said, "Relaxed. Placid. How's Charlotte?"

"Left me after I retired. Just under a year after. There was too much of me around and I . . . maybe I was too placid? Anyway. How are you?"

"Fine."

Twitchy. Anton looked twitchy. I was amused. "Still with the Holy Office?"

"Only citizens call it that, Jack."

"I'm a citizen. Still gives me a kick. How's your chemistry?"

Anton knew what I meant and didn't pretend otherwise. "I'm okay. I'm down."

"Kid, you're looking over both shoulders at once."

Anton managed a credible laugh. "I'm not the kid any more. I'm a weekly."

The ARM had made me a weekly at forty-eight. They couldn't turn me loose at the end of the day any more, because my body chemistry couldn't shift fast enough. So they kept me in the ARM building Monday through Thursday, and gave me all of Thursday afternoon to shed the schitz madness. Another twenty years of that and I was even less flexible, so they retired me.

I said, "You do have to remember. When you're in the ARM building, you're a paranoid schizophrenic. You have to be able to file that when you're outside."

"Hah. How can anyone—"

"You get used to the schitz. After I quit, the difference was *amazing.* No fears, no tension, no ambition."

"No Charlotte?"

"Well . . . I turned boring. And what are you doing here?"

Anton looked around him. "Much the same thing you are, I guess. Jack, am I the youngest one here?"

"Maybe." I looked around, doublechecking. A woman was distracting me, though I could see only her back and a flash of a laughing profile. Her back was slender and strong, and a thick white braid ran down her spine, center, two and a half feet of clean, thick white hair. She was in animated conversation with a blonde companion of Anton's age plus a few.

But they were at a table for two: they weren't inviting company. I forced my attention back. "We're gray singles, Anton. The young ones tend to get the message quick. We're slower than we used to be. We *date*. You want to order?"

Alcohol wasn't popular here. Anton must have noticed, but he ordered guava juice and vodka and drank as if he needed it. This looked worse than Thursday jitters. I let him half finish, then said, "Assuming you can tell me—"

"I don't know anything."

"I know the feeling. What *should* you know?"

A tension eased behind Anton's eyes. "There was a message from the *Angel's Pencil*."

"Pencil . . . oh." My mental reflexes had slowed down. The *Angel's Pencil* had departed twenty years ago for . . . was it Epsilon Eridani? "Come on, kid, it'll be in the boob cubes before you have quite finished speaking. Anything from deep space is public property."

"*Hah!* No. It's restricted. I haven't seen it myself. Only a reference, and it must be more than ten years old."

That was peculiar. And if the Belt stations hadn't spread the news through the solar system, *that* was peculiar. No wonder Anton was antsy. ARMs react that way to puzzles.

Anton seemed to jerk himself back to here and now, back to the gray singles regime. "Am I cramping your style?"

"No problem. Nobody hurries in the Monobloc. If you see someone you like—" My fingers danced over lighted symbols on the rim of the table. "This gets you a map. Locate where she's sitting, put the cursor on it. That gets you a display . . . hmm."

I'd set the cursor on the white-haired lady. I liked the

readout. "Phoebe Garrison, seventy-nine, eleven or twelve years older than you. Straight. Won a Second in the Gray Jumps last year . . . that's the Americas Skiing Matches for seventy and over. She could kick your tail if you don't watch your manners. It says she's smarter than we are, too.

"Point is, she can check you out the same way. Or me. And she probably found this place through the Velvet Net, which is the computer network for unlocked lifestyles."

"So. Two males sitting together—"

"Anyone who thinks we're bent can check if she cares enough. Bends don't come to the Monobloc anyway. But if we want company, we should move to a bigger table."

We did that. I caught Phoebe Garrison's companion's eye. They played with their table controls, discussed, and presently wandered over.

Dinner turned into a carouse. Alcohol was involved, but we'd left the Monobloc by then. When we split up, Anton was with Michiko. I went home with Phoebe.

Phoebe had fine legs, as I'd anticipated, though both knees were teflon and plastic. Her face was lovely even in morning sunlight. Wrinkled, of course. She was two weeks short of eighty and wincing in anticipation. She ate with a cross-country skier's appetite. We told of our lives as we ate.

She'd come to Santa Maria to visit her oldest grandson. In her youth she'd done critical work in nanoengineering. The Board had allowed her four children. (I'd known I was outclassed.) All were married, scattered across the Earth, and so were the grandkids.

My two sons had emigrated to the Belt while still in their twenties. I'd visited them once during an investigation, trip paid for by the United Nations—

"You were an ARM? Really? How interesting! Tell me a story . . . if you can."

"That's the problem, all right."

The interesting tales were all classified. The ARM suppresses dangerous technology. What the ARM buries is supposed to stay buried. I remembered a kind of time compressor, and a field that would catalyze combustion, both centuries old. Both were first used for murder. If turned loose or rediscovered, either would generate more interesting tales yet.

I said, "I don't know anything current. They bounced me out when I got too old. Now I run construction robots at various spaceports."

"Interesting?"

"Mostly placid." She wanted a story? Okay. The ARM enforced more than the killer-tech laws, and some of those tales I could tell.

"We don't get many mother hunts these days. This one was wished on us by the Belt—" And I told her of a lunie who'd sired two clones. One he'd raised on the Moon and one he'd left in the Saturn Conserve. He'd moved to Earth, where one clone is any normal citizen's entire birthright. When we found him he was arranging to culture a third clone. . . .

I dreamed a bloody dream.

It was one of those: I was able to take control, to defeat what had attacked me. In the black of an early Sunday morning the shreds of the dream dissolved before I could touch them; but the sensations remained. I felt strong, balanced, powerful, victorious.

It took me a few minutes to become suspicious of this particular flavor of wonderful;but I'd had practice. I eased out from under Phoebe's arm and leg and out of bed. I lurched into the medical alcove, linked myself up and fell asleep on the table.

Phoebe found me there in the morning. She asked, "Couldn't that wait till after breakfast?"

"I've got four years on you and I'm going for infinity. So I'm careful," I told her. Let her think the tube carried vitamin. It wasn't quite a lie . . . and she didn't quite believe me either.

On Monday Phoebe went off to let her eldest grandson show her the local museums. I went back to work.

In Death Valley a semicircle of twenty lasers points at an axial array of mirrors. Tracks run across the desert to a platform that looks like strands of spun caramel. Every hour or so a spacecraft trundles along the tracks, poses above the mirrors, and rises into the sky on a blinding, searing pillar of light.

Here was where I and three companions and twenty-eight robots worked between emergencies. Emergencies were common enough. From time to time Glenn and Skii and ten or twenty machines had to be shipped off to Outback Field or Baikonur, while I held the fort at Death Valley Field.

All of the equipment was old. The original mirrors had all been slaved to one system, and those had been replaced again and again. Newer mirrors were independently mounted and had their own computers, but even these were up to fifty years old and losing their flexibility. The lasers had to be replaced somewhat more often. Nothing was ready to fall apart, quite.

But the mirrors have to adjust their shapes to match distorting air currents all the way up to vacuum; because the distortions themselves must focus the drive beam. A laser at 99.3 percent efficiency is keeping too much energy, getting too hot. At 99.1 percent something would melt, lost power would blow the laser into shrapnel, and a cargo would not reach orbit.

My team had been replacing mirrors and lasers long before I came on the scene. This circuit was nearly complete. We had already reconfigured some robots to begin replacing track.

The robots worked alone while we entertained ourselves in the monitor room. If the robots ran into anything unfamiliar, they stopped and beeped. Then a story or songfest or poker game would stop just as abruptly.

Usually the beep meant that the robot had found an acute angle, an uneven surface, a surface not strong enough to bear a loaded robot, a bend in a pipe, a pipe where it shouldn't be . . . a geometrical problem. The robots couldn't navigate just anywhere. Sometimes we'd have to unload the robot and move the load to a cart, by hand. Sometimes we had to pick the robot up with a crane and move it or turn it. Lots of what we did was muscle work.

Phoebe joined me for dinner Thursday evening.

She'd whipped her grandson at laser tag. They'd gone through the museum at Edwards AFB. They'd skied . . . he needed to get serious about that, and maybe get some surgery too. . . .

I listened and smiled and presently tried to tell her about my work. She nodded; her eyes glazed. I tried to tell her how good it was, how restful, after all those years in the ARM.

The ARM: that got her interest back. *Stet.* I told her about the Henry Program.

I'd been saving that. It was an embezzling system good enough to ruin the economy. It made Zachariah Henry rich. He might have stayed rich if he'd quit in time . . . and if the system hadn't been so good, so dangerous, he might have ended in prison. Instead . . . well, let his tongue whisper secrets to the ears in the organ banks.

I could speak of it because they'd changed the system. I didn't say that it had happened twenty years before I joined the ARM. But I was still running out of declassified stories. I told her, "If a lot of people know something can be done, somebody'll do it. We can suppress it and suppress it again—"

She pounced. "Like what?"

"Like . . . well, the usual example is the first cold fusion system. They did it with palladium and platinum, but half a dozen other metals work. And organic superconductors: the patents listed a wrong ingredient. Various grad students tried it wrong and still got it. If there's a way to do it, there's probably a lot of ways."

"That was before there was an ARM. Would you have suppressed superconductors?"

"No. What for?"

"Or cold fusion?"

"No."

"Cold fusion releases neutrons," she said. "Sheath the generator with spent uranium, what do you get?"

"Plutonium, I think. So?"

"They used to make bombs out of plutonium."

"Bothers you?"

"Jack, the fission bomb was *it* in the mass murder department. Like the crossbow. Like the Ayatollah's Asteroid." Phoebe's eyes held mine. Her voice had dropped; we didn't want to broadcast this all over the restaurant. "Don't you ever wonder just how *much* of human knowledge is lost in that . . . black Limbo inside the ARM building? Things that could solve problems. Warm the Earth again. Ease us through the lightspeed wall."

"We don't suppress inventions unless they're dangerous," I said.

I could have backed out of the argument; but that too would have disappointed Phoebe. Phoebe liked a good argument. My problem was that what I gave her wasn't good enough. Maybe I couldn't get angry enough . . . maybe my most forceful arguments were classified. . . .

Monday morning, Phoebe left for Dallas and a granddaughter. There had been no war, no ultimatum, but it felt final.

Thursday evening I was back in the Monobloc.

So was Anton. "I've played it," he said. "Can't talk about it, of course."

He looked mildly bored. His hands looked like they

were trying to break chunks off the edge of the table.

I nodded placidly.

Anton shouldn't have told me about the broadcast from *Angel's Pencil*. But he *had;* and if the ARM had noticed, he'd better mention it again.

Company joined us, sampled and departed. Anton and I spoke to a pair of ladies who turned out to have other tastes. (Some bends like to bug the straights.) A younger woman joined us for a time. She couldn't have been over thirty, and was lovely in the modern style . . . but hard, sharply defined muscle isn't my sole standard of beauty. . . .

I remarked to Anton, "Sometimes the vibes just aren't right."

"Yeah. Look, Jack, I have carefully concealed a prehistoric Calvados in my apt at Maya. There isn't really enough for four—"

"Sounds nice. Eat first?"

"Stet. There's *sixteen* restaurants in Maya."

A score of blazing rectangles meandered across the night, washing out the stars. The eye could still find a handful of other space artifacts, particularly around the moon.

Anton flashed the beeper that would summon a taxi. I said, "So you viewed the call. So why so tense?"

Security devices no bigger than a basketball rode the glowing sky, but the casual eye would not find those. One must assume they were there. Patterns in their monitor chips would match vision and sound patterns of a mugging, a rape, an injury, a cry for help. Those chips had gigabytes to spare for words and word patterns the ARM might find of interest.

So: no key words.

Anton said, "Jack, they tell a hell of a story. A . . . foreign vehicle pulled alongside Angela at four-fifths of legal max. It tried to cook them."

I stared. *A spacecraft matched course with the* Angel's

Pencil *at eighty percent of lightspeed? Nothing man-built could do that. And warlike?* Maybe I'd misinterpreted everything. That can happen when you make up your code as you go along.

But how could the Pencil *have escaped?* "How did Angela manage to phone home?"

A taxi dropped. Anton said, "She sliced the bread with the, you know, motor. I said it's a hell of a story."

Anton's apartment was most of the way up the slope of Maya, the pyramidal arcology north of Santa Maria. Old wealth.

Anton led me through great doors, into an elevator, down corridors. He played tour guide: "The Fertility Board was just getting some real power about the time this place went up. It was built to house a million people. It's never been fully occupied."

"So?"

"So we're en route to the east face. Four restaurants, a dozen little bars. And here we stop—"

"This your apt?"

"No. It's empty, it's always been empty. I sweep it for bugs, but the authorities . . . I *think* they've never noticed."

"Is that your mattress?"

"No. Kids. They've got a club that's two generations old. My son tipped me off to this."

"Could we be interrupted?"

"No. *I'm* monitoring *them.* I've got the security system set to let them in, but only when I'm not here. Now I'll set it to recognize you. Don't forget the number: Apt 23309."

"What is the ARM going to think we're doing?"

"Eating. We went to one of the restaurants, then came back and drank Calvados . . . which we will do, later. I can fix the records at Buffalo Bill. Just don't argue about the credit charge, stet?"

"But—Yah, stet." Hope you won't be noticed, that's the real defense. I was thinking of bailing out ... but curiosity is part of what gets you into the ARM. "Tell your story. You said she *sliced the bread with the, you know, motor?*"

"Maybe you don't remember. *Angel's Pencil* isn't your ordinary Bussard ramjet. The field scoops up interstellar hydrogen to feed a fusion-pumped laser. The idea was to use it for communications, too. Blast a message half across the galaxy with that. A Belter crewman used it to cut the alien ship in half."

"There's a communication you can live without. Anton ... what they taught us in school. A sapient species doesn't reach space unless the members learn to cooperate. They'll wreck the environment, one way or another, war or straight libertarianism or overbreeding ... remember?"

"Sure."

"So do you believe all this?"

"I think so." He smiled painfully. "Director Bernhardt didn't. He classified the message and attached a memo, too. Six years of flight aboard a ship of limited size, terminal boredom coupled with high intelligence and too much time, elaborate practical jokes, yadda yadda. Director Harms *left* it classified ... with the cooperation of the Belt. Interesting?"

"But he *had* to have *that.*"

"But they had to agree. There's been more since. *Angel's Pencil* sent us hundreds of detailed photos of the alien ship. It's unlikely they could be faked. There are corpses. Big sort-of cats, orange, more than eight meters tall, big feet and elaborate hands with thumbs. We're in mucking great trouble if we have to face those."

"Anton, we've had three hundred and fifty years of peace. We must be doing something right. The odds say we can negotiate."

"You haven't seen them."

It was almost funny. Jack was trying to make me nervous. Twenty years ago the terror would have been fizzing in my blood. Better living through chemistry! This was all frightening enough; but my fear was a cerebral thing, and I was its master.

I wasn't nervous enough for Anton. "Jack, this isn't just vaporware. A lot of those photos show what's maybe a graviton generator, maybe not. Director Harms set up a lab on the moon to build one for us."

"Funded?"

"Heavy funding. *Somebody* believes in this. But they're getting results! It *works!*"

I mulled it. "Alien contact. As a species we don't seem to handle that too well."

"Maybe this one can't be handled at all."

"What else is being done?"

"Nothing, or damn close. Silly suggestions, career-oriented crap designed to make a bureau bigger . . . nobody wants to use the magic word. *War.*"

"War. Three hundred and fifty years out of practice, we are. Maybe C. Cretemaster will save us." I smiled at Anton's bewilderment. "Look it up in the ARM records. There's supposed to be an alien of sorts living in the cometary halo. He's the force that's been keeping us at peace this past three and a half centuries."

"Very funny."

"Mmm. Well, Anton, this is a lot more real for you than me. *I* haven't yet seen anything upsetting."

I hadn't called him a liar. I'd only made him aware that I knew nothing to the contrary. For Anton there might be elaborate proofs; but I'd seen nothing, and heard only a scary tale.

Anton reacted gracefully. "Of course. Well, there's still that bottle."

Anton's Calvados was as special as he'd claimed, decades old and quite unique. He produced cheese and bread.

Good thing: I was ready to eat his arm off. We managed to stick to harmless topics, and parted friends.

The big catlike aliens had taken up residence in my soul.

Aliens aren't implausible. Once upon a time, maybe. But an ancient ETI in a stasis field had been in the Smithsonian since the opening of the twenty-second century, and a quite different creature—C. Cretemaster's real-life analog—had crashed on Mars before the century ended.

Two spacecraft matching course at near lightspeed, *that* was just short of ridiculous. Kinetic energy considerations . . . why, two such ships colliding might as well be made of antimatter! Nothing short of a gravity generator could make it work. But Anton was *claiming* a gravity generator.

His story was plausible in another sense. Faced with warrior aliens, the ARM would do only what they could not avoid. They would build a gravity generator because the ARM must control such a thing. Any further move was a step toward the unthinkable. The ARM took sole credit (and other branches of the United Nations also took sole credit) for the fact that Man had left war behind. I shuddered to think what force it would take to turn the ARM toward war.

I would continue to demand proof of Anton's story. Looking for proof was one way to learn more, and I resist seeing myself as stupid. But I believed him already.

On Thursday we returned to suite 23309.

"I had to dig deep to find out, but they're not just sitting on their thumbs," he said. "There's a game going in Aristarchus Crater, Belt against flatlander. They're playing peace games."

"Huh?"

"They're making formats for contact and negotiation with hypothetical aliens. The models all have the look of those alien corpses, cats with bald tails, but they all think differently—"

"Good." Here was my proof. I could check this claim.

"Good. Sure. Peace games." Anton was brooding. Twitchy. "What about war games?"

"How would you run one? Half your soldiers would be dead at the end . . . unless you're thinking of rifles with paint bullets. War gets more violent than that."

Anton laughed. "Picture every building in Chicago covered with scarlet paint on one side. A nuclear war game."

"Now what? I mean for us."

"Yah. Jack, the ARM isn't *doing* anything to put the human race back on a war footing."

"Maybe they've done something they haven't told you about."

"Jack, I don't think so."

"They haven't let you read all their files, Anton. Two weeks ago you didn't know about peace games in Aristarchus. But okay. What *should* they be doing?"

"I don't *know.*"

"How's your chemistry?"

Anton grimaced. "How's yours? Forget I said that. Maybe I'm back to normal and maybe I'm not."

"Yah, but you haven't thought of anything. How about weapons? Can't have a war without weapons, and the ARM's been suppressing weapons. We should dip into their files and make up a list. It would save some time, when and if. I know of an experiment that might have been turned into an inertialess drive if it hadn't been suppressed."

"Date?"

"Early twenty-second. And there was a field projector that would make things burn, late twenty-third."

"I'll find 'em." Anton's eyes took on a faraway look. "There's the archives. I don't mean just the stuff that was built and then destroyed. The archives reach all the way back to the early twentieth. Stuff that was proposed, tanks, orbital beam weapons, kinetic energy weapons, biologicals—"

"We don't want biologicals."

I thought he hadn't heard. "Picture crowbars six feet long. A short burn takes them out of orbit, and they steer themselves down to anything with the silhouette you want . . . a tank or a submarine or a limousine, say. Primitive stuff now, but at least it would *do* something." He was really getting into this. The technical terms he was tossing off were masks for horror. He stopped suddenly, then, "Why not biologicals?"

"Nasty bacteria tailored for *us* might not work on warcats. We want *their* biological weapons, and we don't want them to have ours."

" . . . Stet. Now here's one for you. How would you adjust a 'doc to make a normal person into a soldier?"

My head snapped up. I saw the guilt spread across his face. He said, "I had to look up your dossier. *Had* to, Jack."

"Sure. All right, I'll see what I can find." I stood up. "The easiest way is to pick schitzies and train *them* as soldiers. We'd start with the same citizens the ARM has been training since . . . date classified, three hundred years or so. People who need the 'doc to keep their metabolism straight, or else they'll ram a car into a crowd, or strangle—"

"We wouldn't find enough. When you need soldiers, you need thousands. Maybe millions."

"True. It's a rare condition. Well, good night, Anton."

I fell asleep on the 'doc table again.

Dawn poked under my eyelids and I got up and moved toward the holophone. Caught a glimpse of myself in a mirror. Rethought. If David saw me looking like this, he'd be booking tickets to attend the funeral. So I took a shower and a cup of coffee first.

My eldest son looked like I had: decidedly rumpled. "Dad, can't you read a clock?"

"I'm sorry. Really." These calls are so expensive that

there's no point in hanging up. "How are things in Aristarchus?"

"Clavius. We've been moved out. We've got half the space we used to, and we'd need twice the space to hold everything we own. Ah, the time change isn't your fault, Dad, we're all in Clavius now, all but Jennifer. She—" David vanished.

A mechanically soothing voice said, "You have inpinged on ARM police business. The cost of your call will be refunded."

I looked at the empty space where David's face had been. I *was* ARM . . . but maybe I'd already heard enough.

My granddaughter Jennifer is a medic. The censor program had reacted to her name in connection with David.

David said she wasn't with him. The whole family had been moved out but for Jennifer.

If she'd stayed on in Aristarchus . . . or been kept on . . .

Human medics are needed when something unusual has happened to a human body or brain. Then they study what's going on, with an eye to writing more programs for the 'docs. The bulk of these problems are psychological.

Anton's "peace games" must be stressful as Hell.

II

Anton wasn't at the Monobloc Thursday. That gave me another week to rethink and recheck the programs I'd put on a dime disk; but I didn't need it.

I came back the next Thursday. Anton Brillov and Phoebe Garrison were holding a table for four.

I paused—backlit in the doorway, knowing my expression was hidden—then moved on in. "When did you get back?"

"Saturday before last," Phoebe said gravely.

It felt awkward. Anton felt it too; but then, he would.

I began to wish I didn't ever have to see him on a Thursday night.

I tried tact. "Shall we see if we can conscript a fourth?"

"It's not like that," Phoebe said. "Anton and I, we're *together*. We had to tell you."

But I'd never thought . . . I'd never *claimed* Phoebe. Dreams are private. This was coming from some wild direction. "Together as in?"

Anton said, "Well, not married, not yet, but thinking about it. And we wanted to talk privately."

"Like over dinner?"

"A good suggestion."

"I like Buffalo Bill. Let's go there."

Twenty-odd habitues of the Monobloc must have heard the exchange and watched us leave. *Those three long-timers seem friendly enough, but too serious . . . and there's an odd number . . .*

We didn't talk until we'd reached Suite 23309.

Anton closed the door before he spoke. "She's in, Jack. Everything."

I said, "It's really love, then."

Phoebe smiled. "Jack, don't be offended. Choosing is what humans do."

Trite, I thought, and *skip it.* "That bit there in the Monobloc seemed overdone. I felt excessively foolish."

"That was for *them*. My idea," Phoebe said. "After tonight, one of us may have to go away. This way we've got an all-purpose excuse. You leave because your best friend and favored lady closed you out. Or Phoebe leaves because she can't bear to ruin a friendship. Or big, burly Jack drives Anton away. See?"

She wasn't just in, she was taking over. Ah, well. "Phoebe, love, do you believe in murderous cats eight feet tall?"

"Do you have any doubts, Jack?"

"Not any more. I called my son. Something secretive

is happening in Aristarchus, something that requires a medic."

She only nodded. "What have you got for us?"

I showed them my dime disk. "Took me less than a week. Run it in an autodoc. Ten personality choices. The chemical differences aren't big, but . . . infantry, which means killing on foot and doesn't have anything to do with children . . . where was I? Yah. Infantry isn't at all like logistics, and neither is like espionage, and Navy is different yet. We may have lost some of the military vocations over the centuries. We'll have to re-invent them. This is just a first cut. I wish we had a way to try it out."

Anton set a dime disk next to mine, and a small projector. "Mine's nearly full. The ARM's stored an incredible range of dangerous devices. We need to think hard about where to store this. I even wondered if one of us should be emigrating, which is why—"

"To the Belt? Further?"

"Jack, if this all adds up, we won't have *time* to reach another star."

We watched stills and flat motion pictures of weapons and tools in action. Much of it was quite primitive, copied out of deep archives. We watched rock and landscape being torn, aircraft exploding, machines destroying other machines . . . and imagined flesh shredding.

"I could get more, but I thought I'd better show you this first," Anton said.

I said, "Don't bother."

"What? Jack?"

"It only took us a week! Why risk our necks to do work that can be duplicated that fast?"

Anton looked lost. "We need to do *something!*"

"Well, maybe we don't. Maybe the ARM is doing it all for us."

Phoebe gripped Anton's wrist hard, and he swallowed some bitter retort. She said, "Maybe we're missing something. Maybe we're not looking at it right."

"What's on your mind?"

"Let's *find* a way to look at it differently." She was looking straight at me.

I said, "Stoned? Drunk? Fizzed? Wired?"

Phoebe shook her head. "We need the schitz view."

"Dangerous, love. Also, the chemicals you're talking about are massively illegal. *I* can't get them, and Anton would be caught for sure—" I saw the way she was smiling at me. "Anton, I'll break your scrawny neck."

"Huh? Jack?"

"No, no, he didn't tell me," Phoebe said hastily, "though frankly I'd think either of you might have trusted me that much, Jack! I remembered you in the 'doc that morning, and Anton coming down from that twitchy state on a Thursday night, and it all clicked."

"Okay."

"You're a schitz, Jack. But it's been a long time, hasn't it?"

"Thirteen years of peace," I said. "They pick us for it, you know. Paranoid schizophrenics, born with our chemistry screwed up, hair trigger temper and a skewed view of the universe. Most schitzies never have to feel that. We use the 'docs more regularly than you do and that's that. But some of us go into the ARM . . . Phoebe, your suggestion is still silly. Anton's crazy four days out of the week, just like I used to be. Anton's all you need."

"Phoebe, he's right."

"No. The ARM used to be *all* schitzies, right? The genes have thinned out over three hundred years."

Anton nodded. "They tell us in training. The ones who could be Hitler or Napoleon or Castro, they're the ones the ARM wants. They're the ones you can send on a mother hunt, the ones with no social sense . . . but the Fertility Board doesn't let them breed either, unless they've got something special. Jack, you were special, high intelligence or something—"

"Perfect teeth, and I don't get sick in free fall, and Charlotte's people never develop back problems. That helped. Yah . . . but every century there are less of us. So they hire some Antons too, and *make* you crazy—"

"But carefully," Phoebe said. "Anton's not evolved for paranoia, Jack. You are. When they juice Anton up they don't make him too crazy, just enough to get the viewpoint they want. I bet they leave the top management boringly sane. But *you,* Jack—"

"I *see* it." Centuries of ARM tradition were squarely on her side.

"*You* can go as crazy as you like. It's all natural, and medics have known how to handle it since Only One Earth. We need the schitz viewpoint, and we don't have to steal the chemicals."

"Stet. When do we start?"

Anton looked at Phoebe. Phoebe said, "Now?"

We played Anton's tape all the way through, to a running theme of graveyard humor.

"I took only what I thought we could use," Anton said. "You should have seen some of the rest. Agent Orange. Napalm. Murder stuff."

Phoebe said, "Isn't this murder?"

That remark might have been unfair. We were watching this bizarre chunky rotary-blade flyer. Fire leaped from underneath it, once and again . . . weapons of some kind.

Anton said, "Aircraft design isn't the same when you use it for murder. It changes when you expect to be shot at. Here—" The picture had changed. "That's another weapons platform. It's not just fast, it's supposed to hide in the sky. Jack, are you all right?"

"I'm scared green. I haven't felt any effects yet."

Phoebe said, "You need to relax. Anton delivers a terrific massage. I never learned."

She wasn't kidding. Anton didn't have my muscle, but he had big strangler's hands. I relaxed into it, talking as he worked, liking the way my voice wavered as his hands pounded my back.

"It hasn't been that long since a guy like me let his 'doc run out of beta-dammasomething. An indicator light ran out and he didn't notice. He tried to kill his business partner by bombing his partner's house, and got some family members instead."

"We're on watch," Phoebe said. "If you go berserk we can handle it. Do you want to see more of this?"

"We've missed something. Children, I'm a *registered* schitz. If I don't use my 'doc for three days, they'll be trying to find me before I remember I'm the Marsport Strangler."

Anton said, "He's right, love. Jack, give me your door codes. If I can get into your apt, I can fix the records."

"Keep talking. Finish the massage, at least. We might have other problems. Do we want fruit juice? Munchies? Foodlike substances?"

When Anton came back with groceries, Phoebe and I barely noticed.

Were the warcats real? Could we fight them with present tech? How long did Sol system have? And the other systems, the more sparsely settled colony worlds? Was it enough to make tapes and blueprints of the old murder machines, or must we set to building clandestine factories? Phoebe and I were spilling ideas past each other as fast as they came, and I had quite forgotten that I was doing something dangerous.

I noticed myself noticing that I was thinking much faster than thoughts could spill from my lips. I remembered knowing that Phoebe was brighter than I was, and that didn't matter either. But Anton was losing his Thursday edge.

We slept. The old airbed was a big one. We woke to fruit and bread and dived back in.

We re-invented the Navy using only what Anton had recorded of seagoing navies. We had to. There had never been space navies; the long peace had fallen first.

I'm not sure when I slid into schitz mode. I'd spent four days out of seven without the 'doc, every week for forty-one years excluding vacations. You'd think I'd remember the feel of my brain chemistry changing. Sometimes I do; but it's the central *me* that changes, and there's no way to control that.

Anton's machines were long out of date, and none had been developed even for interplanetary war. Mankind had found peace too soon. Pity. But if the warcats' gravity generators·could be copied before the warcats arrived, that alone could save us!

Then again, whatever the cats had for weapons, kinetic energy was likely to be the ultimate weapon, *however* the mass was moved. Energy considerations don't lie . . . I stopped trying to anticipate individual war machines; what I needed was overview. Anton was saying very little.

I realized that I had been wasting my time making medical programs. Chemical enhancement was the most trivial of what we'd need to remake an army. Extensive testing would be needed, and then we might not get soldiers at all unless they retained *some* civil rights, or unless officers killed enough of them to impress the rest. Our limited pool of schitzies had better be trained as our officers. For that matter, we'd better start by taking over the ARM. They had all the brightest schitzies.

As for Anton's work in the ARM archives, the most powerful weapons had been entirely ignored. They were too obvious.

I saw how Phoebe was staring at me, and Anton too, both gape-jawed.

I tried to explain that our task was nothing less than the reorganization of humanity. Large numbers might have to die before the rest saw the wisdom in following our lead. The warcats would teach that lesson . . . but if we waited for them, we'd be too late. Time was breathing hot on our necks.

Anton didn't understand. Phoebe was following me, though not well, but Anton's body language was pulling him back and closing him up while his face stayed blank. He feared me worse than he feared warcats.

I began to understand that I might have to kill Anton. I hated him for that.

We did not sleep Friday at all. By Saturday noon we should have been exhausted. I'd caught cat naps from time to time, we all had, but I was still blazing with ideas. In my mind the pattern of an interstellar invasion was shaping itself like a vast three-dimensional map.

Earlier I might have killed Anton, because he knew too much or too little, because he would steal Phoebe from me. Now I saw that was foolish. Phoebe wouldn't follow him. He simply didn't have the . . . the internal power. As for knowledge, he was our only access to the ARM!

Saturday evening we ran out of food . . . and Anton and Phoebe saw the final flaw in their plan.

I found it hugely amusing. My 'doc was halfway across Santa Maria. They had to get me there. Me, a schitz.

We talked it around. Anton and Phoebe wanted to check my conclusions. Fine: we'd give them the schitz treatment. But for that we needed my disk (in my pocket) and my 'doc (at the apt). So we had to go to my apt. With that in mind, we shaped plans for a farewell bacchanal. Anton ordered supplies. Phoebe got me into a taxi. When I thought of other destinations she was persuasive. And the party was waiting . . .

We were a long time reaching the 'doc. There was beer to be dealt with, and a pizza the size of Arthur's Round Table. We sang, though Phoebe couldn't hold a tune. We took ourselves to bed. It had been years since my urge to rut ran so high, so deep, backed by a sadness that ran deeper yet and wouldn't go away.

When I was too relaxed to lift a finger, we staggered

singing to the 'doc with me hanging limp between them. I produced my dime disk, but Anton took it away. What was this? They moved me onto the table and set it working. I tried to explain: they had to lie down, put the disk here . . . but the circuitry found my blood loaded with fatigue poisons, and put me to sleep.

Sunday noon:

Anton and Phoebe seemed embarrassed in my presence. My own memories were bizarre, embarrassing. I'd been guilty of egotism, arrogance, self-centered lack of consideration. Three dark blue dots on Phoebe's shoulder told me that I'd brushed the edge of violence. But the worst memory was of thinking like some red handed conqueror, and out loud.

They'd never love me again.

But they could have brought me into the apt and straight to the 'doc. Why didn't they?

While Anton was out of the room I caught Phoebe's smile in the corner of my eye, and saw it fade as I turned. An old suspicion surfaced and has never faded since.

Suppose that the women I love are all attracted to Mad Jack. Somehow they recognize my schitz potential, though they find my sane state dull. There must have been a place for madness throughout most of human history. So men and women had sought in each other the capacity for madness . . .

And so what? Schitzies kill. The real Jack Strather is too dangerous to be let loose.

And yet . . . it had been worth doing. From that strange fifty-hour session I remembered one real insight. We spent the rest of Sunday discussing it, making plans, while my central nervous system returned to its accustomed, unnatural state. Sane Jack.

Anton Brillov and Phoebe Garrison held their wedding reception in the Monobloc. I stood as Best Man, bravely,

cheerful, running over with congratulations, staying carefully sober.

A week later I was among the asteroids. At the Monobloc
they said that Jack Strather had fled Earth after his favored
lady deserted him for his best friend.

III

Things ran smoother for me because John Junior had made
a place for himself in Ceres.

Even so, they had to train me. Twenty years ago I'd
spent a week in the Belt. It wasn't enough. Training and
a Belt citizen's equipment used up most of my savings
and two months of my time.

Time brought me to Mercury, and the lasers, eight
years ago.

Lightsails are rare in the inner solar system. Between
Venus and Mercury there are still lightsail races, an
expensive, uncomfortable, and dangerous sport. Cargo
craft once sailed throughout the asteroid belt, until fusion
motors became cheaper and more dependable.

The last refuge of the light-sail is a huge, empty region:
the cometary halo, Pluto, and beyond. The light-sails are
all cargo craft. So far from Sol, their thrust must be aug-
mented by lasers, the same Mercury lasers that sometimes
hurl an unmanned probe into interstellar space.

These were different from the launch lasers I was familiar with. They were enormously larger. In Mercury's lower
gravity, in Mercury's windless environment, they looked
like crystals caught in spiderwebs. When the lasers fired
the fragile support structures wavered like spiderweb in a
wind. Each stood in a wide black pool of solar collector,
as if tar paper had been scattered at random. A collector
sheet that lost fifty percent of power was not removed.
We would add another sheet, but continue to use all the
available power.

Their power output was dangerous to the point of fantasy. For safety's sake the Mercury lasers must be continually linked to the rest of the solar system across a lightspeed delay of several hours. The newer solar collectors also picked up broadcasts from space, or from the control center in Challenger Crater. Mercury's lasers must never lose contact. A beam that strayed where it wasn't supposed to could do untold damage.

They were spaced all along the planet's equator. They were hundreds of years apart in design, size, technology. They fired while the sun was up and feeding their square miles of collectors, with a few fusion generators for backup. They flicked from target to target as the horizon moved. When the sun set, it set for thirty-odd Earth days, and that was plenty of time to make repairs—

"In general, that is." Kathry Perritt watched my eyes to be sure I was paying attention. I felt like a schoolboy again. "In general we can repair and update each laser station in turn and *still* keep ahead of the dawn. But come a quake, we work in broad daylight and like it."

"Scary," I said, too cheerfully.

She looked at me. "You feel nice and cool? That's a million tons of soil, old man, and a layer cake of mirror sheeting on top of that, and these old heat exchangers are still the most powerful ever built. Daylight doesn't scare you? You'll get over that."

Kathry was a sixth generation Belter from Mercury, taller than me by seven inches, not very strong, but extremely dextrous. She was my boss. I'd be sharing a room with her . . . and yes, she rapidly let me know that she expected us to be bedmates.

I was all for that. Two months in Ceres had showed me that Belters respond to social signals I don't know. I had no idea how to seduce anyone.

Sylvia and Myron had been born on Mars in an enclave of areologists digging out the cities beneath the deserts. Companions from birth, they'd married at puberty. They were addicted to news broadcasts. News could get them arguing. Otherwise they behaved as if they could read each other's minds; they hardly talked to each other or to anyone else.

We'd sit around the duty room and wait, and polish our skills as storytellers. Then one of the lasers would go quiet, and a tractor the size of some old Chicago skyscraper would roll.

Rarely was there much of a hurry. One laser would fill in for another until the Monster Bug arrived. Then the robots, riding the Monster Bug like one of Anton's aircraft carriers, would scatter ahead of us and set to work.

Two years after my arrival, my first quake shook down six lasers in four different locations, and ripped a few more loose from the sunlight collectors. Landscape had been shaken into new shapes. The robots had some trouble. Sometimes Kathry could reprogram. Otherwise her team had to muscle them through, with Kathry to shout orders and me to supply most of the muscle.

Of the six lasers, five survived. They seemed built to survive almost anything. The robots were equipped to spin new support structure and to lift the things into place, with a separate program for each design.

Maybe John Junior *hadn't* used influence in my behalf. Flatlander muscles were useful, when the robots couldn't get over the dust pools or through the broken rock. For that matter, maybe it wasn't some Belt tradition that made Kathry claim me on sight. Sylvia and Myron weren't sharing; and I might have been female, or bend. Maybe she thought she was lucky.

After we'd remounted the lasers that survived, Kathry said, "They're all obsolete anyway. They're not being replaced."

"That's not good," I said.

"Well, good and bad. Light-sail cargos are slow. If the light wasn't almost free, why bother? The interstellar probes haven't sent much back yet, and we might as well wait. At least the Belt Speakers think so."

"Do I gather I've fallen into a kind of blind alley?"

She glared at me. "You're an immigrant flatlander. What did you expect, First Speaker for the Belt? You thinking of moving on?"

"Not really. But if the job's about to fold—"

"Another twenty years, maybe. Jack, I'd miss you. Those two—"

"It's all right, Kathry. I'm not going." I waved both arms at the blazing dead landscape and said, "I like it here," and smiled into her bellow of laughter.

I beamed a tape to Anton when I got the chance.

"If I was ever angry, I got over it, as I hope you've forgotten anything I said or did while I was, let's say, running on automatic. I've found another life in deep space, not much different from what I was doing on Earth . . . though that may not last. These light-sail pusher lasers are a blast from the past. Time gets them, the quakes get them, and they're not being replaced. Kathry says twenty years.

"You said Phoebe left Earth, too. Working with an asteroid mining setup? If you're still trading tapes, tell her I'm all right and I hope she is too. Her career choice was better than mine, I expect . . ."

I couldn't think of anything else to do.

Three years after I expected it, Kathry asked. "Why did you come out here? It's none of my business, of course—"

Customs differ: it took her three years in my bed to work up to this. I said, "Time for a change," and "I've got children and grandchildren on the Moon and Ceres and Floating Jupiter."

"Do you miss them?"

I had to say yes. The result was that I took half a year off to bounce around the solar system. I found Phoebe, too, and we did some catching up; but I still came back early. My being away made us both antsy.

Kathry asked again a year later. I said, "What I did on Earth was a lot like this. The difference is, on Earth I'm dull. Here—am I dull?"

"You're fascinating. You won't talk about the ARM, so you're fascinating and mysterious. I can't believe you'd be dull just because of where you are. Why did you leave, really?"

So I said, "There was a woman."

"What was she like?"

"She was smarter than me. I was a little dull for her. So she left, and that would have been okay. But she came back to my best friend." I shifted uncomfortably and said, "Not that they drove me off Earth."

"No?"

"No. I've got everything I once had herding construction robots on Earth, plus one thing that I wasn't bright enough to miss. I lost my sense of purpose when I left the ARM."

I noticed that Myron was listening. Sylvia was watching the holo walls, the three that showed the face of Mercury: rocks blazing like coals, with only the robots and the lasers to give the illusion of life. The fourth we kept changing. Just then it showed a view up the trunk into the waving branches of the tremendous redwood they've been growing for three hundred years, in Hovestraydt City on the moon.

"These are the good times," I said. "You have to notice, or they'll go right past. We're holding the stars together. Notice how much dancing we do? I'd be too old and creaky for that—Sylvia, *what?*"

Sylvia was shaking my shoulder. I heard it as soon as I stopped talking: *"Tombaugh Station relayed this picture, the last broadcast from the* Fantasy Prince. *Once again, the* Fantasy Prince *has apparently been—"*

Starscape glowed within the fourth holo wall. Something came out of nowhere, moving hellishly fast, and stopped so quickly that it might have been a toy. It was egg-shaped, studded with what I remembered as weapons.

Phoebe won't have made her move yet. The warcats will have to be deep in the solar system before her asteroid mining setup can be any deterrent. Then one or another warcat ship will find streams of slag sprayed across its path, impacting at comet speeds.

By now Anton must know whether the ARM actually has plans to repel an interstellar invasion.

Me, I've already done my part. I worked on the computer shortly after I first arrived. Nobody's tampered with it since. The dime disk is in place.

We kept the program relatively simple. Until and unless the warcats destroy something that's being pushed by a laser from Mercury, nothing will happen. The warcats must condemn themselves. Then the affected laser will lock onto the warcat ship . . . and so will every Mercury laser that's getting sunlight. Twenty seconds, then the system goes back to normal until another target disappears.

If the warcats can be persuaded that Sol system is defended, maybe they'll give us time to build defenses.

Asteroid miners dig deep for fear of solar storms and meteors. Phoebe might survive. We might survive here, too, with shielding built to block the hellish sun, and laser cannon to battle incoming ships. But that's not the way to bet.

We might get one ship.

It might be worth doing.

MY ADVICE TO
THE CIVILIZED

John Barnes

*"My Advice to the Civilized" was purchased by
Gardner Dozois, and appeared in the April 1990
issue of* Asimov's, *with an illustration by George
Thompson. It was one of a string of powerful, lit-
erate, and highly inventive stories and novellas that
Barnes sold to* Asimov's *during the '80s, making
him one of our most popular authors. In the compel-
ling story that follows, he takes us to meet a soldier
who is pondering his life on the eve of what might
well be the Last Battle, for a poignant and unsettling
look at just* how *much we have to lose. . . .*

*John Barnes is one of the most popular and inven-
tive of the new generation of "hard SF" writers.
He's a frequent contributor to* Asimov's *and* Analog,
and has also sold fiction to Amazing, *and to other
markets. His novels include the critically acclaimed*
The Man Who Pulled Down the Sky *and* Sin of Origin, *and, most recently, the well-received* Orbital
Resonance, *which was a Nebula Finalist. Barnes
lives in Pittsburgh, Pennsylvania, where he pursues
a triple career as a theater scholar, a computer
modeler, and a science fiction writer.*

The captain says we've got a couple of hours to get letters
written.

A year ago I'd have spent the time writing letters for the younger men. But the literacy class I taught in winter bivouac took care of that. And I have no one to write to, anymore.

So he comes over to my spot at one of the former picnic tables on the former high school gym floor, and tries to cheer me up. Why he wants his company sergeant cheerful, I couldn't say. He's very sincere and sensitive and no help at all, because he can't fix the basic problem—I'm articulate and would love to write, but my family died in the St. Joseph raid, and old friends are all somewhere else, probably dead.

So he gets a dumb idea. "Look, Harry, if I have to I'll order you to do this. Suppose we don't win—maybe that's it for centuries, right? I mean we don't know that any other civilized settlement will make it. But sooner or later people will want to settle down, right, even if all of us are dead? I mean they are human out there. Or maybe some other settlement will make it all come together. And when civilization gets going again, they'll do archeology, just like Before."

I agree that all this is plausible because Dave can argue trivia to death.

"Well, then," he goes on, "write a letter to the future. You're a historian—tell the historians of the future what they'll want to know."

"I don't have their ZIP code. Maybe you would know it?"

His eyes widen. His fingers clench. He must be on edge; you don't mention what somebody did Before, like teaching college history. And I must be on edge too, because when someone is rude that way, you don't compound it by being rude back—like by alluding to the fact that Dave used to be a mailman. He sees we're headed for trouble, so he starts back to the big desk in the corner we share—the "Company Office."

He was just trying to help, and I feel bad for him, so I

walk after him and say I'll do it. "We'll bury it in a plastic bag someplace before I get on the plane. If we win I can always dig it up and continue it."

I pick up the pen and begin.

I don't know how Before became After. The big cities were smashed and burned first thing, but radio reports from the settlements that can afford expeditions say that there's no detectable radioactivity around Kansas City, Caracas, Honolulu, or Detroit. So it probably wasn't a nuclear war. Things just got violent and ugly one day, or within a week, but communications was the first thing to go, so all we have is the word of some ham and military radio operators that everything went to shit everywhere at about the same time.

Ernwood, a physicist, said he'd been up at the observatory that day and all the instruments went weird, a lot of them burning out. He thought maybe some solar event caused a giant global EMP (I forget what that stands for but it was connected with nuclear winter or something), starting fires wherever conductors ran.

But that didn't explain why some engines and a few radios and so forth still worked, or why nothing in our little huddle of valleys did anything like that—I'd assume my wristwatch would have charred my wrist.

When I asked Ernwood about that, he started talking fast, drawing pictures in the dirt, and his red hair and the flutter of his hands reminded me so much of Cynthia that I got fascinated and couldn't remember what he said afterwards. (This was just after I lost Margie and the kids at St. Joseph, and I couldn't seem to get my mind off Cynthia.)

Anyway, if it will help you, I'm pretty sure Ernwood used words like "shadowing effects," "bounceback," "reradiation," and "induced opaqueness." Science was my dead worst subject, but if that gives you a clue, maybe you'll find a surviving library somewhere to put it all together.

I'd have Ernwood write something for you, but he died in the defense of Providence Falls when we lost it eight weeks ago to Thrasher's Horde. Because of his red hair, his was about the only head we recognized in the big box they sent to us.

What I can tell you, anyway, is that I got up one Wednesday and there was no electricity, no water, no gas, nothing on the radio, no phone. A few days after, hundreds of refugees came up the highway with wild stories of looting and fighting, cities on fire and towns deserted.

As I re-read what I've written so far, I realize that I'm leaving you the sort of cryptic document that the Dark Ages specialists I knew could spend ages arguing about. My problem is I'm a historian, and no one can write history in these circumstances—history is interpretation, the choice and expression of a view. There's plenty of material for historiographers, establishers of facts and data, in the last decade, but nothing yet for historians.

They announce at least two hours' delay. Fine with me. I feel better about the odds going after dark. So do a lot of the men—they're sacking out all over—but I can't sleep. Might as well keep writing, especially after the promise I was making when I was interrupted.

Anyway, for you historiographers, you grubby fact-grinding establishers of names, dates, and places:

Before

Late XXth century A.D., USA, up until 199-

After

The current period. We are in the ninth year After, which will become the tenth year After five weeks after the next spring solstice. I'm very proud of myself for remembering a word like "solstice" and that that's what starts spring, so you'll have an accurate date to work from.

Civilization

That's what we call ourselves. Politically we're a republic constituted from the old county government of Carson-Bridger County. We used to control about 2500 square miles. We are now down to less than 1000 square miles, which Thrasher penetrated yesterday. He's being slowed by harassment for the moment. The plan is to get him a long way in before we spring what we hope will be a trap.

(Units of measure in above)

Mile = a little over 5000 feet, I think. The number 1760 comes to mind, too, but I can't remember why, and I don't think it's right. Use the land mile—nautical miles are different. One foot (the plural is feet) = 12 inches, I'm sure. One inch = I---------------I. (I copied that from an old ruler).

Basic geography

This will be buried at Gallatin High Barracks, which is our main military encampment. One half of a mile west of us is the old UMW Hall, where the Legislature meets, and that's across the street from the old County Courthouse, which is where the President and the Speaker have their offices.

St. Joseph

Nearest town east of here. Clorox's Horde surprise-raided it at the beginning of summer in the year 8. They killed everyone, took all the Before stuff they could carry, and torched the rest. We caught them and killed about fifty, three miles beyond Frederickstein Pass. The next spring they were wiped out by Excess's Horde.

Horde

Gang of raiders. Always named after their leaders. North of us is Wanker's Horde, and then clockwise from them there's Banger's, Excess's, Rover's (due south), Nitrofucker's, Fun Boy's, and Thrasher's. Thrasher seems to be the successful Attila type—Wanker, Banger, and Fun Boy have all been forced to swear some kind of fealty to him in the last couple of years.

The Company

I am in the Northwest Company. In better days we guarded Angel Break Pass. Now the whole Army will try to drive Thrasher's Horde (and its allies) back toward the pass. Northwest Company will try to seal it against them, so the Army—with the help of a couple of other surprises—can corner them for a massacre.

Army

Eleven companies, down from fourteen. They're about the size of US Army companies, Before. We have a colonel, Bob Peterin, and under him there are eleven captains, of whom David Lipowicz is mine. I'm his company sergeant and de facto XO—we've decided civilization can survive without lieutenants, at least for a while. The President is Mrs. Roberta Gibson, and the Speaker of the Legislature is Tiffany Ann Hutchinson, both of the Democratic/No Quarter Party. My party, by the way.

That was off the subject of my annotations, but I couldn't stand the thought that you might know the names of the Hordes' leaders and not ours.

• • •

Well, that used up twenty minutes. I stretch and flex my hand, numb from the unaccustomed strain of writing so much in a room that's rapidly getting cold.

The phone beeps. I pick it up. It's Samuelson with confirmation that the plans are go. I still can't believe that our little Cessna was able to get enough parts from other airfields so that we could get all four Dash-8's to fly, after all this time, or even that we managed to make enough methanol, and find enough kerosene, to fuel them.

So strange to think I'll be flying again!

Out the window, the sun has almost set. Dusk has that wonderful October gold color that Margie and I used to walk in for hours. The last fall we had together, Joshua was big enough to walk with us too, not having to be picked up and carried.

I can't believe I'll be flying again, and yet I used to fly into Salt Lake weekly when Harris and I were working on that silly paper about Reconstruction government opposition parties.

Will it all work? Supposedly we'll fly out low, away from Thrasher's Horde, and circle around to land in Angel Break Pass on the old interstate. That will give us most of the night to dig in. But we've had no rehearsals.

I look up from my thoughts. Three men, waiting patiently for me to notice them, want me to witness their wills. I do it, and talk with them for a couple of minutes. They go back to their benches to get some sleep. I should write more if I want to finish before we go, but instead I stand up and stretch.

The October gold fades to indefinite gray, and I look out the window, past the old football stadium, to the airfield. There's an indistinct dark lump out there.

It's a Q-hut, and it contains a collection of scuba tanks, soda machine cylinders, propane tanks, and so forth, all loaded with the nerve gas Bernie Klipfer was finally allowed to make after we won the election. (Well, the party won. I lost to a Democratic Christian by eight votes.) I helped attach the farm-dynamite heads and the bedsheet-strip tails.

So strange to imagine that those crude devices could end the threat within a few days. I wonder what the B-29 crew thought—really thought, not said later to journalists—when they first saw Little Boy? But then they had been winning.

The map of the region swims up in my head, with a red arrow, the kind newspapers used Before, stabbing like a spearhead into the soft, breastlike northwest bulge of civilization. I picture Angel Break Pass at the base of the arrow, and the Army as a dark bar in front of it.

Had we been able to do this last year, we could have dealt with all the Hordes by Dash-8. As it is, we must beat Thrasher or it's all for nothing.

But if we do beat Thrasher—then gas will fall on the other Hordes' winter encampments, some clear night in January when nothing can move far. We'll follow it up with fire bombs that same night, then pneumococcus a week later if Ralph Rogers can get it isolated and into a workable bomb by then. We may have to content ourselves with cholera in their streams in the spring, and with brucellosis in their cattle.

I've never been religious, but I pray now, offering thanks for all three, nerve gas and napalm and germs, my head down on the desk, the wood cool against my forehead.

And then I pray for us as well. The phone beeps again.

There was business to take care of, and we've had one more delay, so it's two hours since I last wrote and we go in about an hour. Now that the annotations are all written, I find myself wanting to tell you things, but I have no order, no scheme, no vision to put them into. As I said before, history isn't yet possible.

The main thing we learn from history is that no one learns anything from history. Somebody said that but I forget who.

Now that I've written all those dusty facts down for the pedants, I'll take what time I've got to say what I think.

Someone is crying, very quietly, in the southeast corner of the gym. It's very dark away from the desk. Maybe I miss electric lights most. It's dusty—no men to spare for cleaning this past month. I don't want to sneeze and draw attention. Besides, I might wake someone.

It's my youngest squad leader, Rodney, who is sixteen. He got his men to go to sleep and then felt bad himself afterward.

We know his age because when we found him seven years ago he had a passport. Back when we still did rescue, and we were still absolutely the good guys.

If it hadn't happened, he'd have been here, or somewhere like it, on a Friday night in October, at a basketball game or a dance.

I ask what's wrong. Just nerves, and a bad dream. He'll be fine—he's been through the whole summer's campaign already. Anyone can get scared. Since he's okay, I go back to the desk.

It's a long way back to the candle. I go slowly, avoiding stepping on people; moments from Before swarm up in me. I remember the cold floors on my way to the bathroom in my pj's, back when all I had to fear was monsters.

Dave doesn't look up from his map. He's asleep with his head in his hands. I sit down in the little pool of red-gold flickering light and pick up the pen again. Beyond our smear of light, it's absolutely dark. I hear only the soft white noise of many people breathing.

Sorry about the time taken from writing to you. I had to comfort a crying kid. I can't help that—I grew up in civilization.

But you understand. Either you're civilized or you're trying—otherwise you would use this to start a fire, not read it.

Unless you've found this *very* late, when you're already dreaming of the lost charms of barbarism. Then no one will read this except some pedant who will grind it up to count how many different verbs I use and the frequency of misspelled words.

That too is civilized.

All I will do now is let myself ramble. I might be decades or centuries older than you are, and you know old people are garrulous.

The moonlight is coming in the window now. Before I begin to write, I go over to look at it. Almost, except for the dead streetlight, this could be the same town, Before.

My Advice to the Civilized

One. *Write down a lot of stuff that doesn't matter.*

Civilization itself isn't much more than accumulated stuff we like that doesn't matter. All that *really* matters is getting enough to eat, sleeping safe and warm, and having somebody to talk to. If you're less strict, there are other things that also matter: politics, GNP, armies moving. Let somebody else write all that down.

Write down stuff that *doesn't* matter.

Like that Margie married me because she liked the University but hated being a grad student. And that I asked her because I knew I wouldn't do any better at my age and salary. And that we had Josh because our birth control stockpile finally ran out.

About the time he was born, we fell in love again. Or maybe just one of us did, and the other was gracious about it. That's how we had Sally.

Graciousness is attention to small details—which you should write down. When Josh learned to hang icicles one at a time and not just hurl them at the tree, he was learning graciousness.

I don't know now why I think of Cynthia so often, but she was gracious, too, and this truly can't matter in the future—it doesn't even matter now—so it's a perfect example.

When she decided the romance was over, she remembered how strongly I associated places with things that happened there, so she made sure she told me in a place I wouldn't ever have to see again.

Even now remembering Larry's Family Dining hurts, but I have no idea whether it was still standing even ten years Before. Just a formica/steel place off the freeway with twenty-four-hour breakfast, a coffee pot on every table, and everything-creme pie.

Cynthia told me as we ate. Uncharacteristically plain in jeans, sweatshirt, and no makeup, she still wore her trademark plastic earrings that looked like a cross between fishing lures and IUDs. Rain thumped against the window next to us and slid down in lumpy sheets.

We had gone in my car: her way of saying she trusted me.

The full moon is higher now. In London in the 40s they called the Harvest Moon (normally the longest full moon in the year) the Bomber's Moon because it made it easy for planes to operate.

I hope it still works. The rhombus of moonlight on the floor is divided by the crosspiece shadows and I think of the end of *Mrs. Miniver*.

I try to concentrate on something serious, but my own advice, scribbled on the candle-shadowed, flickering page before me, disagrees. If I had life to live over, I would think more about whatever popped into my head, and much less about what I was supposed to. The only thing worth doing I did in grade school was daydream.

I look back to the shadowed cross in the dust-yellowed moonlight on the floor and I see the end of *Mrs. Miniver,* again. Greer Garson's face glows, tilted up toward the crossed beams in the bomb hole in the church. Cut to four Spitfires roaring across the sky seen through the upper left corner of the cross—the basic shape of an American flag (= hope?) overlaid on a cross.

I get up to look out the window. There have been some hundreds of days of fighting across the past several years. There will be more if we win. Dave talks about doing what Powell or Pike or Lewis and Clark did, a real exploration of the territory, "once things settle down." He's promised to take me.

As I turn back to the desk, the moonbeam is so bright dust specks shine in it. My shadow blanks them like the Black Thing in *A Wrinkle in Time*.

When I was seven or eight, at Grandma's house, I discovered that if I watched closely enough I could follow a speck out of the sunlight and into the surrounding shadow. As long as I didn't look away I could stay with it. I followed one speck all the way into the hallway and the sunlight of another window. There it was lost in the busy swirl of other specks.

Here's something else that doesn't matter. Margie never learned to love *Mrs. Miniver* the way I did. Probably because it had been Cynthia's and my movie. Some couples have songs (Margie and I had "Scotch and Soda") and foods (one of my roommates and his girlfriend felt that pineapple and green pepper pizza twice a week was mandatory) but Cynthia and I were the only couple I knew who had a movie.

It showed as part of the classic film series, at 7:00 and 9:30 for two nights, every semester. We made it to all eight showings junior year, and six the year before.

Cynthia and I used to fantasize constantly about our

living in the *"Mrs. Miniver* Universe." She would be a British Army nurse, because she had always wanted to be British, and I would be a former Okie who had hoboed and worked for the CCC, because I had always wanted a romantic tough background even though (because?) I'd grown up in the suburbs. "Now"—circa 1942 or '43, MMU—I would be a ball turret gunner on a B-17. (I'd rather have flown a Mustang but that was more middle than working class.)

It went on for more than a year. We carried it as far as learning ballroom jitterbug and taking a lot of history courses covering the New Deal period, World War II, and occasionally the early Cold War. Some forties-style stuff was in fashion so we could sort of dress the part. If there had been Lucky Strikes available then, we'd have started smoking.

You see what I mean. Write down stuff that doesn't matter. If you don't see what I mean, you'll probably just burn this, or wipe your ass with it.

Dave's right. I can't stand the idea.

Two. *Keep the roads open.*

That's what we're trying to do.

Barbarians travel, but *they* only open roads for them-selves, just carving holes through human geography and continuing on their lice-ridden way. The Vandals moved a lot by fifth and sixth century standards, but they made it tough and dangerous for anyone else to try. Civilization requires that people who aren't bothering other people have a safe, easy way to go other places. You've got to know the world isn't your village, and you've got to be surrounded by people who know that.

I guess we were losing, Before. In 1910 you could have gone from Shanghai to Capetown, north to Stockholm, and all the way back east to Vladivostok, mostly by land with no problems on the way. Even in 1970 you could still drive from Scotland to India, and from Alaska to Tierra del Fuego, though that was getting dangerous. By the time the big change came, the same trips would have ended in Ankara and in Mexico City.

Anyway, we're going to re-open the roads north and south next spring. There are still a lot of "holds"—ranches with forts—out there, that could feed us if we got the roads safe again.

Gunfire.

I lift the phone to my ear. The connection's always open so I just say "Northwest here. What's the shooting?"

"No problem," Samuelson says. It's his standard answer to everything. "That's our guys. We want them real nervous, so some guys from South Company ambushed a scouting party that was dumb enough to walk up a road. Radio report is six dead, nine to be Plan B'd."

Plan B is what got Mrs. Gibson my vote. Instead of trying to rehabilitate the wounded (they take off as soon as they're well) or exchange prisoners (Hordes don't take any), we hang them, naked, and mutilate the corpses, on the approaches to town. We'd held off on doing that this summer, saving it for shock value.

I voted for Plan B, but I didn't urge anyone else to. Civilization is built on those small ethical distinctions, made repeatedly and recorded.

The rising moon looks smaller now, against stars instead of trees and hills. There are footprints on it. I remember my father shook me awake, made me come downstairs in my T-shirt and pajama bottoms, because there would only be a first time *once*.

Dad was really into the antiwar movement, and the room was full of his students, but unlike any other time I could recall, it was dead silent.

Armstrong bounced around like a kangaroo, sharp-edged with no air to soften it. It was so much like a marionette show under a bright spotlight, like *Thunderbirds* or *Supercar*, that I unconsciously looked for the thin white lines of the strings.

There's no more gunfire. I think of Providence Falls and St. Joseph, and my stomach rolls and my heart pounds to be out there, cutting at their corpses, and to see Thrasher's face when he sees them.

The Hordes would not bother to kill a person before starting to cut—another small, important distinction.

I sit down to write more, but the guns start going again. I pick up the phone.

"No problem. Spiders," Samuelson explains. Those are the young teenagers whose job is to fire a few shots from ambush at the first enemy they see and then get out. It forces the invaders to stop and duck each time, slowing their advance. "Now that they're between Thrasher and his forward scouts, they can slow him down a lot. They can shoot and scoot all night." Samuelson sounds as happy as he ever does.

I thank him, sit down, and pick up the pen.

People who plan roads, bridges, sewers, and so forth are called civil engineers. Civilization happens in cities, where civil society is possible, because of civil engineers. Cities are fed by roads, drained by sewers, watered by pipes that they lay down.

There have been barbarian poets and composers, even painters and some lawyers, but never a barbarian civil engineer. You have to be civilized to care about roads.

I used to take walking tours, from hotel to hotel on foot with just a knapsack. I backpacked too and enjoyed that but it wasn't the same thing. Backpackers walk to see empty useless land; walking tourists walk to see people—where they live and work, what they offer, threaten, sing, or shout to each other along the road. Backpackers say fuck you to people and commune with nature like gibbering savages; walking tourists commune with people.

Backpackers like trails, walking tourists like roads. Roads are civilized. Almost all walking tourists like backpacking but few backpackers like walking tours. Civilized people can enjoy barbaric pleasures, but not vice versa.

Cynthia got me into walking tours, the two summers we were dating. A decade later I got Margie into them.

Cynthia's whole family did walking tours, so there wasn't much choice if I wanted to see her for those two weeks. Besides, I liked her family. We walked in Vermont one year, and Minnesota the next.

I remember Cynthia swinging along on a dirt road through some state park in Vermont. She wore a black, stretchy sleeveless dress and hiking boots. She said it was comfortable; I told her she looked like Olive Oyl, though with her thick red hair hanging down in that French braid, there was no resemblance at all.

Her other dress was blue. Nightly showers, and always being around laundromats in the evening, meant never being more than one day dirty. If you've been backpacking

(will your civilization do such things? I hope so!

Three. *When you no longer* must *walk, walk for fun.*)

As I was saying, if you've been backpacking, you can imagine the pleasures of being clean every day.

One morning, on a deserted back road, when the rest of her family had gotten well ahead, Cynthia and I stopped to fuck. We'd done this often enough to have the technique perfected. For an hour, we'd been talking dirty to each other, quietly, in between some intense kissing—we called it "oral foreplay." We were both ready at the first good spot.

She pulled the black dress off over her head and dropped it on the grass, skinned down her panties, and leaned against a tree in only her bra, hiking boots, and wool socks. I took a rubber from the side pocket in my pack that held the survival kit ("put the stuff that you may need suddenly there," her father had said), and pulled off my shorts and underwear. She put the rubber on me.

As I slipped into her, pressing her against the tree, she gasped, choking down the loud moans she used to make in my frat house room, and pressed her face against my shoulder.

I looked away. Her fifteen-year-old sister Elaine was watching us, standing a few feet away on the trail.

She smiled and gestured for me to go on. As I went harder and faster into Cynthia, her hands clutching my buttocks, Elaine and I stared into each other's eyes. I even moved a little to the side, and Elaine came closer and squatted, so she could get a better look.

As I finished, Elaine stepped into a little side trail and disappeared. I had not thought of Cynthia at all, the whole time.

For the rest of the trip, Elaine would smile at me at odd times. Once she flashed a bare breast at me. I did not know how to respond.

Maybe in penance, or maybe because I didn't want anything else to happen, I didn't fuck Cynthia for the remaining four days of the trip.

When I told Margie about it, years later, she seemed confused and upset. Months later she asked if I wanted to do it outdoors with her, or while someone watched.

I said what she wanted to hear. I would gladly do it with her under any circumstances, but I didn't feel any need to repeat my youthful experiences.

As I said it, I felt disappointment. Margie was affectionate rather than dramatic, and I had always liked drama.

Four. *Enjoy lying, scandal, hypocrisy, and manners.*

Barbarians speak the truth all the time. Thrasher's last message to us was "I am coming. I want loot. I want pussy. Fuck you."

When I was in college the bathroom graffiti used to say hypocrisy was the vaseline of social intercourse. And most manners boil down to hypocrisy—doing a thing the way that pleases others, not the way that comes naturally.

Only barbarians are always honest. Had I been honest

with Dave about this busywork, I'd never have enjoyed writing it.

The phone beeps. I pick it up and say "Yeah, Northwest."

"Ready for go in twenty?"

"Sure." Go will mean lining up and crossing the field to board. I hang up. I'll wake the men in ten—they all sleep with boots on and packs loaded, and there's bound to be another delay at the airfield.

I set my watch alarm. In five years at the very most, the last batteries for watches will all be dead.

Gunfire far away—a harassing party shooting up Thrasher's rear?

Has Thrasher found the mutilated corpses? How did he react?

Thrasher's message was all honesty because barbarians rejoice in the rough honesty of discomfort—hair shirts, vision quests, war, gang rape, miserliness, all the ways of injuring yourself to propitiate the Big Booga-Booga in the Sky.

People think honesty is morally correct because all societies are barbarian in their early years, when their moral foundations are laid.

When I learned of Margie's affair with Robertson—an education professor, of all things—I threw the TA who was trying to tell me about it down a flight of stairs, and was disappointed that his arm didn't break. I cried all night after talking with Margie. I spat in Robertson's face when I met him in a bar. (A good move as it turned out—he was not tenured and I was, and the University decided he would be the easier problem to eliminate.)

All that was stupid. There was no style to any of it. I was a stupid jerk instead of the suave, controlled sophisticate I wanted to be.

Five. *Act like who you'd rather be, not who you are.*

• • •

I check my watch. Sixteen minutes left. The moon is high; our little town glows. I feel in my bones that this will work.

Six. *Dress well.* Junior year, the night of my frat's May Formal, Cynthia wore a perfectly white strapless dress that clung to her, and elbow-length white gloves. I wore a straight black dinner jacket, ruffled shirt, and black tie.

We moved like perfectly poised dolls or statues through the evening. It was only the next day that I realized I had *been* sophisticated, rather than just feeling it.

I remember that the stench of cigars and the sweet piercing scent of gin plus sweat in the crowded hotel ballroom drove us out onto the terrace.

We kissed, once, lightly, in the moonlight. There were a few other couples out there, along the wall, none near us. The lilacs stung the other smells from my nose, and the alcohol burned in my brain.

A wind came up—it would later become a thunderstorm, and lead to our taking a room in the hotel and spending the night making love in the flashes and thunder, but that came later and didn't matter as much, now that I look back. Right now the wind was still just a warm brushing of spring-soft boughs.

The band played Chad and Jeremy's "Summer Song." I took Cynthia in my arms, very formally, for a foxtrot, and we danced there on the terrace.

Her face was pale and deeply shadowed in the moonlight. When I kissed her at the end of the song, her skin was cool, her breath hot, on my cheek.

I knew then, as surely as I knew anything, that I was going to marry her. I was wrong, but I really knew it.

Ten minutes. I blow the whistle and people start moving. I pull out a plastic bag from the desk, but I won't bury my letter. It should be fine if I just put it in the bag, in the inside pocket of my coat. Raiders will take my watch and wedding ring, but they won't bother with paper, if it comes to that.

This way, if it does come to that, the words might have my body to go with them.

As I fold it I realize I'm not done.

I knew a lot of things. I knew Josh would be a big strong kid and drive me crazy by being a jock. I knew Margie would eventually love me. I knew the power would come back on and the phones start working, by the end of the first week After.

Seven. (Almost forgot!) *Make wine.*

And all good and beautiful things.

And especially make love, in the teeth of the odds.

Time.

I seal the bag, zip it in, and start bellowing at the company now forming up.

RHIP—I'm getting a window seat. I still don't believe, after all these years, an airplane.

THE PEACE SPY

Gene Wolfe

"The Peace Spy" was purchased by Gardner Dozois, and appeared in the January 1987 issue of Asimov's, *with an illustration by George Thompson. Wolfe is another of those writers who doesn't appear in the magazine nearly as often as we'd like, but he has had a number of excellent stories published here, starting under the editorship of George Scithers—including the sly and subtle story that follows, an unsettling look into a* very odd profession. . . .

Gene Wolfe is perceived by many critics to be one of the best—perhaps the best—SF and fantasy writers working today. His most acclaimed work is the tetralogy The Book of the New Sun, *individual volumes of which have won the Nebula Award, the World Fantasy Award, and the John W. Campbell Memorial Award, and which is widely considered to be one of the seminal works of the '80s. His other books include the novels* Peace, Soldier in the Mist, Free Live Free, The Urth of the New Sun, Soldier of Arete, *and* There Are Doors, *and the collections* The Island of Doctor Death and Other Stories, Gene Wolfe's Book of Days, Endangered Species, *and* Storeys from the Old Hotel. *His most recent books are* Castleview *and* Pandora by Holly Hollander.

"Hello, Mr. Percival," the young woman said, "so nice of you to come." She shut the door again, and Krasilnikov heard the rattle of a security chain before she opened it wide.

He stepped inside, and she closed the door behind him, threw the bolt and reattached the chain. "This is my business," he said. "I've gone to see people in places a lot farther from Washington than Alexandria."

"Won't you sit down?" She made a graceful gesture, and Krasilnikov reflected that she had not yet forgotten her manners; she was not yet so Americanized as all that.

He sat. "I admire your taste, Ms. Aralov." He smiled as he patted the arm of the stiff, tapestry-covered chair. "This is good antique furniture."

She shook her head. "It is Russian. No, it is not Russian, but it is as near to Russian furniture as I could discover here. I wished to say to the Americans, not 'I am an American,' but 'Look, I am a Soviet citizen living with you.' Surely you have seen such furnishings in other apartments. Would you care for tea?"

Krasilnikov nodded. "Sure, I've seen furniture of the same type, but it wasn't as nice as this—the red and gray color scheme. Most Russians go for red and black."

She smiled again, bitterly this time, before she bent in front of the steaming samovar in the corner. "Red for our country, black for death. We are so dramatic. Only I say red for our country, gray for no peace and no war. I say that because I like red and gray better." She presented him with a fragrant glass of tea.

He sipped. "You've got to understand, Ms. Aralov, that I don't do all my business with people like you. A lot of it's with Americans and American companies. The next biggest is with foreigners who want American citizenship."

"But you have handled such cases as mine before?"

"Sure," Krasilnikov said. He rattled off names, making some of them up.

"Ah, I know Lebedev, he was one of the early ones, one of the first of us."

"That's right."

"The others, they did not live here, not in Washington? Because I know all those in Washington, I think."

Krasilnikov reflected that her knowledge was not as complete as she believed. "No," he said. "Denikin was in New York, Nina Mikhalevo down in Florida."

"And you are not an attorney." She was looking at his card again, and he traced the raised black letters in his mind as she followed them with her remarkable gray eyes. The card read, *C. C. Percival*, and on the next line, *Expediter*, followed by an address and a telephone number. He was proud of that card.

"No," he told her. "A lawyer would bring suit in District Court, and the Federal Government would stall it as long as they could. The Government can stall things for a long, long time here, Ms. Aralov."

"In my country, too. Here, how long?"

He shrugged. "Maybe five years, if you were lucky and had a good lawyer."

"And with you? How long?"

"Five weeks, if we're lucky. Five months if we're not."

For the first time, she too sat, perching on the edge of her high-backed divan. "Then with you is better."

Krasilnikov smiled. "I like to think so."

"And your fees?"

He knew how much she had in the bank, and he told her. After a moment he added, "That's the retainer. I keep it all, no matter how fast I get you back to Russia. If things don't move that fast, then you've hired me, at three hundred a week, until the retainer's used up or I've got you home. Of course you realize I won't be working for you exclusively, only as needed. I have other clients."

She nodded slowly. "The retainer. It is so much."

He was firm. "Frankly, I'm giving you a break, Ms. Aralov, because I like you and I like what you've done. If you were some fat Arab who needed an American passport, it would be a lot more."

"I have to live while you work. I will have to buy my ticket."

Indeed. Indeed. "Your father's the Minister of Marine?"

She nodded again. "You would say the Secretary of the Navy here."

"I know. Surely you can call on him for help."

"Once, yes. Not any more. I—"

He cut her off. "First the retainer, Ms. Aralov. Then we'll talk about your father. Maybe I can do something."

"I understand." She stood, smoothing the soft, gray-blue fabric of her skirt. "I must get my checkbook. If you will excuse me."

"Sure."

He wanted to search for the American listening devices he knew must be there, but he was too well trained for that. He took some papers from the breast pocket of his jacket instead; when she returned, he appeared to be studying them.

"Here is your retainer," she said. "It is nearly all I have."

He said thank you, crossing his legs, refolding his papers and replacing them before he accepted her check. "Now sit down and tell me about your father, Ms. Aralov."

She sat, this time on the footstool. "It was so strange, so terrible . . ."

Her eyes had filled with tears, and he felt something he had thought dead since childhood move inside him. He said, "Perhaps it isn't really as strange as you think, Ms. Aralov. Or as terrible. Start at the beginning."

She nodded and blew her nose in one of the tiny handkerchiefs women used here. "It started with that dancer . . ."

She was groping for the dancer's name. He supplied, "The President's son."

"Yes. He went to Moscow on a tourist visa, remember? And he said he would stay there until his father was no longer President, that he would be our security against nuclear attack. It was just after our Party Secretary had said *we* would never fire the first missile."

"And then others came."

She added, no longer sniffling. "Janet Johnson was one of them. I met her in Moscow. Her father is something in the cabinet here."

He sipped his tea and waited.

"Then we thought we should do the same thing, and we did." She threw back her hair, her eyes gleaming, and he thrilled as if to the call of a trumpet. "Oh, they tried to stop us, but they could not send us to the *gulag*—to the camps. Our fathers were in the Politburo, and we said we would go to the American embassy. Then they had to let us go, and they did."

He said, "But now you want to go back."

"Yes, there is the fighting in the east." She hesitated. "I could do something. With training I might become a nurse. Our grandmothers fought the Germans beside their men. I would even do that."

He waited, staring out the window at the bland, blank brick face of the apartment building across the street.

"And I am so lonely here."

Tonelessly he said, "There are other Russians around Washington."

"Not enough, and they are going back too, or trying to." After a moment she added, "I want to see my mother and father, my brother and my sister and my aunt. Can't you understand?"

"It seems that your father doesn't want to see you."

"He was so angry! The letters I got from him were terrible! Yet he sent money, so I would not be in need. Then just when I had decided to come back . . ."

"The money stopped."

"Yes! I wrote to him. I said, 'I am coming home, Little Father, please forgive me.' There was nothing."

"Nothing?"

"No more letters, no more money."

His hand touched hers. "Has it ever occurred to you that perhaps your father doesn't really want you to return to Russia?"

For a moment she stared at him. "It was *before* I had told him I was coming home. He had ordered me a hundred times, called me traitor, the vilest names."

Carefully Krasilnikov said, "His position in your government would force him to do that, wouldn't it? How do you know he's not secretly proud of you?"

"But this was before! Before I had told him I wanted to come home."

"He might have guessed it just the same, from the tone of your letters. Or like I said, there are a lot of Russians around Washington. Couldn't one of them have tipped him off?"

She sighed, her eyes on the carpet. "You do not understand how it is in our country, how it is in our families."

He should have been proud, and he told himself to be proud; but the thing that had awakened was weeping in his chest. "I guess I don't," he told her. "But it seems to me that if you were proud of yourselves when you did what you did, your father might be proud of you, even if he couldn't say it out loud. I know we were all proud of the President's son, and the ones who went after him too."

She shook her head, eyes still averted.

He said, "If you want your check back, you can have it. Or I'll tear it up, if you want me to."

She looked up at that. "You aren't really an evil man, are you, Mr. Percival? I had hoped to employ an evil man, because I thought an evil man might get me what I wanted."

He smiled. "Evil enough, if you still want it. And call me Charlie, Ms. Aralov. If you still want to go back home, we'll be seeing a lot of each other." That was perfectly true, and ridiculous though it was, knowing it was true made him feel better.

"All right, Charlie. I am Sonja. Yes, I am going home."

"You don't have a passport?"

She shook her head. "We burned them when we arrived; that was part of our pledge that we would stay. You will say it was so foolish, and you will be right."

He shook his head. "I never fret over the past, Sonja. It uses up too much energy."

"But my real troubles are not with our government, but with the government here. They do not wish me to go. They have put every possible obstacle in my path. There is the court order—" She told him about it, swiftly and inaccurately.

When she was through he said, "All right, the first thing is to get you a Green Card."

"A Green Card?"

"So you can work here. You said you didn't have much money, Sonja, and your father won't send you any more. You're going to have to eat while I'm getting you out."

She shook her head. "No."

"And pay the rent on this apartment and maybe some legal fees. If I'm going to help you, you'll have to do what I say, or it's no use."

She rose from the footstool, angry and imperious. "What could I do here? Do you wish me to wait on tables?"

"That's a beautiful dress."

A breath and she was relaxed and smiling. "Oh, do you like it? I think I have some taste in clothes. Most of our women do not; they are *muzhiks*, peasants."

He said, "I want you to change it. The people who give out Green Cards don't like pretty dresses. Put on the dress you wear when you clean the kitchen."

"I have told you—"

"Have you thought of modeling, Sonja?" He saw at once that she had not. "You're tall, and with that face and that accent . . ." He let it hang. "I know a woman who runs an agency here. You might have to lose ten pounds or so."

"You think that?" At once her attention was on her body, her hands caressing her waist, lingering at her hips.

"Not for a man, Sonja. But for a modeling agency, maybe. We'll let Madamè Deppe decide."

"Not in the clothes in which I clean my oven!"

"You'll have plenty of time to change and bathe before we see Madame," he explained patiently. "But it's no use seeing her without the Green Card."

She hesitated, though he knew he had won. At last, "All right. It will not harm to try. You will wait while I change?"

"Of course," Krasilnikov said.

When she was gone, he rose and went to the window. It was hot out; he remembered how the heat had struck his face when he had stepped from his car. There was so much good climate in this country, yet they had built their capital here.

The telephone rang. She called from the bedroom, "Would you get that, please? It is probably a mistake— a wrong number."

He said, "All right," and picked up the telephone. "Sonja Aralov's apartment."

"It is me, Wilson. And you are?"

"C. C. Percival."

"They are sending Ipatiev."

"The film star?"

"Yes. I can hardly believe it, but that is what they say. He will hold her."

Half to himself he whispered, "Unless he goes to Hollywood."

"You said? I could not hear you."

She called, "Was it not a wrong number?"

He covered the mouthpiece with his hand. "It was for me. I let my secretary know I'd be here." He told the mouthpiece, "Thank you," and hung up.

"I am not too long?"

"No hurry." There was a copy of *Time* on the shelf under the little table beside the samovar. He thought, Why do all of us subscribe to it? They could trace every agent just from that—from *Time's* subscription list. Of course, we want them to know; agents count for something too. Not much, perhaps, but something.

He picked it up. The Chinese were in Kazakhstan, the Red Army had been stopped before Paris. It was still better than the old days, he decided. Better than when we were all so afraid, though at least we had peace.

HARDFOUGHT

Greg Bear

"Hardfought" was purchased by Shawna McCarthy toward the beginning of her regime, and appeared in the February 1983 issue of Asimov's, *with illustrations by H. R. Van Dongen. It was the first* Asimov's *story to carry a "warning label"—usually a notice that the story contains explicit sexual material and/or "hard" language; in the case of "Hardfought," it was not so much used for that as to warn people that what they were about to read was wildly unlike anything that had ever appeared in* Asimov's *before—vauntingly ambitious, stunningly complex, and staggering in scope. The purchase of "Hardfought" was a real gamble on McCarthy's part, and one that paid off handsomely. "Hardfought" became one of the most critically acclaimed stories of the year, hailed everywhere as a "breakthrough" novella, a step forward in the evolution of the genre. It went on to win a Nebula Award that year, as did Bear's "Blood Music," from our sister publication,* Analog. *Bear has not appeared subsequently in* Asimov's, *alas, but we intend to keep after him.*

Born in San Diego, California, Greg Bear made his first sale at the age of fifteen to Robert Lowndes's Famous Science Fiction, *and has subsequently established himself as one of the top professionals in the genre. His books include the novels* Hegira,

Psychlone, Beyond Heaven's River, Strength of
Stones, The Infinity Concerto, The Serpent Mage,
Eon, Eternity, *and* The Forge of God, *and the
collections* Wind From a Burning Woman *and*
Tangents. *His most recent novel is the critically
acclaimed* Queen of Angels.

Humans called it the Medusa. Its long twisted ribbons
of gas strayed across fifty parsecs, glowing blue, yellow,
and carmine. Its central core was a ghoulish green flecked
with watery black. Half a dozen protostars circled the core,
and as many more dim conglomerates pooled in dimples
in the nebula's magnetic field. The Medusa was a huge
womb of stars—and disputed territory.

Whenever Prufrax looked at it in displays or through the
ship's ports, it seemed malevolent, like a zealous mother
displaying an ominous face to protect her children. Prufrax
had never had a mother, but she had seen them in some of
the fibs.

At five, Prufrax was old enough to know the *Mellangee*'s
mission and her role in it. She had already been through
four ship-years of indoctrination. Until her first battle she
would be educated in both the Know and the Tell. She
would be exercised and trained in the Mocks; in sleep
she would dream of penetrating the huge red-and-white
Senexi seedships and finding the brood mind. "Zap, Zap,"
she went with her lips, silent so the tellman wouldn't think
her thoughts were straying.

The tellman peered at her from his position in the center
of the spherical classroom. Her mates stared straight at
the center, all focusing somewhere around the tellman's
spiderlike teaching desk, waiting for the trouble, some
fidgeting. "How many branch individuals in the Senexi
brood mind?" he asked. He looked around the classroom.
Peered face by face. Focused on her again. "Pru?"

"Five," she said. Her arms ached. She had been pumped full of moans the wake before. She was already three meters tall, in elfstate, with her long, thin limbs not nearly adequately fleshed out and her fingers still crisscrossed with the surgery done to adapt them to the gloves.

"What will you find in the brood mind?" the tellman pursued, his impassive face stretched across a hammer-head as wide as his shoulders. Some of the fems thought tellmen were attractive. Not many—and Pru was not one of them.

"Yoke," she said.

"What is in the brood-mind yoke?"

"Fibs."

"More specifically? And it really isn't all fib, you know."

"Info. Senexi data."

"What will you do?"

"Zap," she said, smiling.

"Why, Pru?"

"Yoke has team gens-memory. Zap yoke, spill the life of the team's five branch inds."

"Zap the brood, Pru?"

"No," she said solemnly. That was a new instruction, only in effect since her class's inception. "Hold the brood for the supreme overs." The tellmen did not say what would be done with the Senexi broods. That was not her concern.

"Fine," said the tellman. "You tell well, for someone who's always half-journeying."

She was already five, soon six. Old. Some saw Senexi by the time they were four.

"Zap, Zap," she went with her lips.

Aryz skidded through the thin layer of liquid ammonia on his broadest pod, considering his new assignment. He knew the Medusa by another name, one that conveyed all the time and effort the Senexi had invested in it.

The protostar nebula held few mysteries for him. He and his four branch-mates, who along with the all-important brood mind made up one of the six teams aboard the seedship, had patrolled the nebula for ninety-three orbits, each orbit—including the timeless periods outside status geometry—taking some one hundred and thirty human years. They had woven in and out of the tendrils of gas, charting the infalling masses and exploring the rocky accretion disks of stars entering the main sequence. With each measure and update, the brood minds refined their view of the nebula as it would be a hundred generations hence when the Senexi plan would finally mature.

The Senexi were nearly as old as the galaxy. They had achieved spaceflight during the time of the starglobe when the galaxy had been a sphere. They had not been a quick or brilliant race. Each great achievement had taken thousands of generations, and not just because of their intellectual handicaps. In those times elements heavier than helium had been rare, found only around stars that had greedily absorbed huge amounts of primeval hydrogen, burned fierce and blue, and exploded early, permeating the ill-defined galactic arms with carbon and nitrogen, lithium and oxygen. Elements heavier than iron had been almost nonexistent. The biologies of cold gas-giant worlds had developed with a much smaller palette of chemical combinations in producing the offspring of the primary Population II stars.

Aryz, even with the limited perspective of a branch ind, was aware that, on the whole, the humans opposing the seedship were more adaptable, more vital. But they were not more experienced. The Senexi with their billions of years had often matched them. And Aryz's perspective was expanding with each day of his new assignment.

In the early generations of the struggle, Senexi mental stasis and cultural inflexibility had made them avoid contact with the Population I species. They had never begun a program of extermination of the younger, newly life-forming worlds; the task would have been monumental and probably useless. So when spacefaring cultures developed, the Senexi had retreated, falling back into the redoubts of old stars even before engaging with the new kinds. They had retreated for three generations, about thirty thousand human years, raising their broods on cold nestworlds around red dwarfs, conserving, holding back for the inevitable conflicts.

As the Senexi had anticipated, the younger Population I races had found need of even the aging groves of the galaxy's first stars. They had moved in savagely, voraciously, with all the strength and mutability of organisms evolved from a richer soup of elements. Biology had, in some ways, evolved in its own right and superseded the Senexi.

Aryz raised the upper globe of his body, with its five silicate eyes arranged in a cross along the forward surface. He had memory of those times, and times long before, though his team hadn't existed then. The brood mind carried memories selected from the total store of nearly twelve billion years' experience, an awesome amount of knowledge, even to a Senexi. He pushed himself forward with his rear pods.

Through the brood mind Aryz could share the memories of a hundred thousand past generations, yet the brood mind itself was younger than its branch individuals. For a time in their youth, in their liquid-dwelling larval form, the branch inds carried their own sacs of data, each a fragment of the total necessary for complete memory. The branch inds swam through ammonia seas and wafted through thick warm gaseous zones, protoplasmic blobs three to four meters in diameter, developing their personalities under the weight of the past—and not even a complete past. No wonder they were inflexible, Aryz thought. Most branch inds were aware enough to see that—especially when they were allowed to compare histories with the Population I species, as he was doing—but there was nothing to be done. They were content the way they were. To change would be unspeakably repugnant. Extinction was preferable . . . almost.

But now they were pressed hard. The brood mind had begun a number of experiments. Aryz's team had been selected from the seedship's contingent to oversee the experiments, and Aryz had been chosen as the chief investigator. Two orbits past, they had captured six human embryos in a breeding device, as well as a highly coveted memory storage center. Most Senexi engagements had been with humans for the past three or four generations. Just as the Senexi dominated Population II species, humans were ascendant among their kind.

Experiments with the human embryos had already been conducted. Some had been allowed to develop normally; others had been tampered with, for reasons Aryz was not aware of. The tamperings had not been very successful.

The newer experiments, Aryz suspected, were going to take a different direction, and the seedship's actions now focused on him; he believed he would be given complete authority over the human shapes. Most branch inds would have dissipated under such a burden, but not Aryz. He found the human shapes rather interesting, in their own horrible way. They might, after all, be the key to Senexi survival.

The moans were toughening her elfstate. She lay in pain for a wake, not daring to close her eyes; her mind was changing and she feared sleep would be the end of her. Her nightmares were not easily separated from life; some, in fact, were sharper.

Too often in sleep she found herself in a Senexi trap, struggling uselessly, being pulled in deeper, her hatred wasted against such power. . . .

When she came out of the rigor, Prufrax was given leave by the subordinate tellman. She took to the

Mellangee's greenroads, walking stiffly in the shallow gravity. Her hands itched. Her mind seemed almost empty after the turmoil of the past few wakes. She had never felt so calm and clear. She hated the Senexi double now; once for their innate evil, twice for what they had made her overs put her through to be able to fight them. She was growing more mature wake by wake. Fight-budding, the tellman called it, hate coming out like blooms, synthesizing the sunlight of his teaching into pure fight.

The greenroads rose temporarily beyond the labyrinth shields and armor of the ship. Simple transparent plastic-and-steel geodesic surfaces formed a lacework over the gardens, admitting radiation necessary to the vegetation growing along the paths.

Prufrax looked down on the greens to each side of the paths without much comprehension. They were *beautiful*. Yes, one should say that, think that, but what did it mean? Pleasing? She wasn't sure what being pleased meant, outside of thinking Zap. She sniffed a flower that, the signs explained, bloomed only in the light of young stars not yet fusing. They were near such a star now, and the greenroads were shiny black and electric green with the blossoms. Lamps had been set out for other plants unsuited to such darkened conditions. Some technic allowed suns to appear in selected plastic panels when viewed from certain angles. Clever, the technicals.

She much preferred the looks of a technical to a tellman, but she was common in that. She wished a technical were on the greenroads with her. The moans had the effect of making her receptive—what she saw, looking in mirrors, was a certain shine in her eyes—but there was no chance of a breeding liaison. She was quite unreproductive in this moment of elfstate.

She looked up and saw a figure at least a hundred meters away, sitting on an allowed patch near the path. She walked casually, as gracefully as possible with the stiffness. Not a technical, she saw soon, but she was not disappointed. Too calm.

"Over," he said as she approached.

"Under," she replied. But not by much—he was probably six or seven ship-years old and not easily classifiable.

"Such a fine elfstate," he commented. His hair was black. He was shorter than she, but something in his build reminded her of the glovers. He motioned for her to sit, and she did so with a whuff, massaging her knees.

"Moans?" he asked.

"Bad stretch," she said.

"You're a glover." He was looking at the fading scars on her hands.

"Can't tell what you are," she said.

"Noncombat," he said. "Tuner of the mandates."

She knew very little about the mandates, except that law decreed every ship carry one, and few of the crew were ever allowed to peep. "Noncombat, hm?" She mused. She didn't despise him for that; one never felt strong negatives for a crew member.

"Been working on ours this wake," he said. "Too hard, I guess. Told to talk." Overzealousness in work was considered an erotic trait aboard the *Mellangee*. Still, she didn't feel too receptive toward him.

"Glovers walk after a rough growing," she said.

He nodded. "My name's Clevo."

"Prufax."

"Combat soon?"

"Hoping. Waiting forever."

"I know. Just been allowed access to the mandate for a half-dozen wakes. All new to me. Very happy."

"Can you talk about it?" she asked. Information about the ship not accessible in certain rates was excellent barter.

"Not sure," he said, frowning. "I've been told caution."

"Well, I'm listening."

He could come from glover stock, she thought, but probably not from technical. He wasn't very muscular, but he wasn't as tall as a glover, or as thin, either.

"If you'll tell me about gloves."

With a smile she held up her hands and wriggled the short, stumpy fingers. "Sure."

The brood mind floated weightless in its tank, held in place by buffered carbon rods. Metal was at a premium aboard the Senexi ships, more out of tradition than actual material limitations.

Aryz floated before the brood mind, all these thoughts coursing through his tissues. He had no central nervous system, no truly differentiated organs except those that dealt with the outside world—limbs, eyes, permea. The brood mind, however, was all central nervous system, a thinly buffered sac of viscous fluids about ten meters wide.

"Have you investigated the human memory device yet?" the brood mind asked.

"I have."

"Is communication with the human shapes possible for us?"

"We have already created interfaces for dealing with their machines. Yes, it seems likely we can communicate."

"Does it strike you that in our long war with humans, we have made no attempt to communicate before?"

This was a complicated question. It called for several qualities that Aryz, as a branch ind, wasn't supposed to have. Inquisitiveness, for one. Branch inds did not ask questions. They exhibited initiative only as offshoots of the brood mind.

He found, much to his dismay, that the question had occurred to him. "We have never captured a human memory store before," he said, by way of incomplete answer. "We could not have communicated without such an extensive source of information."

"Yet, as you say, even in the past we have been able to use human machines."

"The problem is vastly more complex."

The brood mind paused. "Do you think the teams have been prohibited from communicating with humans?"

Aryz felt the closest thing to anguish possible for a branch ind. Was he being considered unworthy? Accused of conduct inappropriate to a branch ind? His loyalty the brood mind was unshakeable. "Yes."

"And what might our reasons be?"

"Avoidance of pollution."

"Correct. We can no more communicate with them and remain untainted than we can walk on their worlds, breathe their atmosphere." Again, silence. Aryz lapsed into a mode of inactivity. When the brood mind readdressed him, he was instantly aware.

"Do you know how you are different?" it asked.

"I am not . . ." Again, hesitation. Lying to the brood mind was impossible for him. He signaled his distress.

"You are useful to the team," the brood mind said. Aryz calmed instantly. His thoughts became sluggish, receptive. There was a possibility of redemption. But how was he different? "You are to attempt communication with the shapes yourself. You will not engage in any discourse with your fellows while you are so involved." He was banned. "And after completion of this mission and transfer of certain facts to me, you will dissipate."

Aryz struggled with the complexity of the orders. "How am I different, worthy of such a commission?"

The surface of the brood mind was as still as an undisturbed pool. The indistinct black smudges that marked its radiating organs circulated slowly within the interior, then returned, one above the other, to focus on him. "You will grow a new branch ind. It will not have your flaws, but, then again, it will not be useful to me should such a situation come a second time. Your dissipation will be a relief, but it will be regretted."

"How am I different?"

"I think you know already," the brood mind said. "When the time comes, you will feed the new branch ind all your memories but those of human contact. If you do not survive to that stage of its growth, you will pick your fellow who will perform that function for you."

A small pinkish spot appeared on the back of Aryz's globe. He floated forward and placed his largest permeum against the brood mind's cool surface. The key and command were passed, and his body became capable of reproduction. Then the signal of dismissal was given. He left the chamber.

Flowing through the thin stream of liquid ammonia lining the corridor, he felt ambiguously stimulated. His was a position of privilege and anathema. He had been blessed—and condemned. Had any other branch ind experienced such a thing?

Then he knew the brood mind was correct. He was different from his fellows. None of them would have asked such questions. None of them could have survived the suggestion of communicating with human shapes. If this task hadn't been given to him, he would have had to dissipate anyway.

The pink spot grew larger, then began to make grayish flakes. It broke through the skin, and casually, almost without thinking, Aryz scraped it off against a bulkhead. It clung, made a radiofrequency emanation something like a sigh, and began absorbing nutrients from the ammonia.

Aryz went to inspect the shapes.

She was intrigued by Clevo, but the kind of interest she felt was new to her. She was not particularly receptive. Rather, she felt a mental gnawing as if she were hungry or had been injected with some kind of brain moans. What Clevo told her about the mandates opened up a topic she

had never considered before. How did all things come to
be—and how did she figure in them?

The mandates were quite small, Clevo explained, each
little more than a cubic meter in volume. Within them
was the entire history and culture of the human species,
as accurate as possible, culled from all existing sources.
The mandate in each ship was updated whenever the ship
returned to a contact station.

Clevo had been assigned small tasks—checking data
and adding ship records—that had allowed him to sample
bits of the mandate. "It's mandated that we have records,"
he explained, "and what we have, you see, is *man-data*."
He smiled. "That's a joke," he said. "Sort of."

Prufrax nodded solemnly. "So where do we come
from?"

"Earth, of course," Clevo said. "Everyone knows that."

"I mean, where do *we* come from—you and I, the
crew."

"Breeding division. Why ask? You know."

"Yes." She frowned, concentrating. "I mean, we don't
come from the same place as the Senexi. The same way."

"No, that's foolishness."

She saw that it was foolishness—the Senexi were different all around. What was she struggling to ask? "Is their
fib like our own?"

"Fib? History's not a fib. Not most of it, anyway. Fibs
are for unreal. History is over fib."

She knew, in a vague way, that fibs were unreal. She
didn't like to have their comfort demeaned, though. "Fibs
are fun," she said. "They teach Zap."

"I suppose," Clevo said dubiously. "Being noncombat,
I don't see Zap fibs."

Fibs without Zap were almost unthinkable to her. "Such
dull," she said.

"Well, of course you'd say that. I might find Zap fibs
dull—think of that?"

"We're different," she said. "Like Senexi are different."

Clevo's jaw hung open. "No way. We're crew. We're human. Senexi are . . ." He shook his head as if fed bitters.

"No, I mean . . ." She paused, uncertain whether she was entering unallowed territory. "You and I, we're fed different, given different moans. But in a big way we're different from Senexi. They aren't made, nor act, as you and I. But . . ." Again it was difficult to express. She was irritated. "I don't want to talk to you anymore."

A tellman walked down the path, not familiar to Prufrax. He held out his hand for Clevo, and Clevo grasped it. "It's amazing," the tellman said, "how you two gravitate to each other. Go, elfstate," he addressed Prufrax. "You're on the wrong greenroad."

She never saw the young researcher again. With glover training under way, the itches he aroused soon faded, and Zap resumed its overplace.

The Senexi had ways of knowing humans were near. As information came in about fleets and individual cruisers less than one percent nebula diameter distant, the seedship seemed warmer, less hospitable. Everything was UV with anxiety, and the new branch ind on the wall had to be shielded by a special silicate cup to prevent distortion. The brood mind grew a corniculum automatically, though the toughened outer membrane would be of little help if the seedship was breached.

Aryz had buried his personal confusion under a load of work. He had penetrated the human memory store deeply enough to find instructions on its use. It called itself a *mandate* and even the simple preliminary directions were difficult for Aryz. It was like swimming in another family's private sea, though of course infinitely more alien; how could he connect with experiences never had, problems and needs never encountered by his kind?

He observed the new branch ind once or twice each watch period. Never before had he seen an induced replacement. The normal process was for two brood minds to exchange plasm and form new team buds, then to exchange and nurture the buds. The buds were later cast free to swim as individual larvae. While the larvae swam through the liquid and gas atmosphere of a Senexi world often for thousands, even tens of thousands of kilometers, inevitably they returned to gather with the other buds of their team. Replacements were selected from a separately created pool of "generic" buds only if one or more originals had been destroyed during their wanderings. The destruction of a complete team meant reproductive failure.

In a mature team, only when a branch ind was destroyed did the brood mind induce a replacement. In essence, then, Aryz was already considered dead.

Yet he was still useful. That amused him, if the Senexi emotion could be called amusement. Restricting himself from his fellows was difficult, but he filled the time by immersing himself, through the interface, in the mandate.

The humans were also connected with the mandate through their surrogate parent, and in this manner they were quiescent.

He reported infrequently to the brood mind. Until he had established communication, there was little to report.

And throughout his turmoil, like the others he could sense a fight was coming. It could determine the success or failure of all their work in the nebula. In the grand scheme, failure here might not be crucial. But the Senexi had taken the long view too often in the past.

And he knew himself well enough to doubt he would fail.

He could feel an affinity for the humans already, peering at them through the thick glass wall in their isolated chamber, his skin paling at the thought of their heat, their poisonous chemistry. A diseased affinity. He hated himself for it. And reveled in it. It was what made him particularly useful to the team. If he was defective, and this was the only way he could serve, then so be it.

The other branch inds observed his passings from a distance, making no judgments. Aryz was dead, though he worked and moved. His sacrifice had been fearful. Yet he would not be a hero. His kind could never be emulated.

It was a horrible time, a horrible conflict.

She floated in language, learned it in a trice; there were no distractions. She floated in history and picked up as much as she could, for the source seemed inexhaustible. She tried to distinguish between eyes-open—the barren, pale gray-brown chamber with the thick green wall, beyond which floated a murky roundness—and eyes-shut, when she dropped back into language and history with no fixed foundation.

Eyes-open, she saw the Mam with its comforting limbs and its soft voice, its tubes and extrusions of food and its hissings and removal of waste. Through Mam's wires she learned. Mam also tended another like herself, and another unlike either of them, more like the shape beyond the green wall.

She was very young, and it was all a mystery.

At least she knew her name. And what she was supposed to do. She took small comfort in that.

They fitted Prufrax with her gloves, and she went into the practice chamber, dragged by her gloves almost, for she hadn't yet knitted the plug-in nerves in her right index digit and her pace control was uncertain.

There, for six wakes straight, she flew with the other glovers back and forth across the dark spaces like elfstate comets. Constellations and nebula aspects flashed at random on the distant walls, and she oriented to them like a night-flying bird. Her glovemates were Ornin, an especially slender male, and Ban, a redhaired female, and the special-projects sisters Ya, Trice, and Damu, new from the breeding division.

When she let the gloves have their way, she was freer than she had ever felt before. Control was somewhere uncentered, behind her eyes and beyond her fingers, as if she were drawn on a beautiful silver wire where it was best to go. Doing what was best to do. She barely saw the field that flowed from the grip of the thick, solid gloves or felt its caressing, life-sustaining influence. Truly, she hardly saw or felt anything but situations, targets, opportunities, the success or failure of the Zap. Failure was an acute pain. She was never reprimanded for failure; the reprimand was in her blood, and she felt as if she wanted to die. But then the opportunity would improve, the Zap would succeed, and everything around her—stars, Senexi seedship, the *Mellangee*, everything—seemed part of a beautiful dream all her own.

She was intense in the Mocks.

Their initial practice over, the entry play began.

One by one, the special-projects sisters took their hyperbolic formation. Their glove fields threw out extensions, and they combined force. In they went, the mock Senexi seedship brilliant red and white and UV and radio and hateful before them. Their tails swept through the seedship's outer shields and swirled like long silky hair laid on water; they absorbed fantastic energies, grew bright like violent little stars against the seedship outline. They were engaged in the drawing of the shields, and sure as topology, the spirals of force had to have a dimple on the opposite side that would iris wide enough to let in glovers. The sisters twisted the forces, and Prufrax could see the dimple stretching out under them—

The exercise ended. The elfstate glovers were cast into sudden dark. Prufrax came out of the mock unprepared, her mind still bent on the Zap. The lack of orientation drove her as mad as a moth suddenly flipped from night to day. She careened until gently mitted and channeled. She flowed down a tube, the field slowly neutralizing, and came to a halt still gloved, her body jerking and tingling.

"What the breed happened?" she screamed, her hands beginning to hurt.

"Energy conserve," a mechanical voice answered. Behind Prufrax the other elfstate glovers lined up in the catch tube, all but the special-projects sisters. Ya, Trice, and Damu had been taken out of the exercise early and replaced by simulations. There was no way their functions could be mocked. They entered the tube ungloved and helped their comrades adjust to the overness of the real.

As they left the mock chamber, another batch of glovers, even younger and fresher in elfstate, passed them. Ya held her hands up, and they saluted in return. "Breed more every day," Prufrax grumbled. She worried about having so many crew she'd never be able to conduct a satisfactory Zap herself. Where would the honor of being a glover go if everyone was a glover?

She wriggled into her cramped bunk, feeling exhilarated and irritated. She replayed the mocks and added in the missing Zap, then stared gloomily at her small narrow feet.

Out there the Senexi waited. Perhaps they were in the same state as she—ready to fight, testy at being reined in. She pondered her ignorance, her inability to judge whether such things were even possible among the enemy. She thought of the researcher, Clevo. "Blank," she murmured. "Blank, blank." Such thoughts were unnecessary, and humanizing Senexi was unworthy of a glover.

Aryz looked at the instrument, stretched a pod into it, and willed. Vocal human language came out the other end, thin and squeaky in the helium atmosphere. The sound disgusted and thrilled him. He removed the instrument from the gelatinous strands of the engineering wall and pushed it into his interior through a stretched permeum. He took a thick draft of ammonia and slid to the human-shapes chamber again.

He pushed through the narrow port into the observation room. Adjusting his eyes to the heat and bright light beyond the transparent wall, he saw the round mutated shape first—the result of their unsuccessful experiments. He swung his sphere around and looked at the others.

For a time he couldn't decide which was uglier—the mutated shape or the normals. Then he thought of what it would be like to have humans tamper with Senexi and try to make them into human forms. . . . He looked at the round human and shrank as if from sudden heat. Aryz had had nothing to do with the experiments. For that, at least, he was grateful.

Aryz placed the tip of the vocalizer against a sound-transmitting plate and spoke.

"Zello," came the sound within the chamber. The mutated shape looked up. It lay on the floor, great bloated stomach backed by four almost useless pods. It usually made high-pitched sounds continuously. Now it stopped and listened, straining on the tube that connected it to the breed-supervising device.

"Hello," replied the *male*. It sat on a ledge across the chamber, having unhooked itself.

The machine that served as surrogate parent and instructor stood in one corner, an awkward parody of a human, with limbs too long and head too small. Aryz could see the unwillingness of the designing engineers to examine human anatomy too closely.

"I am called—" Aryz said, his name emerging as a meaningless stretch of white noise. He would have to do better than that. He compressed and adapted the frequencies. "I am called Aryz."

"Hello," the young female said.

"What are your names?" He knew them well enough, having listened many times to their conversations.

"Prufrax," the female said. "I'm a glover."

The human shapes contained very little genetic memory. As a kind of brood marker, Aryz supposed, they had been equipped with their name, occupation, and the rudiments of environmental knowledge.

"I'm a teacher, Prufrax," Aryz said.

"I don't understand you," the female replied.

"You teach me, I teach you."

"We have the Mam," the male said, pointing to the machine. "She teaches us." The Mam, as they called it, was hooked into the mandate.

"Do you know where you are?" Aryz asked.

"Where we live," Prufrax said. "Eyes-open."

"Don't talk to it," the male said. "Mam talks to us." Aryz consulted the mandate for some understanding of the name they had given to the breed-supervising machine. Mam, it explained, was probably a natural expression for womb-carrying parent. Aryz severed the machine's power.

"Mam is no longer functional," he said. He would have the engineering wall put together another less identifiable machine to link them to the mandate and to their nutrition. He wanted them to associate comfort and completeness with nothing but himself.

The machine slumped, and the female shape pulled herself free of the hookup. She started to cry, a reaction quite mysterious to Aryz. His link with the mandate had not been intimate enough to answer questions about the wailing and moisture from the eyes. After a time the male and female lay down and became dormant.

The mutated shape made more soft sounds and tried to approach the transparent wall. It held up its thin arms as if beseeching. The others would have nothing to do with it; now it wished to go with him. Perhaps the biologists had partially succeeded in their attempt at transformation; perhaps it was more Senexi than human.

Aryz quickly backed out through the port, into the cool and security of the corridor beyond.

It was an endless orbital dance, this detection and matching of course, moving away and swinging back, deceiving and revealing, between the *Mellangee* and the Senexi seedship.

Filled with her skill and knowledge, Prufrax waited, feeling like a ripe fruit about to fall from the tree. At this point in their training, just before the application, elfstates were most receptive. She was allowed to take a lover, and they were assigned small separate quarters near the outer greenroads.

The contact was satisfactory, as far as it went. Her mate was an older glover named Kumnax, and as they lay back in the cubicle, soothed by air-dance fibs, he told her stories about past battles, special tactics, how to survive.

"Survive?" she asked, puzzled.

"Of course." His long brown face was intent on the view of the greenroads through the cubicle's small window.

"I don't understand," she said.

"Most glovers don't make it," he said patiently.

"I will."

He turned to her. "You're six," he said. "You're very young. I'm ten. I've seen. You're about to be applied for the first time, you're full of confidence. But most glovers won't make it. They breed thousands of us. We're expendable. We're based on the best glovers of the past but even the best don't survive."

"I will," Prufrax repeated, her jaw set.

"You always say that," he murmured.

Prufrax stared at him for a moment.

"Last time I knew you," he said, "you kept saying that. And here you are, fresh again."

"What last time?"

"Master Kumnax," a mechanical voice interrupted.

He stood, looking down at her. "We glovers always have big mouths. They don't like us knowing, but once we know, what can they do about it?"

"You are in violation," the voice said. "Please report to

S."

"But now, if you last, you'll know more than the tellman tells."

"I don't understand," Prufrax said slowly, precisely, looking him straight in the eye.

"I've paid my debt," Kumnax said. "We glovers stick. Now I'm going to go get my punishment." He left the cubicle. Prufrax didn't see him again before her first application.

The seedship buried itself in a heating protostar, raising shields against the infalling ice and stone. The nebula had congealed out of a particularly rich cluster of exploded fourth- and fifth-generation stars, thick with planets, the detritus of which now fell on Aryz's ship like hail.

Aryz had never been so isolated. No other branch ind addressed him; he never even saw them now. He made his reports to the brood mind, but even there the reception was warmer and warmer, until he could barely endure to communicate. Consequently—and he realized this was part of the plan—he came closer to his charges, the human shapes.

The brood mind was interested in one question: how successfully could they be planted aboard a human ship? Would they be accepted until they could carry out their sabotage, or would they be detected? Already Senexi instructions were being coded into their teachings.

"I think they will be accepted in the confusion of an engagement," Aryz answered. He had long since guessed the general outlines of the brood mind's plans. Communication with the human shapes was for one purpose only, to use them as decoys, insurgents. They were weapons. Knowledge of human activity and behavior was not an end in itself; seeing what was happening to him, Aryz fully understood why the brood mind wanted such study to proceed no further.

He would lose them soon, he thought, and his work

would be over. He would be much too human-tainted.
He would end, and his replacement would start a new
existence, very little different from Aryz's—but, he rea-
soned, adjusted. The replacement would not have Aryz's
peculiarity.

He approached his last meeting with the brood mind,
preparing himself for his final work, for the ending. In
the cold liquid-filled chamber, the great red-and-white sac
waited, the center of his team, his existence. He adored it.
There was no way he could criticize its action.

Yet—

"We are being sought," the brood mind radiated. "Are
the shapes ready?"

"Yes," Aryz said. "The new teaching is firm. They
believe they are fully human." And, except for the new
teaching, they were. "They defy sometimes." He said
nothing about the mutated shape. It would not be used. If
they won this encounter, it would probably be placed with
Aryz's body in a fusion torch for complete purging.

"Then prepare them," the brood mind said. "They will
be delivered to the vector for positioning and transfer."

Darkness and waiting. Prufrax nested in her delivery tube
like a freshly chambered round. Through her gloves she
caught distant communications murmurs that resembled
voices down hollow pipes. The *Mellangee* was coming
to full readiness.

Huge as her ship was, Prufrax knew that it would be
dwarfed by the seedship. She could recall some hazy
details about the seedship's structure, but most of that
information was stored securely away from interference
by her conscious mind.

More information would be fed to her just before the
launch, but she knew the general procedure. The seedship
was deep in a protostar, hiding behind the distortion of
geometry and the complete hash of electromagnetic energy. The *Mellangee* would approach, collide if need be.

Penetrate. Release. Find. Zap. Her fingers ached. Sometime before the launch she would also be fed her final
moans—the tempers—and she would be primed to leave
elfstate. She would be a mature glover. She would be a
woman.

If she returned

will return.

Her fingers ached worse.

The tempers came, moans tiding in, then the battle
data. As it passed into her subconscious, she caught a
flash of—

Rocks and ice, a thick cloud of dust and gas glowing
red but seeming dark, no stars, no constellation guides
this time. The beacon came on. That would be her only
way to orient once the gloves stopped inertial and locked
onto the target.

The seedship

was like

a shadow within a shadow

twenty-two kilometers across, yet

carrying

only six

teams

LAUNCH *she flies!*

Data: The *Mellangee* has buried herself in the seedship,
plowed deep into the interior like a carnivore's muzzle
looking for vitals

Instruction a swarm of seeks is dashing through the
seedship, looking for the brood minds, for the brood cham-
bers, for branch inds. The glovers will follow.

Prufrax sees herself clearly now. She is the great aveng-
ing comet, bringer of omen and doom, like a knife moving
through the glass and ice and thin, cold helium as if they
weren't there, the chambered round fired and tearing at
hundreds of kilometers an hour through the Senexi vessel,
following the seeks.

The seedship cannot withdraw into higher geometries

now. It is pinned by the *Mellangee*. It is hers.

Information floods her, pleases her immensely. She swoops down orange-and-gray corridors, buffeting against the walls like a ricocheting bullet. Almost immediately she comes across a branch ind, sliding through the ammonia film against the out-rushing wind, trying to reach an armored cubicle. Her first Zap is too easy, not satisfying, nothing like what she thought. In her wake the branch ind becomes scattered globules of plasma. She plunges deeper.

Aryz delivers his human charges to the vectors that will launch them. They are equipped with simulations of the human weapons, their hands encased in the hideous gray gloves.

The seedship is in deadly peril; the battle has almost been lost at one stroke. The seedship cannot remain whole. It must self-destruct, taking the human ship with it, leaving only a fragment with as many teams as can escape.

The vectors launch the human shapes. Aryz tries to determine which part of the ship will be elected to survive; he must not be there. His job is over, and he must die.

The glovers fan out through the seedship's central hollow, demolishing the great cold drive engines, bypassing the shielded fusion flare and the reprocessing plant, destroying machinery built before their Earth was formed.

The special-projects sisters take the lead. Suddenly they are confused. They have found a brood mind, but it is not heavily protected. They surround it, prepare for the Zap—

It is sacrificing itself, drawing them into an easy kill and away from another portion of the seedship. Power is concentrating elsewhere. Sensing that, they kill quickly and move on.

Aryz's brood mind prepares for escape. It begins to wrap itself in flux bind as it moves through the ship toward the frozen fragment. Already three of its five branch inds are dead; it can feel other brood minds dying. Aryz's bud replacement has been killed as well.

Following Aryz's training, the human shapes rush into corridors away from the main action. The special-projects sisters encounter the decoy male, allow it to fly with them . . . until it aims its weapons. One Zap almost take out Trice. The others fire on the shape immediately. He goes to his death weeping, confused from the very moment of his launch.

The fragment in which the brood mind will take refuge encompasses the chamer where the humans had been nurtured, where the mandate is still stored. All the other brood minds are dead, Aryz realizes; the humans have swept down on them so quickly. What shall he do?

Somewhere, far off, he feels the distressed pulse of another branch ind dying. He probes the remains of the seedship. He is the last. He cannot dissipate now; he must ensure the brood mind's survival.

Prufrax, darting through the crumbling seedship, searching for more opportunities, comes across an injured glover. She calls for the mediseek and pushes on.

The brood mind settles into the fragment. Its support system is damaged; it is entering the time-isolated state, the flux bind, more rapidly than it should. The seals of foamed electric ice cannot quite close off the fragment before Ya, Trice, and Damu slip in. They frantically call for bind cutters and preservers; they have instructions to capture the last brood mind, if possible.

But a trap falls upon Ya, and snarling fields tear her from her gloves. She is flung down a dark disintegrating shaft, red cracks opening all around as the seedship's integrity fails. She trails silver dust and freezes, hits a barricade, shatters.

The ice seals continue to close. Trice is caught between them and pushes out frantically, blundering into the region of the intensifying flux bind. Her gloves break into hard bits, and she is melded into an ice wall like an insect trapped on the surface of a winter lake.

Damu sees that the brood mind is entering the final phase of flux bind. After that they will not be able to touch it. She begins a desperate Zap.

and is too late.

Aryz directs the subsidiary energy of the flux against her. Her Zap deflects from the bind region, she is caught in an interference pattern and vibrates until her tiniest particles stop their knotted whirlpool spins and she simply becomes

space and searing light.

The brood mind, however, has been damaged. It is losing information from one portion of its anatomy. Desperate for storage, it looks for places to hold the information before the flux bind's last wave.

Aryz directs an interface onto the brood mind's surface. The silvery pools of time binding flicker around them both. The brood mind's damaged sections transfer their data into the last available storage device—the human mandate.

Now it contains both human and Senexi information.

The silvery pools unite, and Aryz backs away. No longer can he sense the brood mind. It is out of reach but not yet safe. He must propel the fragment from the remains of the seedship. Then he must wrap the fragment in its own flux bind, cocoon it in physics to protect it from the last ravages of the humans.

Aryz carefully navigates his way through the few remaining corridors. The helium atmosphere has almost completely dissipated, even there. He strains to remember all the procedures. Soon the seedship will explode, destroying the human ship. By then they must be gone.

Angry red, Prufrax follows his barely sensed form, watching him behind barricades of ice, approaching the moment of a most satisfying Zap. She gives her gloves their way

and finds a shape behind her, wearing gloves that are not gloves, not like her own, but capable of grasping her in tensed fields, blocking the Zap, dragging them together. The fragment separates, heat pours in from the protostar cloud. They are swirled in their vortex of power, twin locked comets—one red, one sullen gray.

"Who are you?" Prufrax screams as they close in on each other in the fields. Their environments meld. They grapple. In the confusion, the darkening, they are drawn out of the cloud with the fragment, and she sees the other's face.

Her own.

The seedship self-destructs. The fragment is propelled from the protostar, above the plane of what will become planets in their orbits, away from the crippled and dying *Mellangee*.

Desperate, Prufrax uses all her strength to drill into the fragment. Helium blows past them, and bits of dead branch inds.

Aryz catches the pair immediately in the shapes chamber, rearranging the fragment's structure to enclose them with the mutant shape and mandate. For the moment he has time enough to concentrate on them. They are dangerous. They are almost equal to each other, but his shape is weakening faster than the true glover. They float, bouncing from wall to wall in the chamber, forcing the mutant to crawl into a corner and howl with fear.

There may be value in saving the one and capturing the other. Involved as they are, the two can be carefully dissected from their fields and induced into a crude kind of sleep before the glover has a chance to free her weapons. He can dispose of the gloves—fake and real—and hook them both to the Mam, reattach the mutant shape as well. Perhaps something can be learned from the failure of the experiment.

The dissection and capture occur faster than the planning. His movement slows under the spreading flux bind. His last action, after attaching the humans to the Mam, is to make sure the brood mind's flux bind is properly nested within that of the ship.

The fragment drops into simpler geometries.

It is as if they never existed.

The battle was over. There were no victors. Aryz became aware of the passage of time, shook away the sluggishness, and crawled through painfully dry corridors to set the environmental equipment going again. Throughout the fragment, machines struggled back to activity.

How many generations? The constellations were unrecognizable. He made star traces and found familiar spectra and types, but advanced in age. There had been a malfunction in the overall flux bind. He couldn't find the nebula where the battle had occurred. In its place were comfortably middle-aged stars surrounded by young planets.

Aryz came down from the makeshift observatory. He slid through the fragment, established the limits of his new home, and found the solid mirror surface of the brood mind's cocoon. It was still locked in flux bind, and he knew of no way to free it. In time the bind would probably wear off—but that might require life spans. The seedship was gone. They had lost the brood chamber, and with it the stock.

He was the last branch ind of his team. Not that it mattered now; there was nothing he could initiate without a brood mind. If the flux bind was permanent, then he might as well be dead.

He closed his thoughts around him and was almost completely submerged when he sensed an alarm from the shapes chamber. The interface with the mandate had turned itself off; the new version of the Mam was malfunctioning. He tried to repair the equipment, but without the engineer's wall he was almost helpless. The best he could do was rig a temporary nutrition supply through the old human-form Mam. When he was done, he looked at the captive and the two shapes, then at the legless, armless Mam that served as their link to the interface and life itself.

• • •

She had spent her whole life in a room barely eight by ten meters, and not much taller than her own height. With her had been Grayd and the silent round creature whose name—if it had any—they had never learned. For a time there had been Mam, then another kind of Mam not nearly as satisfactory. She was hardly aware that her entire existence had been miserable, cramped, in one way or another incomplete.

Separated from them by a transparent partition, another round shape had periodically made itself known by voice or gesture.

Grayd had kept her sane. They had engaged in conspiracy. Removing themselves from the interface—what she called "eyes-shut"—they had held onto each other, tried to make sense out of what they knew instinctively, what was fed them through the interface, and what the being beyond the partition told them.

First they knew their names, and they knew that they were glovers. They knew that glovers were fighters. When Aryz passed instruction through the interface on how to fight, they had accepted it eagerly but uneasily. It didn't seem to jibe with instructions locked deep within their instincts.

Five years under such conditions had made her introspective. She expected nothing, sought little beyond experience in the eyes-shut. Eyes-open with Grayd seemed scarcely more than a dream. They usually managed to ignore the peculiar round creature in the chamber with them; it spent nearly all its time hooked to the mandate and the Mam.

Of one thing only was she completely sure. Her name was Prufrax. She said it in eyes-open and eyes-shut, her only certainty.

Not long before the battle, she had been in a condition resembling dreamless sleep, like a robot being given instructions. The part of Prufrax that had taken on personality during eyes-shut and eyes-open for five years had

been superseded by the fight instructions Aryz had programmed. She had flown as glovers must fly (though the
gloves didn't seem quite right). She had fought, grappling
(she thought) with herself, but who could be certain of
anything?

She had long since decided that reality was not to be
sought too avidly. After the battle she fell back into the
mandate—into eyes-shut—all too willingly.

But a change had come to eyes-shut, too. Before the
battle, the information had been selected. Now she could
wander through the mandate at will. She seemed to smell
the new information, completely unfamiliar, like a whiff
of ocean. She hardly knew where to begin. She stumbled
across:

**—that all vessels carry one, no matter what their size
or class, just as every individual carries the map of a
species. The mandate shall contain all the information
of our kind, including accurate and uncensored history, for if we have learned anything, it is that censored
and untrue accounts distort the eyes of the leaders.
Unders are told lies. Leaders must seek and be provided with accounts as accurate as possible, or we will
be weakened and fall—**

What wonderful dreams the *leaders* must have had. And
they possessed some intrinsic gift called *truth*, through the
use of the *mandate*. Prufrax could hardly believe that. As
she made her tentative explorations through the new fields
of eyes-shut, she began to link the word *mandate* with
what she experienced. That was where she was.

And she was alone. Once, she had explored with Grayd.
Now there was no sign of Grayd.

She learned quickly. Soon she walked along a beach
on Earth, then a beach on a world called Myriadne, and
other beaches, fading in and out. By running through the
entries rapidly, she came up with a blurred *eidos* and so
learned what a beach was in the abstract. It was a boundary between one kind of eyes-shut and another, between

water and land, neither of which had any corollary in eyes-open.

Some beaches had sand. Some had clouds—the *edios* of clouds was quite attractive. And one—

had herself running scared, screaming.

She called out, but the figure vanished. Prufrax stood on a beach under a greenish-yellow star, on a world called Kyrene, feeling lonelier than ever.

She explored further, hoping to find Grayd, if not the figure that looked like herself. Grayd wouldn't flee from her. Grayd would—

The round thing confronted her, its helpless limbs twitching. Now it was her turn to run, terrified. Never before had she met the round creature in eyes-shut. It was mobile; it had a purpose. Over land, clouds, trees, rocks, wind, air, equations, and an edge of physics she fled. The farther she went, the more distant from the round one with hands and small head, the less afraid she was.

She never found Grayd.

The memory of the battle was fresh and painful. She remembered the ache of her hands, clumsily removed from the gloves. Her environment had collapsed and been replaced by something indistinct. Prufrax had fallen into a deep slumber and had dreamed.

The dreams were totally unfamiliar to her. If there was a left-turning in her arc of sleep, she dreamed of philosophies and languages and other things she couldn't relate to. A right-turning led to histories and sciences so incomprehensible as to be nightmares.

It was a most unpleasant sleep, and she was not at all sorry to find she wasn't really asleep.

The crucial moment came when she discovered how to slow her turnings and the changes of dream subject. She entered a pleasant place of which she had no knowledge but which did not seem threatening. There was a vast expanse of water, but it didn't terrify her. She couldn't even identify it as water until she scooped up a handful. Beyond the water was a floor of shifting particles. Above both was an open expanse, not black but obviously space, drawing her eyes into intense pale blue-green. And there was that figure she had encountered in the seedship. Herself. The figure pursued. She fled.

Right over the boundary into Senexi information. She knew then that what she was seeing couldn't possibly come from within herself. She was receiving data from another source. Perhaps she had been taken captive. It was possible she was now being forcibly debriefed. The tellman had discussed such possibilities, but none of the glovers had been taught how to defend themselves in specific situations. Instead it had been stated—in terms that brooked no second thought—that self-destruction was the only answer. So she tried to kill herself.

She sat in the freezing cold of a red-and-white room, her feet meeting but not touching a fluid covering on the floor. The information didn't fit her senses—it seemed blurred, inappropriate. Unlike the other data, this didn't allow participation or motion. Everything was locked solid.

She couldn't find an effective means of killing herself. She resolved to close her eyes and simply will herself into dissolution. But closing her eyes only moved her into a deeper or shallower level of deception—other categories, subjects, visions. She couldn't sleep, wasn't tired, couldn't die.

Like a leaf on a stream, she drifted. Her thoughts untangled, and she imagined herself floating on the water called ocean. She kept her eyes open. It was quite by accident that she encountered:

Instruction. Welcome to the introductory use of the mandate. As a noncombat processor, your duties are to maintain the mandate, provide essential information for your overs, and, if necessary, protect or destroy the mandate. The mandate is your immediate over. If it requires maintenance, you will oblige. Once linked

with the mandate, as you are now, you may explore any aspect of the information by requesting delivery. To request delivery, indicate the core of your subject—

Prufrax! she shouted silently. What is Prufrax?

A voice with different tone immediately took over.

Ah, now that's quite a story. I was her biographer, the organizer of her life tapes (ref. GEORGE MACKNAX), and knew her well in the last years of her life. She was born in the Ferment 26468. Here are selected life tapes. Choose emphasis. Analyses follow.

—Hey! Who are you? There's someone here with me . . .

—Shh! Listen. Look at her. Who is she?

They looked, listened to the information.

—Why, she's *me* . . . sort of.

—She's *us*.

She stood two and a half meters tall. Her hair was black and thick, though cut short; her limbs well muscled though drawn out by the training and hormonal treatments. She was seventeen years old, one of the few birds born in the solar system, and for the time being she had a chip on her shoulder. Everywhere she went, the birds asked about her mother, Jay-ax. "You better than her?"

Of course not! Who could be? But she was good; the instructors said so. She was just about through training, and whether she graduated to hawk or remained bird she would do her job well. Asking Prufrax about her mother was likely to make her set her mouth tight and glare.

On Mercior, the Grounds took up four thousand hectares and had its own port. The Grounds was divided into Land, Space, and Thought, and training in each area was mandatory for fledges, those birds embarking on hawk training. Prufrax was fledge three. She had passed Land—though she loathed downbound fighting—and was two years into Space. The tough part, everyone said, was not passing Space, but lasting through four years of Thought after the action in nearorbit and planetary.

Since she had been a little girl, no more than five—

—Five! Five what?

and had seen her mother's ships and fightsuits and fibs, she had known she would never be happy until she had ventured far out and put a seedship in her sights, had convinced a Senexi of the overness of end—

—The Zap! She's talking the Zap!

—What's that?

—You're me, you should know.

—I'm not you, and we're not her.

The Zap, said the mandate, and the data shifted.

"Tomorrow you receive your first implants. These will allow you to coordinate with the zero-angle phase engines and find your targets much more rapidly than you ever could with simple biologic. Are there any questions?"

"Yes, sir." Prufrax stood at the top of the spherical classroom, causing the hawk instructor to swivel his platform. "I'm having problems with the zero-angle phase maths. Reduction of the momenta of the real."

Other fledge threes piped up that they, too, had had trouble with those maths. The hawk instructor sighed. "We don't want to install cheaters in all of you. It's bad enough needing implants to supplement biologic. Individual learning is much more desirable. Do you request cheaters?" That was a challenge. They all responded negatively, but Prufrax had a secret smile. She knew the subject. She just took delight in having the maths explained again. She could reinforce an already thorough understanding. Others not so well versed would benefit. She wasn't wasting time. She was in the pleasure of her weapon—the weapon she would be using against the Senexi.

"Zero-angle phase is the temporary reduction of the momenta of the real." Equations and plexes appeared before each student as the instructor went on. "Nested unreals can conflict if a barrier is placed between the participator princip and the assumption of the real. The

effectiveness of the participator can be determined by a
convenience model we call the angle of phase. Zero-angle
phase is achieved by an opaque probability field according
to modified Fourier of the separation of real waves. This
can also be caused by the reflection of the beam—an
effective counter to zero-angle phase, since the beam is
always compoundable and the compound is always time-
reversed. Here are the true gedanks—"

—Zero-angle phase. She's learning the Zap.

—She hates them a lot, doesn't she?

—The Senexi? They're Senexi.

—I think . . . eyes-open is the world of the Senexi.
What does that mean?

—That we're prisoners. You were caught before me.

—Oh.

The news came as she was in recovery from the
implant. Seedships had violated human space again,
dropping cuckoos on thirty-five worlds. The worlds had
been young colonies, and the cuckoos had wiped out all
life, then tried to reseed with Senexi forms. The overs had
reacted by sterilizing the planets' surfaces. No victory, loss
to both sides. It was as if the Senexi were so malevolent
they didn't care about success, only about destruction.

She hated them. She could imagine nothing worse.

Prufrax was twenty-three. In a year she would be quali-
fied to hawk on a cruiser/raider. She would demonstrate
her hatred.

Aryz felt himself slipping into endthought, the mind
set that always preceded a branch ind's self-destruction.
What was there for him to do? The fragment had survived, but at what cost, to what purpose? Nothing had
been accomplished. The nebula had been lost, or he supposed it had. He would likely never know the actual
outcome.

He felt a vague irritation at the lack of a spectrum of
responses. Without a purpose, a branch ind was nothing
more than excess plasm.

He looked in on the captive and the shapes, all hooked to the mandate, and wondered what he would do with them. How would humans react to the situation he was in? More vigorously, probably. They would fight on. They always had. Even without leaders, with no discernible purpose, even in defeat. What gave them such stamina? Were they superior, more deserving? If they were better, then was it right for the Senexi to oppose their triumph?

Aryz drew himself tall and rigid with confusion. He had studied them too long. They had truly infected him. But here at least was a hint of purpose. A question needed to be answered.

He made preparations. There were signs the brood mind's flux bind was not permanent, was in fact unwinding quite rapidly. When it emerged, Aryz would present it with a judgment, an answer.

He realized, none too clearly, that by Senexi standards he was now a raving lunatic.

He would hook himself into the mandate, improve the somewhat isolating interface he had used previously to search for selected answers. He, the captive, and the shapes would be immersed in human history together. They would be like young suckling on a Population I mother-animal—just the opposite of the Senexi process, where young fed nourishment and information into the brood mind.

The mandate would nourish, or poison. Or both.

—Did she love?
—What—you mean, did she receive?
—No, did she—we—I—give?
—I don't know what you mean.
—I wonder if *she* would know what I mean . . .
Love, said the mandate, and the data proceeded.

Prufrax was twenty-nine. She had been assigned to a cruiser in a new program where superior but untested fighters were put into thick action with no preliminary.

The Cruiser was a million-ton raider, with a hawk contingent of fifty-three and eighty regular crew. She would be used in a second wave attack, following the initial hardfought.

She was scared. That was good; fright improved basic biologic, if properly managed. The cruiser would make a raid into Senexi space and retaliate for past cuckoo-seeding programs. They would come up against thornships and seedships, probably.

The fighting was going to be fierce.

The raider made its final denial of the overness of the real and pipsqueezed into an arduous, nasty sponge space. It drew itself together again and emerged far above the galactic plane.

Prufrax sat in the hawks wardroom and looked at the simulated rotating snowball of stars. Red-coded numerals flashed along the borders of known Senexi territory, signifying where they had first come to power when the terrestrial sun had been a mist-wrapped youngster. A green arrow showed the position of the raider.

She drank sponge-space supplements with the others but felt isolated because of her firstness, her fear. Everyone seemed so calm. Most were fours or fives—on their fourth of fifth battle call. There were ten ones and an upper scatter of experienced hawks with nine to twenty-five battles behind them. There were no thirties. Thirties were rare in combat; the few that survived so many engagements were plucked off active and retired to PR service under the polinstructors. They often ended up in fibs, acting poorly, looking unhappy.

Still, when she had been more naive, Prufrax's heros had been a man-and-woman thirty team she had watched in fib after fib—Kumnax and Arol. They had been better actors than most.

Day in, day out, they drilled in their fightsuits. While the crew bustled, hawks were put through implant learning, what slang was already calling the Know, as opposed to the Tell, of classroom teaching. Getting background, just enough to tickle her curiosity, not enough to stimulate morbid interest.

—There it is again. Feel?

—I know it. Yes. The round one, part of eyes-open . . .

—Senexi?

—No, brother without name.

—Your . . . brother?

—No . . . I don't know.

Still, there were items of information she had never received before, items privileged only to the fighters, to assist them in their work. Older hawks talked about the past, when data had been freely available. Stories circulated in the wardroom about the Senexi, and she managed to piece together something of their origins and growth.

Senexi worlds, according to a twenty, had originally been large, cold masses of gas circling bright young suns nearly metal-free. Their gas-giant planets had orbited the suns at hundreds of millions of kilometers and had been dusted by the shrouds of neighboring dead stars; the essential elements carbon, nitrogen, silicon, and fluorine had gathered in sufficient quantities on some of the planets to allow Population II biology.

In cold ammonia seas, lipids had combined in complex chains. A primal kind of life had arisen and flourished. Across millions of years, early Senexi forms had evolved. Compared with evolution on Earth, the process at first had moved quite rapidly. The mechanisms of procreation and evolution had been complex in action, simple in chemistry.

There had been no competition between life forms of different genetic bases. On Earth, much time had been spent selecting between the plethora of possible ways to pass on genetic knowledge.

And among the early Senexi, outside of predation there had been no death. Death had come about much later, self-imposed for social reasons. Huge colonies of protoplasmic individuals had gradually resolved into the team-forms now familiar.

Soon information was transferred through the budding of branch inds; cultures quickly developed to protect the integrity of larvae, to allow them to regroup and form a new brood mind. Technologies had been limited to the rare heavy materials available, but the Senexi had expanded for a time with very little technology. They were well adapted to their environment, with few predators and no need to hunt, absorbing stray nutrients from the atmosphere and from layers of liquid ammonia. With perceptions attuned to the radio and microwave frequencies, they had before long turned groups of branch inds into radio telescope chains, piercing the heavy atmosphere and probing the universe in great detail, especially the very active center of the young galaxy. Huge jets of matter, streaming from other galaxies and emitting high-energy radiation, had provided laboratories for their vicarious observations. Physics was a primitive science to them.

Since little or no knowledge was lost in breeding cycles, cultural growth was rapid at times; since the dead weight of knowledge was often heavy, cultural growth often slowed to a crawl.

Using water as a building material, developing techniques that humans still understood imperfectly, they prepared for travel away from their birthworlds.

Prufrax wondered, as she listened to the older hawks, how humans had come to know all this. Had Senexi been captured and questioned? Was it all theory? Did anyone really know—anyone she could ask?

—She's weak.

—Why weak?

—Some knowledge is best for glovers to ignore. Some questions are best left to the supreme overs.

—Have you thought that in here, you can answer her questions, our questions?

—No. No. Learn about me—us—first.

In the hour before engagement, Prufrax tried to find a place alone. On the raider, this wasn't difficult. The ship's size was overwhelming of the number of hawks and crew aboard. There were many areas where she could put on an environs and walk or drift in silence, surrounded by the dark shapes of equipment wrapped in plexerv.

She pulled herself through the cold G-less tunnels, feeling slightly awed by the loneness, the quiet. One tunnel angled outboard, toward the hull of the cruiser. She hesitated, peering into its length with her environs beacon, when a beep warned her she was near another crew member. She was startled to think someone else might be as curious as she. She scooted expertly up the tunnel, spreading her arms and tucking her legs as she would in a fightsuit.

The tunnel was filled with a faint milky green mist, absorbing her environs beam. It couldn't be much more than a couple of hundred meters long, however, and it was quite straight. The signal beeped louder.

Ahead she could make out a dismantled weapons blister. That explained the fog: a plexerv aerosol diffused in the low pressure. Sitting in the blister was a man, his environs glowing a pale violet. He had deopaqued a section of the blister and was staring out at the stars. He swiveled as she approached and looked her over dispassionately. He seemed to be a hawk—he had fightform, tall, thin with brown hair above hull-white skin, large eyes with pupils so dark she might have been looking through his head into space beyond.

"Under," she said as their environs met and merged.

"Over. What are you doing here?"

"I was about to ask you the same."

"You should be getting ready for the fight," he admonished.

"I am. I need to be alone for a while."

"Yes." He turned back to the stars. "I used to do that, too."

"You don't fight now?"

He shook his head. "Retired. I'm a researcher."

She tried not to look impressed. Crossing rates was almost impossible. A bitalent was unusual in the service.

"What kind of research?" she asked.

"I'm here to correlate enemy finds."

"Won't find much of anything, after we're done with the zero phase."

It would have been polite for him to say, "Power to that," or offer some other encouragement. He said nothing.

"Why would you want to research them?"

"To fight an enemy properly, you have to know what they are. Ignorance is defeat."

"You research tactics?"

"Not exactly."

"What, then?"

"You'll be in tough hardfought this wake. Make you a proposition. You fight well, observe, come to me, and tell me what you see. Then I'll answer your questions."

"Brief you before my immediate overs?"

"I have the authority," he said. No one had ever lied to her; she didn't even suspect he would. "You're eager?"

"Very."

"You'll be doing what?"

"Engaging Senexi fighters, then hunting down branch inds and brood minds."

"How many fighters going in?"

"Twelve."

"Big target, eh?"

She nodded.

"While you're there, ask yourself—what are they fighting for? Understand?"

"I—"

"Ask, what are they fighting for. Just that. Then come back to me."

"What's your name?"

"Not important," he said. "Now go."

She returned to the prep center as the sponge-space warning tones began. Overhawks went among the fighters in the lineup, checking gear and giveaway body points for mental orientation. Prufrax submitted to the molded sensor mask being slipped over her face. "Ready!" the overhawk said. "Hardfought!" He clapped her on the shoulder. "Good luck."

"Thank you, sir." She bent down and slid into her fightsuit. Along the launch line, eleven other hawks did the same. The overs and other crew left the chamber, and twelve red beams delineated the launch tube. The fightsuits automatically lifted and aligned on their individual beams. Fields swirled around them like silvery tissue in moving water, then settled and hardened into cold scintillating walls, pulsing as the launch energy built up.

The tactic came to her. The ship's sensors became part of her information net. She saw the Senexi thornship—twelve kilometers in diameter, cuckoos lacing its outer hull like maggots on red fruit, snakes waiting to take them on.

She was terrified and exultant, so worked up that her body temperature was climbing. The fightsuit adjusted her balance.

At the count of ten and nine, she switched from biologic to cyber. The implant—after absorbing much of her thought processes for weeks—became Prufrax.

For a time there seemed to be two of her. Biologic continued, and in that region she could even relax a bit, as if watching a fib.

With almost dreamlike slowness, in the electronic time of cyber, her fightsuit followed the beam. She saw the stars and oriented herself to the cruiser's beacon, using both for reference, plunging in the sword-flower formation to assault the thornship. The cuckoos retreated in the vast red hull like worms withdrawing into an apple. Then hundreds of tiny black pinpoints appeared in the quadrant closest to the sword flower.

Snakes shot out, each piloted by a Senexi branch ind. "Hardfought!" she told herself in biologic before that portion gave over completely to cyber.

Why were we flung out of dark
through ice and fire, a shower of
sparks? a puzzle;
Perhaps to build hell

We strike here, there;
Set brief glows, fall through
and cross round again.

By our dimming, we see what
Beatitude we have.
In the circle, kindling
together, we form an
exhausted Empyrean.
We feel the rush of
igniting winds but still
grow dull and wan.

New rage flames, new light,
dropping like sun through muddy
ice and night and fall
Close, spinning blue and bright.

In time they, too,
Tire. Redden.
We join, compare pasts
cool in huddled paths,
turn gray.

And again.
We are a companion flow

of ash, in the slurry,
out and down.
We sleep.

Rivers form above and below.
Above, iron snakes twist,
clang and slice, chime,
helium eyes watching, seeing
Snowflake hawks,
signaling adamant muscles and
energy teeth. What hunger
compels our venom spit?

It flies, strikes the crystal
flight, making mist gray-green
with ammonia rain.

Sleeping we glide,
and to each side
unseen shores wait
with the moans of an
unseen tide.

    —She wrote that. We. One of her—our—poems.
    —Poem?
    —A kind of fib, I think.
    —I don't see what it says.
    —Sure you do! She's talking hardfought.
    —Do you understand it?
    —Not all . . .

She lay back in the bunk, legs crossed, eyes closed, feeling the receding dominance of the implant—the overness of cyber—and the almost pleasant ache in her back. She had survived her first. The thornship had retired, severely damaged, its surface seared and scored so heavily it would never release cuckoos again.

It would become a hulk, a decoy. Out of action. *Satisfaction/out of action/ Satisfaction . . .*

Still, with eight of the twelve fighters lost, she didn't quite feel the exuberance of the rhyme. The snakes had fought very well. Bravely, she might say. They lured, sacrificed, cooperated, demonstrating teamwork as fine as that in her own group. Strategy was what made the cruiser's raid successful. A superior approach, an excellent tactic. And perhaps even surprise, though the final analysis hadn't been posted yet.

Without those advantages, they might have all died.

She opened her eyes and stared at the pattern of blinking lights in the ceiling panel, lights with their secret codes that repeated every second, so that whenever she looked at them, the implant deep inside was debriefed, reinstructed. Only when she fought would she know what she was now seeing.

She returned to the tunnel as quickly as she was able. She floated up toward the blister and found him there, surrounded by packs of information from the last hardfought. She waited until he turned his attention to her.

"Well?" he said.

"I asked myself what they are fighting for. And I'm very angry."

"Why?"

"Because I don't know. I *can't* know. They're Senexi."

"Did they fight well?"

"We lost eight. Eight." She cleared her throat.

"Did they fight well?" he repeated, an edge in his voice.

"Better than I was ever told they could."

"Did they die?"

"Enough of them."

"How many did you kill?"

"I don't know." But she did. Eight.

"You killed eight," he said, pointing to the packs. "I'm analyzing the battle now."

"You're behind what we read, what gets posted?" she asked.

"Partly," he said. "You're a good hawk."

"I knew I would be," she said, her tone quiet, simple.

"Since they fought bravely—"

"How can Senexi be brave?" she asked sharply.

"Since," he repeated, "they fought bravely, why?"

"They want to live, to do their . . . work. Just like me."

"No," he said. She was confused, moving between extremes in her mind, first resisting, then giving in too much. "They're Senexi. They're not like us."

"What's your name?" she asked, dodging the issue.

"Clevo."

Her glory hadn't even begun yet, and already she was well into her fall.

Aryz made his connection and felt the brood mind's emergency cache of knowledge in the mandate grow up around him like ice crystals on glass. He stood in a static scene. The transition from living memory to human machine memory had resulted in either a coding of data or a reduction of detail; either way, the memory was cold, not dynamic. It would have to be compared, recorrelated, if that would ever be possible.

How much human data had had to be dumped to make space for this?

He cautiously advanced into the human memory, calling up topics almost at random.

He backed away from sociological data, trying to remain within physics and mathematics. There he could make conversions to fit his understanding without too much strain.

Then something unexpected happened. He felt the brush of another mind, a gentle inquiry from a source made even stranger by the hint of familiarity. It made what passed for a Senexi greeting, but not in the proper form, using what one branch ind of a team would radiate to a fellow; a gross breach, since it was obviously not from his team or even from his family. Aryz tried to withdraw. How was it possible for minds to meet in the mandate? As he retreated, he pushed into a broad region of incomprehensible data. It had none of the characteristics of the other human regions he had examined.

—This is for machines, the other said.—Not all cultural data are limited to biologic. You are in the area where programs and cyber designs are stored. They are really accessible only to a machine hooked into the mandate.

—What is your family? Aryz asked, the first step-question in the sequence Senexi used for urgent identity requests.

—I have no family. I am not a branch ind. No access to active brood minds. I have learned from the mandate.

—Then what are you?

—I don't know, exactly. Not unlike you.

It was the mind of the mutated shape, the one that had remained in the chamber, beseeching when he approached the transparent barrier.

—I must go now, the shape said. Aryz was alone again in the incomprehensible jumble. He moved slowly, carefully, into the Senexi sector, calling up subjects familiar to him. If he could encounter one shape, doubtless he could encounter the others—perhaps even the captive.

The idea was dreadful—and fascinating. So far as he knew, such intimacy between Senexi and human had never happened before. Yet there was something very Senexi-like in the method, as if branch inds attached to the brood mind were to brush mentalities while searching in the ageless memories.

The dread subsided. There was little worse that could happen to him, with his fellows dead, his brood mind in flux bind, his purpose uncertain.

What Aryz was feeling, for the first time, was a small measure of *freedom*.

The story of the original Prufrax continued.

In the early stages she visited Clevo with a barely concealed anger. His method was aggravating, his goals never precisely spelled out. What did he want with her, if anything?

And she with him? Their meetings were clandestine, though not precisely forbidden. She was a hawk one now with considerable personal liberty between exercises and engagements. There were no monitors in the closed-off reaches of the cruiser, and they could do whatever they wished. The two met in areas close to the ship's hull, usually in weapons blisters that could be opened to reveal the stars; there they talked.

Prufrax was not accustomed to prolonged conversation. Hawks were neither raised to be voluble, nor selected for their curiosity. Yet the exhawk Clevo talked a great deal and was the most curious person she had met, herself included, and she regarded herself as uncharacteristically curious.

Often he was infuriating, especially when he played the "leading game," as she called it. Leading her from one question to the next, like an instructor, but without the trappings or any clarity of purpose. "What do you think of your mother?"

"Does that matter?"

"Not to me."

"Then why ask?"

"Because you matter."

Prufrax shrugged. "She was a fine mother. She bore me with a well-chosen heritage. She raised me as a hawk candidate. She told me her stories."

"Any hawk I know would envy you for listening at Jay-ax's knee."

"I was hardly at her knee."

"A speech tactic."

"Yes, well, she was important to me."

"She was a preferred single?"

"Yes."

"So you have no father."

"She selected without reference to individuals."

"Then you are really not that much different from a Senexi."

She bristled and started to push away. "There! You insult me again."

"Not at all. I've been asking one question all this time, and you haven't even heard. How well do you know the enemy?"

"Well enough to destroy them." She couldn't believe that was the only question he'd been asking. His speech tactics were very odd.

"Yes, to win battles, perhaps. But who will win the war?"

"It'll be a long war," she said softly, floating a few meters from him. He rotated in the blister, blocking out a blurred string of stars. The cruiser was preparing to shift out of status geometry again. "They fight well."

"They fight with conviction. Do you believe them to be evil?"

"They destroy us."

"We destroy them."

"So the question," she said, smiling at her cleverness, "is who began to destroy?"

"Not at all," Clevo said. "I suspect there's no longer a clear answer to that. We are the new, they are the old. The old must be superseded.

"That's the only way we're different? They're old, we're not so old? I don't understand."

"Nor do I, entirely."

"Well, finally!"

"The Senexi," Clevo continued, unperturbed, "long ago needed only gas-giant planets like their homeworlds. They lived in peace for billions of years before our world was formed. But as they moved from star to star, they learned uses for other types of worlds. We were most interested in rocky Earth-like planets. Gradually we found uses for gas giants, too. By the time we met, each of us encroached on the other's territory. Their technology is so improbable, so unlike ours, that when we first encountered them we thought they must come from another geometry."

"Where did you learn all this?" Prufrax squinted at him suspiciously.

"I'm no longer a hawk," he said, "but I was too valuable just to discard. My experience was too broad, my abilities too useful. So I was placed in research. It seems a safe place for me. Little contact with my conrades." He looked directly at her. "We must try to know our enemy, at least a little."

"That's dangerous," Prufrax said, almost instinctively.

"Yes, it is. What you know, you cannot hate."

"We must hate," she said. "It makes us strong. Senexi hate."

"They might," he said. "But, sometime, wouldn't you like to . . . sit down and talk with one, after a battle? Talk with a fighter? Learn its tactic, how it bested you in one move, compare—"

"No!" Prufrax shoved off rapidly down the tube. "We're shifting now. We have to get ready."

—She's smart. She's leaving him. He's crazy.

—Why do you think that?

—He would stop the fight, end the Zap.

—But he was a hawk.

—And hawks became glovers, I guess. But glovers go wrong, too. Like you.

—?

—Did you know they used you? How you were used?

—That's all blurred now.

—She's doomed if she stays around him. Who's that?

—Someone is listening with us.

The next battle was bad enough to fall into the hellfought. Prufrax was in her fightsuit, legs drawn up as if about to kick off. The cruiser exited sponge space and plunged into combat before sponge space supplements could reach full effectiveness. She was dizzy, disoriented. The overhawks could only hope that a switch from biologic to cyber would cure the problem.

She didn't know what they were attacking. Tactic was flooding the implant, but she was only receiving the wash of that; she hadn't merged yet. She sensed that things were confused. That bothered her. Overs did not feel confusion.

The cruiser was taking damage. She could sense at least that, and she wanted to scream in frustration. Then she was ordered to merge with the implant. Biologic became cyber. She was in the Know.

The cruiser had reintegrated above a gas-giant planet. They were seventy-nine thousand kilometers from the upper atmosphere. The damage had come from ice mines—chunks of Senexi-treated water ice, altered to stay in sponge space until a human vessel integrated near by. Then they emerged, packed with momentum and all the residual instability of an unsuccessful return to status geometry. Unsuccessful for a ship, that is—very successful for a weapon.

The ice mines had given up the overness of the real within range of the cruiser and had blasted out whole sections of the hull. The launch lanes had not been damaged. The fighters lined up on their beams and were peppered out into space, spreading in the famous sword flower.

The planet was a cold nest. Over didn't know what the atmosphere contained, but Senexi activity had been high in the star system, concentrating on this world. Over had decided to take a chance. Fighters headed for the atmosphere. The cruiser began planting singularity eggs. The eggs went ahead of the fighters, great black grainy ovoids that seemed to leave a trail of shadow—the wake of a birthing disruption in status geometry that could turn a gas giant into a short-lived sun.

Their time was limited. The fighters would group on entry sleds and descend to the liquid water regions where Senexi commonly kept their upwelling power plants. The fighters would first destroy any plants, loop into the liquid ammonia regions to search for hidden cuckoos, then see what was so important about the world.

She and five other fighters mounted the sled. Growing closer, the hazy clear regions of the atmosphere sparkled with Senexi sensors. Spiderweb beams shot from the six sleds to down the sensors. Buffet began. Scream, heat, then a second flower from the sled at a depth of two hundred kilometers. The sled slowed and held station. It would be their only way back. The fightsuits couldn't pull out of such a large gravity well.

She descended deeper. The pale, bloated beacon of the red start was dropping below the second cloudtops, limning the strata in orange and purple. At the liquid ammonia level she was instructed to key in permanent memory of all she was seeing. She wasn't "seeing" much, but other sensors were recording a great deal, all of it duly processed in her implant. "There's life here," she told herself. Indigenous life. Just another example of Senexi disregard for basic decency: they were interfering with a world developing its own complex biology.

The temperature rose to ammonia vapor levels, then to liquid water. The pressure on the fightsuit was enormous, and she was draining her stores much more rapidly than expected. At this level the atmosphere was particularly thick with organics.

Senexi snakes rose from below, passed them in altitude, then doubled back to engage. Prufrax was designated the deep diver; the others from her sled would stay at this level in her defense. As she fell, another sled group moved in behind her to double the cover.

She searched for the characteristic radiation curve of an upwelling plant. At the lower boundary of the liquid water level, below which her suit could not safely descend, she found it.

The Senexi were tapping the gas giant's convection from greater depths than usual. Above the plant, almost indetectable, was another object with an uncharacteristic curve. They were separated by ten kilometers. The power plant was feeding its higher companion with tight energy beams.

She slowed. Two other fighters, disengaged from the brief skirmish above, took positions as backups a few dozen kilometers higher than she. Her implant searched for an appropriate tactic. She would avoid the zero-angle phase for the moment, go in for reconnaissance. She could feel sound pouring from the plant and its companion—rhythmic, not waste noise, but deliberate. And homing in on that sound were waves of large vermiform organisms, like chains of gas-filled sausage. They were dozens of meters long, two meters at their greatest thickness, shaped vaguely like the Senexi snake fighters. The vermiforms were native, and they were being lured into the uppermost floating structure. None were emerging. Her backups spread apart, descended, and drew up along her flanks.

She made her decision almost immediately. She could see a pattern in the approach of the natives. If she fell into the pattern, she might be able to enter the structure unnoticed.

—It's a grinder. She doesn't recognize it.

—What's a grinder?

—She should make the Zap! It's an ugly thing; Senexi use them all the time. Net a planet with grinders, like a cuckoo, but for larger operations.

The creatures were being passed through separator fields. Their organics fell from the bottom of the construct, raw material for new growth—Senexi growth. Their heavier elements were stored for later harvest.

With Prufrax in their midst, the vermiforms flew into the separator. The interior was hundreds of meters wide, lead-white walls with flat gray machinery floating in a dust haze, full of hollow noise, the distant bleats of vermiforms being slaughtered. Prufrax tried to retreat, but she was caught in a selector field. Her suit bucked and she was whirled violently, then thrown into a repository for examination. She had been screened from the separator; her plan to record, then destroy, the structure had been foiled by an automatic filter.

"Information sufficient." Command logic programmed into the implant before launch was now taking over. "Zero-angle phase both plant and adjunct." She was drifting in the repository, still slightly stunned. Something was fading. Cyber was hissing in and out; the over logic-commands were being scrambled. Her implant was malfunctioning and was returning control to biologic. The selector fields had played havoc with all cyber functions, down to the processors in her weapons.

Cautiously she examined the down systems one by one, determining what she could and could not do. This took as much as thirty seconds—an astronomical time on the implant's scale.

She still could use the phase weapon. If she was judicious and didn't waste her power, she could cut her way out of the repository, maneuver and work with her escorts to destroy both the plant and the separator. By the time they returned to the sleds, her implant might have rerouted itself and made sufficient repairs to handle defense. She had no way of knowing what was waiting for her if—when—she escaped, but that was the least of her concerns for the moment.

She tightened the setting of the phase beam and swung her fightsuit around, knocking a cluster of junk ice and silty phosphorescent dust. She activated the beam. When she had a hole large enough to pass through, she edged the suit forward, beamed through more walls and obstacles, and kicked herself out of the repository into free fall. She swiveled and laid down a pattern of wide-angle beams, at the same time relaying a message on her situation to the escorts.

The escorts were not in sight. The separator was beginning to break up, spraying debris through the almost opaque atmosphere. The rhythmic sound ceased, and the crowds of vermiforms began to disperse.

She stopped her fall and thrust herself several kilometers higher—directly into a formation of Senexi snakes. She had barely enough power to reach the sled, much less fight and turn her beams on the upwelling plant.

Her cyber was still down.

The sled signal was weak. She had no time to calculate its direction from the inertial guidance cyber. Besides, all cyber was unreliable after passing through the separator.

Why do they fight so well? Clevo's question clogged her thoughts. Cursing, she tried to blank and keep all her faculties available for running the fightsuit. *When evenly matched, you cannot win against your enemy unless you understand them. And if you truly understand, why are you fighting and not talking?* Clevo had never told her that—not in so many words. But it was part of a string of logic all her own.

Be more than an automation with a narrow range of choices. Never underestimate the enemy. Those were old Grounds dicta, not entirely lost in the new training, but only emphasized by Clevo.

If they fight as well as you, perhaps in some ways they fight-think like you do. Use that.

Isolated, with her power draining rapidly, she had no choice. They might disregard her if she posed no danger. She cut her thrust and went into a diving spin. Clearly she was on her way to a high-pressure grave. They would sense her power levels, perhaps even pick up the lack of field activity if she let her shields drop. She dropped the shields. If they let her fall and didn't try to complete the kill—if they concentrated on active fighters above—she had enough power to drop into the water vapor regions, far below the plant, and silently ride a thermal into range. With luck, she could get close enough to lay a web of zero-angle phase and take out the plant.

She had minutes in which to agonize over her plan. Falling, buffeted by winds that could knock her kilometers out of range, she spun like a vagrant flake of snow.

She couldn't even expend the energy to learn if they were scanning her, checking out her potential.

Perhaps she underestimated them. Perhaps they would be that much more thorough and take her out just to be sure. Perhaps they had unwritten rules of conduct like the ones she was using, taking hunches into account. Hunches were discouraged in Grounds training—much less reliable than cyber.

She fell. Temperature increased. Pressure on her suit began to constrict her air supply. She used fighter trancing to cut back on her breathing.

Fell.

And broke the trance. Pushed through the dense smoke of exhaustion. Planned the beam web. Counted her reserves. Nudged into an updraft beneath the plant. The thermal carried her, a silent piece of paper in a storm, drifting back and forth beneath the objective. The huge field intakes pulsed above, lightning outlining their invisible extension. She held back on the beam.

Nearly faded out. Her suit interior was almost unbearably hot.

She was only vaugely aware of laying down the pattern. The beams vanished in the murk. The thermal pushed her through a layer of haze, and she saw the plant, riding high above clear-atmosphere turbulence. The zero-angle phase had pushed through the field intakes, into their source nodes and the plant body, surrounding it with bright blue Tcherenkov. First the surface began to break up, then the middle layers, and finally key supports. Chunks vibrated away with the internal fury of their molecular, then atomic, then particle disruption. Paraphrasing Grounds description of beam action, the plant became less and less convinced of its reality. "Matter dreams," an instructor had said a decade before. "Dreams it is real, maintains the dream by shifting rules with constant results. Disturb the dreams, the shifting of the rules results in inconstant results. Things cannot hold."

She slid away from the updraft, found another; wondering idly how far she would be lifted. Curiosity at the last. Let's just see, she told herself; a final experiment.

Now she was cold. The implant was flickering, showing signs of reorganization. She didn't use it. No sense expanding the amount of time until death. No sense at all.

The sled, maneuvered by one remaining fighter, glided up beneath her almost unnoticed.

Aryz waited in the stillness of a Senexi memory, his thinking temporarily reduced to a faint susurrus. What he waited for was not clear.

—Come.

The form of address was wrong, but he recognized the voice. His thoughts stirred, and he followed the nebulous presence out of Senexi territory.

—Know your enemy.

Prufrax . . . the name of one of the human shapes sent out against their own kind. He could sense her presence in the mandate, locked into a memory store. He touched on the store and caught the essentials—the grinder, the updraft plant, the fight from Prufrax's viewpoint.

—Know how your enemy knows you.

He sensed a second presence, similar to that of Prufrax. It took him some time to realize that the human captive was another form of the shape, a reproduction of the . . .

Both were reproductions of the female whose image was in the memory store. Aryz was not impressed by threes—Senexi mysticism, what had ever existed of it, had been preoccupied with fives and sixes—but the coincidence was striking.

—Know how your enemy sees you.

He saw the grinder processing organics—the vermiform natives—in preparation for a widespread seeding of deuterium gatherers. The operation had evidently been conducted for some time; the vermiform populations were greatly reduced from their usual numbers. Vermiforms were a common type-species on gas giants of the sort depicted. The mutated shape nudged him into a particular channel of the memory, that which carried the original Prufrax's emotions. She had reacted with *disgust* to the Senexi procedure. It was a reaction not unlike what Aryz might feel when coming across something forbidden in Senexi behavior. Yet eradication was perfectly natural, analogous to the human cleansing of *food* before *eating*.

—It's in the memory. The vermiforms are intelligent. They have their own kind of civilization. Human action on this world prevented their complete extinction by the Senexi.

—So what matter they were *intelligent*? Aryz responded. They did not behave or think like Senexi, or like any species Senexi find compatible. They were therefore not desirable. Like humans.

—You would make humans extinct?

—We would protect ourselves from them.

—Who damages the other most?

Aryz didn't respond. The line of questioning was incomprehensible. Instead he flowed into the memory of Prufrax, propelled by another aspect of complete freedom, confusion.

The implant was replaced. Prufrax's damaged limbs and skin were repaired or regenerated quickly, and within four wakes, under intense treatment usually reserved only for overs, she regained all her reflexes and speed. She requested liberty of the cruiser while it returned for repairs. Her request was granted.

She first sought Clevo in the designated research area. He wasn't there, but a message was, passed on to her by a smiling young crew member. She read it quickly:

"You're free and out of action. Study for a while, then come find me. The old place hasn't been damaged. It's less private, but still good. Study! I've marked highlights."

She frowned at the message, then handed it to the crew member, who duly erased it and returned to his duties. She wanted to talk with Clevo, not study.

But she followed his instructions. She searched out highlighted entries in the ship's memory store. It was not nearly as dull as she had expected. In fact, by following the highlights, she felt she was learning more about Clevo and about the questions he asked.

Old literature was not nearly as graphic as fibs, but it was different enough to involve her for a time. She tried to create imitations of what she read, but erased them. Nonfib stories were harder than she suspected. She read about punishment, duty; she read about places called heaven and hell, from a writer who had died tens of thousands of years before. With ed supplement guidance, she was able to comprehend most of what she read. Plugging the store into her implant, she was able to absorb hundreds of volumes in an hour.

Some of the stories were losing definition. They hadn't been used in decades, perhaps centuries.

Halfway through, she grew impatient. She left the research area. Operating on another hunch, she didn't go to the blister as directed, but straight to memory central, two decks inboard the research area. She saw Clevo there, plugged into a data pillar, deep in some aspect of ship history. He noticed her approach, unplugged, and swiveled on his chair. "Congratulations," he said, smiling at her.

"Hardfought," she acknowledged, smiling.

"Better than that, perhaps," he said.

She looked at him quizzically. "What do you mean, better?"

"I've been doing some illicit tapping on over channels."

"So?"

—He *is dangerous*!

"For what?"

"You may have a valuable genetic assortment. Overs think you behaved remarkably well under impossible conditions."

"Did I?"

He nodded. "Your type may be preserved."

"Which means?"

"There's a program being planned. They want to take the best fighters and reproduce them—clone them—to make uniform top-grade squadrons. It was rumored in my time—you haven't heard?"

She shook her head.

"It's not new. It's been done, off and on, for tens of thousands of years. This time they believe they can make it work."

"You were a fighter, once," she said. "Did they preserve your type?"

Clevo nodded. "I had something that interested them, but not, I think, as a fighter."

Prufrax looked down at her stubby-fingered hands. "It was grim," she said. "You know what we found?"

"An extermination plant."

"You want me to understand them better. Well, I can't. I refuse. How could they do such things?" She looked disgusted and answered her own question. "Because they're Senexi."

"Humans," Clevo said, "have done much the same, sometimes worse."

"No!"

—No!

"Yes," he said firmly. He sighed. "We've wiped Senexi worlds, and we've even wiped worlds with intelligent species like our own. Nobody is innocent. Not in this universe."

"We were never taught that."

"It wouldn't have made you a better hawk. But it might make a better human of you to know. Greater depth of character. Do you want to be more aware?"

"You mean, study more?"

He nodded.

"What makes you think *you* can teach me?"

"Because you thought about what I asked you. About how Senexi thought. And you survived where some other hawk might not have. The overs think it's in your genes. It might be. But it's also in your head."

"Why not tell the overs?"

"I have," he said. He shrugged.

"They wouldn't want me to learn from you?"

"I don't know," Clevo said. "I suppose they're aware you're talking to me. They could stop it if they wanted."

"And if I learn from you?"

"Not from me, actually. From the past. From history, what other people have thought. I'm really not any more capable than you . . . but I know history, small portions of it. I won't teach you so much as guide."

"I did use your questions," Prufrax said. "But will I ever need to use them—think that way—again?"

Clevo nodded. "Of course."

—You're quiet.

—She's giving in to him.

—She gave in a long time ago.

—She should be afraid.

—Were you—we—ever really afraid of a challenge?

—No.

—Not Senexi, not forbidden knowledge.

Clevo first led her through the history of past wars, judging that was appropriate considering her occupation. She was attentive enough, though her mind wandered; sometimes he was didactic, but she found she didn't mind that much.

She saw that in all wars, the first stage was to dehuman-ize the enemy, reduce the enemy to a lower level so that

he might be killed without compunction. When the enemy
was not human to begin with, the task was easier. As wars
progressed, this tactic frequently led to an underestimation
of the enemy, with disastrous consequences. "We aren't
exactly underestimating the Senexi," Clevo said. "The
overs are too smart for that. But we refuse to understand
them, and that could make the war last indefinitely."

"Then why don't the overs see that?"

"Because we're being locked into a pattern. We've been
fighting for so long, we've begun to lose ourselves. And
it's getting worse." He assumed his didactic tone, and she
knew he was reciting something he'd formulated years
before and repeated to himself a thousand times. "There
is no war so important that, to win it, we must destory our
minds."

She didn't agree with that; losing the war with the
Senexi would mean extinction, as she understood things.

Most often they met in the single unused weapons
blister that had not been damaged. They met when the
ship was basking in the real between sponge-space jaunts.
He brought memory stores with him in portable modules,
and they read, listened, experienced together. She never placed a great deal of importance in the things she
learned; her interest was focused on Clevo. Still, she
learned.

The rest of her time she spent training. She was aware
of a growing isolation from the hawks, which she attribu-
ted to her uncertain rank status. Was her genotype going
to be preserved or not? The decision hadn't been made.
The more she learned, the less she wanted to be singled
out for honor. Attracting that sort of attention might be
dangerous, she thought. Dangerous to whom, or what, she
could not say.

Clevo showed her how hero images had been used to
indoctrinate birds and hawks in a standard of behavior
that was ideal, not realistic. The results were not always
good; some tragic blunders had been made by fighters

trying to be more than anyone possibly could or refusing to be flexible.

The war was certainly not a fib. Yet more and more the overs seemed to be treating it as one. Unable to bring about strategic victories against the Senexi, the overs had settled in for a long war of attrition and were apparently bent on adapting all human societies to the effort.

"There are overs we never hear of, who make decisions that shape our entire lives. Soon they'll determine whether or not we're even born, if they don't already."

"That sounds paranoid," she said, trying out a new word and concept she had only recently learned.

"Maybe so."

"Besides, it's been like that for ages—not knowing all our overs."

"But it's getting worse," Clevo said. He showed her the projections he had made. In time, if trends continued unchanged, fighters and all other combatants would be treated more and more mechanically, until they became the machines the overs wished them to be.

—No.

—Quiet. How does he feel toward her?

It was inevitable that as she learned under his tutelage, he began to feel responsible for her changes. She was an excellent fighter. He could never be sure that what he was doing might reduce her effectiveness. And yet he had fought well—despite similar changes—until his billet switch. It had been the overs who had decided he would be more effective, less disruptive, elsewhere.

Bitterness over that decision was part of his motive. The overs had done a foolish thing, putting a fighter into research. Fighters were tenacious. If the truth was to be hidden, then fighters were the ones likely to ferret it out. And pass it on. There was a code among fighters, seldom revealed to their immediate overs, much less to the supreme overs parsecs distant in their strategospheres. What one fighter learned that could be of help to another had to be passed on, even under penalty. Clevo was simply following that unwritten rule.

Passing on the fact that, at one time, things had been different. That war changed people, governments, societies, and that societies could effect an enormous change on their constituents, especially now—change in their lives, their thinking. Things could become even more structured. Freedom of fight was a drug, an illusion—

—No!

used to perpetuate a state of hatred.

"Then why do they keep all the data in stores?" she asked. "I mean, you study the data, everything becomes obvious."

"There are still important people who think we may want to find our way back someday. They're afraid we'll lose our roots, but—" His face suddenly became peaceful. She reached out to touch him, and he jerked slightly, turning toward her in the blister. "What is it?" she asked.

"It's not organized. We're going to lose the information. Ship overs are going to restrict access more and more. Eventually it'll decay, like some already has in these stores. I've been planning for some time to put it all in a single unit—"

—*He* built the mandate!

"and have the overs place one on every ship, with researchers to tend it. Formalize the loose scheme still in effect, but dying. Right now I'm working on the fringes. At least I'm allowed to work. But soon I'll have enough evidence that they won't be able to argue. Evidence of what happens to societies that try to obscure their histories. They go quite mad. The overs are still rational enough to listen; maybe I'll push it through." He looked out the transparent blister. The stars were smudging to one side as the cruiser began probing for entrances to sponge space. "We'd better get back."

"Where are you going to be when we return? We'll all be transferred."

"That's some time removed. Why do you want to know?"

"I'd like to learn more."

He smiled. "That's not your only reason."

"I don't need someone to tell me what my reasons are," she said testily.

"We're so reluctant," he said. She looked at him sharply, irritated and puzzled. "I mean," he continued, "we're hawks. Comrades. Hawks couple like *that*." He snapped his fingers. "But you and I sneak around it all the time."

Prufrax kept her face blank.

"Aren't you receptive toward me?" he asked, his tone almost teasing.

"It's just that that's not all," she said, her tone softening.

"Indeed," he said in a barely audible whisper.

In the distance they heard the alarms.

—It was never any different.

—What?

—Things were never any different before me.

—Don't be silly. It's all here.

—If Clevo made the mandate, then he put it here. It isn't true.

—Why are you upset?

—I don't like hearing that everything I believe is a . . . fib.

—I've never known the difference, I suppose. Eyes-open was never all that real to me. This isn't real, you aren't . . . this is eyes-shut. So why be upset? You and I . . . we aren't even whole people. I feel you. You wish the Zap, you fight, not much else. I'm just a shadow, even compared to you. But she is whole. She loves him. She's less a victim than either of us. So something has to have changed.

—You're saying things have gotten worse.

—If the mandate is a lie, that's all I am. You refuse to accept. I *have* to accept, or I'm even less than a shadow.

—I don't refuse to accept. It's just hard.

—You started it. You thought about love.

—You did!

—Do you know what love is?

—Reception.

They first made love in the weapons blister. It came as no surprise; if anything, they approached it so cautiously they were clumsy. She had become more and more receptive, and he had dropped his guard. It had been quick, almost frantic, far from the orchestrated and drawn-out ballet the hawks prided themselves for. There was no pretense. No need to play the roles of artists interacting. They were depending on each other. The pleasure they exchanged was nothing compared to the emotions involved.

"We're not very good with each other," Prufrax said.

Clevo shrugged. "That's because we're shy."

"Shy?"

He explained. In the past—at various times in the past, because such differences had come and gone many times—making love had been more than a physical exchange or even an expression of comradeship. It had been the acknowledgment of a bond between people.

She listened, half-believing. Like everything else she had heard, that kind of love seemed strange, distasteful. What if one hawk was lost, and the other continued to love? It interfered with the hardfought, certainly. But she was also fascinated. Shyness—the fear of one's presentation to another. The hesitation to present truth, or the inward confusion of truth at the awareness that another might be important, more important than one thought possible.

Complex emotion was not encouraged either at the Grounds or among hawks on station. Complex emotion degraded complex performance. The simple and direct was desirable.

"But all we seem to do is talk—until now," Prufrax said, holding his hand and examining his fingers one by one. They were very little different from her own, though extended a bit from hawk fingers to give greater versatility with key instruction.

"Talking is the most human thing we can do."

She laughed. "I know what you are," she said, moving up until her eyes were even with his chest. "You're an instructor at heart. You make love by telling." She felt peculiar, almost afraid, and looked up at his face. "Not that I don't enjoy your lovemaking, like this. Physical."

"You receive well," he said. "Both ways."

"What we're saying," she whispered, "is not truth-speaking. It's amenity." She turned into the stroke of his hand through her hair. "Amenity is supposed to be decadent. That fellow who wrote about heaven and hell. He would call it a sin."

"Amenity is the recognition that somebody may see or feel differently than you do. It's the recognition of individuals. You and I, we're part of the end of all that."

"Even if you convince the overs?"

He nodded. "They want to repeat success without risk. New individuals are risky, so they duplicate past success. There will be more and more people, fewer individuals. More of you and me, less of others. The fewer individuals, the fewer stories to tell. The less history. We're part of the death of history."

She floated next to him, trying to blank her mind as she had done before, to drive out the nagging aware-ness that he was right. She thought she understood the social structure around her. Things seemed new. She said as much.

"It's a path we're taking," Clevo said. "Not a place we're at."

—It's a place *we're* at. How different are *we*?

—But there's so much history in here. How can it be over for us?

—I've been thinking. Do we know the last event record-ed in the mandate?

—Don't, we're drifting from Prufrax now. . . .

• • •

Aryz felt himself drifting with them. They swept over
countless millennia, then swept back the other way. And
it became evident that as much change had been wrapped
in one year of the distant past as in a thousand years of
the closing entries in the mandate. Clevo's voice seemed
to follow them, though they were far from his period, far
from Prufrax's record.

"Tyranny is the death of history. We fought the Senexi
until we became like them. No change, youth at an end,
old age coming upon us. There is no important change,
merely elaborations in the pattern."

—How many times have we been here, then? How
many times have we died?

Aryz wasn't sure, now. *Was* this the first time humans
had been captured? Had he been told everything by the
brood mind? Did the Senexi have no *history*, whatever
that was—

**The accumulated lives of living, thinking beings.
Their actions, thoughts, passions, hopes**.

The mandate answered even his confused, nonhuman
requests. He could understand action, thought, but not
passion or hope. Perhaps without those there was no *history*.

—You have no history, the mutated shape told him.
There have been millions like you, even millions like
the brood mind. What is the last event recorded in
the brood mind that is not duplicated a thousand
times over, so close they can be melded together for
convenience?

—How do you understand that—because we made you
between human and Senexi?

—Not only that.

The requests of the twin captives and shape were moving them back once more into the past, through the dim
gray millennia of repeating ages. History began to manifest again, differences in the record.

• • •

On the way back to Mercior, four skirmishes were fought. Prufrax did well in each. She carried something special with her, a thought she didn't even tell Clevo, and she carried the same thought with her through their last days at the Grounds.

Taking advantage of hawk liberty, she opted for a posthardfought residence just outside the Grounds, in the relatively uncrowded Daughter of Cities zone. She wouldn't be returning to fight until several issues had been decided—her status most important among them.

Clevo began making his appeal to the middle overs. He was given Grounds duty to finish his proposals. They could stay together for the time being.

The residence was sixteen square meters in area, not elegant—*natural*, as rentOpts described it.

On the last day she lay in the crook of Clevo's arm. They had done a few hours of nature sleep. He hadn't come out yet, and she looked up at his face, reached up with a hand to feel his arm.

It was different from the arms of others she had been receptive toward. It was unique. The thought amused her. There had never been a reception like theirs. This was the beginning. And if both were to be duplicated, this love, this reception, would be repeated an infinite number of times. Clevo meeting Prufrax, teaching her, opening her eyes.

Somehow, even though repetition contributed to the death of history, she was pleased. This was the secret thought she carried into fight. Each time she would survive, wherever she was, however many duplications down the line. She would receive Clevo, and he would teach her. If not now—if one or the other died—then in the future. The death of history might be a good thing. Love could go on forever.

She had lost even a rudimentary apprehension of death, even with present pleasure to live for. Her functions had sharpened. She would please him by doing all the things he could not. And if he was to enter that state he frequently found him in, that state of introspection, of reliving his own battles and of envying her activity, then that wasn't bad. All they did to each other was good.

—*Was* good

—*Was*

She slipped from his arm and left the narrow sleeping quarter, pushing through the smoke-colored air curtain to the lounge. Two hawks and an over she had never seen before were sitting there. They looked up at her.

"Under," Prufrax said.

"Over," the woman returned. She was dressed in tan and green, Grounds colors, not ship.

"May I assist?"

"Yes."

"My duty, then?"

The over beckoned her closer. "You have been receiving a researcher."

"Yes," Prufrax said. The meetings could not have been a secret on the ship, and certainly not their quartering near the Grounds. "Has that been against duty?"

"No." The over eyed Prufrax sharply, observing her perfected fightform, the easy grace with which she stood, naked, in the middle of the small compartment. "But a decision has been reached. Your status is decided now."

She felt a shiver.

"Prufrax," said the elder hawk. She recognized him from fibs, and his companion: Kumnax and Arol. Once her heroes. "You have been accorded an honor, just as your partner has. You have a valuable genetic assortment—"

She barely heard the rest. They told her she would return to fight, until they deemed she had had enough experience and background to be brought into the polinstruc division. Then her fighting would be over. She would serve better as an example, a hero.

Heroes never partnered out of function. Hawk heroes could not even partner with exhawks.

Clevo emerged from the air curtain. "Duty," the over said. "The residence is disbanded. Both of you will have separate quarters, separate duties."

They left. Prufrax held out her hand, but Clevo didn't take it. "No use," he said.

Suddenly she was filled with anger. "You'll give it up? Did I expect too much? *How strongly*?"

"Perhaps even more strongly than you," he said. "I knew the order was coming down. And still I didn't leave. That may hurt my chances with the supreme overs."

"Then at least I'm worth more than your breeding history?"

"Now you are history. History the way they make it."

"I feel like I'm dying," she said, amazement in her voice. "What is that, Clevo? What did you do to me?"

"I'm in pain, too," he said.

"You're hurt?"

"I'm confused."

"I don't believe that," she said, her anger rising again. "You knew, and you didn't do anything?"

"That would have been counter to duty. We'll be worse off if we fight it."

"So what good is your great, exalted history?"

"History is what you have," Clevo said. "I only record."

—Why did they separate them?

—I don't know. You didn't like him, anyway.

—Yes, but now . . .

—I don't understand.

—We don't. Look what happens to her. They took what was best out of her. Prufrax.

went into battle eighteen more times before dying as heroes often do, dying in the midst of what she did best. The question of what made her better before the separation—for she definitely was not as fine a fighter

after—has not been settled. Answers fall into an extinct classification of knowledge, and there are few left to interpret, none accessible to this device.

—So she went out and fought and died. They never even made fibs about her. This killed her?

—I don't think so. She fought well enough. She died like other hawks died.

—And she might have lived otherwise.

—How can I know that, any more than you?

—They—we—met again, you know. I met a Clevo once, on my ship. They didn't let me stay with him long.

—How did you react to him?

—There was so little time, I don't know.

—Let's ask. . . .

In thousands of duty stations, it was inevitable that some of Prufrax's visions would come true, that they should meet now and then. Clevos were numerous, as were Prufraxes. Every ship carried complements of several of each. Though Prufrax was never quite as successful as the original, she was a fine type. She—

—She was never quite as successful. They took away her edge. They didn't even know it!

—They must have known.

—Then they didn't want to win!

—We don't know that. Maybe there were more important considerations.

—Yes, like killing history.

Aryz shuddered in his warming body, dizzy as if about to bud, then regained control. He had been pulled from the mandate, called to his own duty.

He examined the shapes and the human captive. There was something different about them. How long had they been immersed in the mandate? He checked quickly, frantically, before answering the call. The reconstructed Mam had malfunctioned. None of them had been nourished. They were thin, pale, cooling.

Even the bloated mutant shape was dying; lost, like the others, in the mandate.

He turned his attention away. Everything was confusion. Was he human or Senexi now? Had he fallen so low as to understand them? He went to the origin of the call, the ruins of the temporary brood chamber. The corridors were caked with ammonia ice, burning his pod as he slipped over them. The brood mind had come out of flux bind. The emergency support systems hadn't worked well; the brood mind was damaged.

"Where have you been?" it asked.

"I assumed I would not be needed until your return from the flux bind."

"You have not been watching!"

"Was there any need? We are so advanced in time, all our actions are obsolete. The nebula is collapsed, the issue is decided."

"We do not know that. We are being pursued."

Aryz turned to the sensor wall—what was left of it— and saw that they were, indeed, being pursued. He had been lax.

"It is not your fault," the brood mind said. "You have been set a task that tainted you and ruined your function. You will dissipate."

Aryz hesitated. He had become so different, so tainted, that he actually *hesitated* at a direct command from the brood mind. But it was damaged. Without him, without what he had learned, what could it do? It wasn't reasoning correctly.

"There are facts you must know, important facts—"

Aryz felt a wave of revulsion, uncomprehending fear, and something not unlike human anger radiate from the brood mind. Whatever he had learned and however he had changed, he could not withstand that wave.

Willingly, and yet against his will—it didn't matter— he felt himself liquefying. His pod slumped beneath him, and he fell over, landing on a pool of frozen ammonia. It burned, but he did not attempt to lift himself. Before he ended, he saw with surprising clarity what it was to be a branch ind, or a brood mind, or a human. Such a valuable insight, and it leaked out of his permea and froze on the ammonia.

The brood mind regained what control it could of the fragment. But there were no defenses worthy of the name. Calm, preparing for its own dissipation, it waited for the pursuit to conclude.

The Mam set off an alarm. The interface with the mandate was severed. Weak, barely able to crawl, the humans looked at each other in horror and slid to opposite corners of the chamber.

They were confused: which of them was the captive, which the decoy shape? It didn't seem important. They were both bone-thin, filthy with their own excrement. They turned with one motion to stare at the bloated mutant. It sat in its corner, tiny head incongruous on the huge thorax, tiny arms and legs barely functional even when healthy. It smiled wanly at them.

"We felt you," one of the Prufraxes said. "You were with us in there." Her voice was a soft croak.

"That was my place," it replied. "My only place."

"What function, what name?"

"I'm . . . I know that. I'm a researcher. In there, I knew myself in there."

They squinted at the shape. The head. Something familiar, even now. "You're a Clevo . . ."

There was noise all around them, cutting off the shape's weak words. As they watched, their chamber was sectioned like an orange, and the wedges peeled open. The illumination ceased. Cold enveloped them.

A naked human female, surrounded by tiny versions of herself, like an angel circled by fairy kin, floated into the chamber. She was thin as a snake. She wore nothing but silver rings on her wrists and a thin torque around her waist. She glowed blue-green in the dark.

The two Prufraxes moved their lips weakly but made no sound in the near vacuum. *Who are you?*

She surveyed them without expression, then held out her arms as if to fly. She wore no gloves, but she was of their type.

As she had done countless times before on finding such Senexi experiments—though this seemed older than most—she lifted one arm higher. The blue-green intensified, spread in waves to the mangled walls, surrounded the freezing, dying shapes. Perfect, angelic, she left the debris behind to cast its fitful glow and fade.

They destroyed every portion of the fragment but one. They left the mandate behind unharmed.

Then they continued, millions of them thick like mist, working the spaces between the stars, their only master the overness of the real.

They needed no other masters. They would never malfunction.

The mandate drifted in the dark and cold, its memory going on, but its only life the rapidly fading tracks where minds had once passed through it. The trails writhed briefly, almost as if alive, but only following the quantum rules of diminished energy states. Briefly, a small memory was illuminated.

Prufrax's last poem, explained the mandate reflexively.

How the fires grow! Peace passes
All memory lost.
Somehow we always miss that single door,
Dooming ourselves to circle.

Ashes to stars, lies to souls,
Let's spin 'round the sinks and holes.

Kill the good, eat the young.
Forever and more
You and I are never done.

The track faded into nothing. Around the mandate, the universe grew old very quickly.